H. P. Lovecraft is today u
as the twentieth century's
story of supernatural horr
lifetime he suffered relativ
out a living almost as muc
revising the manuscripts o
experienced authors as by his own writing. However, among his clients were writers interested in occult and macabre fiction – Lovecraft's own special field of interest – and the stories sent to him by these writers interested him more than all his other revision work. In a small number of cases, he undertook nothing less than a complete rewriting of those tales he considered to be particularly worth while: these have been gathered here and in *The Horror in the Burying Ground* (also available in Panther Books) for the benefit of the ever-growing number of Lovecraft enthusiasts and for all readers who relish the nerve-tingling taste of total terror . . .

Here are such memorable stories as Zealia Bishop's short novel *The Mound*, a tale of secret, subterranean K'n-Yan and Yoth . . . the title story by Hazel Heald, one of the classic stories in the famous Cthulhu Mythos . . . C. M. Eddy Jr.'s *The Loved Dead* which profoundly shocked the authorities when it first appeared in the magazine *Weird Tales* . . . and other nightmare offerings shaped by the hand of the century's most accomplished creator of occult terror, H. P. Lovecraft.

Also available in Panther Books

At the Mountains of Madness and other novels of terror
by H. P. Lovecraft

The Haunter of the Dark and other tales
by H. P. Lovecraft

The Lurking Fear and other stories
by H. P. Lovecraft

Dagon and other macabre tales
by H. P. Lovecraft

The Tomb and other tales
by H. P. Lovecraft

The Case of Charles Dexter Ward
by H. P. Lovecraft

The Shuttered Room and other tales
by H. P. Lovecraft & August Derleth

The Lurker at the Threshold
by H. P. Lovecraft & August Derleth

Tales of the Cthulhu Mythos: Volume 1
by H. P. Lovecraft & others

Tales of the Cthulhu Mythos: Volume 2
by H. P. Lovecraft & others

The Horror in the Burying Ground
by H. P. Lovecraft & others

H. P. Lovecraft
and others

The Horror in the Museum

and other tales

Panther

Granada Publishing Limited
First published in Great Britain in 1975 by
Panther Books Ltd
Frogmore, St Albans, Herts AL2 2NF

Published by arrangement with Arkham House

Made and printed in Great Britain by
Hazel Watson & Viney Ltd
Aylesbury, Bucks
Set in Intertype Times

CONTENTS

LOVECRAFT'S 'REVISIONS'

However paradoxical it may seem, in view of his present posthumous fame as a master of the macabre, Howard Phillips Lovecraft made his scant living principally by revising and correcting manuscripts of prose and poetry sent to him by a variety of hopeful writers. The greater number of his clients seldom achieved publication in any but amateur press magazines, but his revision of the work of a small group of writers with reasonably strong themes but a concomitant lack of writing skills or prose style enlisted a greater share of his interest and assistance – amounting often to the complete rewriting of a submitted story – and so found their way into print.

Lovecraft's revision work divided into two classes – the bulk of it amounted to little more than professional correction of the language, syntax, punctuation, etc., but a minority of tales in the domain of the macabre aroused his personal interest to the extent of active participation. Even this small group of tales was sub-divided into groups of lesser and major interest. Some, as in the case of Sonia Greene's stories, the early work of Hazel Heald, and the tales of his old Providence friend, Clifford M. Eddy, Jr., required less drastic revision and more or less advisory assistance. Writing on September 30, 1944 of one such story, *The Man of Stone*†, the late Hazel Heald admitted, 'Lovecraft helped me on this story as much as on the others, and did actually rewrite paragraphs. He would criticize paragraph after paragraph and pencil remarks beside them, and then make me rewrite them until they pleased him.' But of course Lovecraft did considerably more with Hazel Heald's later stories – he rewrote them from beginning to end, so that they are essentially Lovecraft stories, retaining only the plot or story-line of the writer whose byline appeared over the story – and not even this in every case. The kind of revision to which Mrs Heald here referred is illustrated in the manuscript of Robert E. Barlow's tale, *'Till All the Seas'*†, in the Lovecraft Collection of the John Hay Memorial Library of Brown University in Providence, Rhode Island.

†Included in this volume.

Zealia Bishop, writing in her memoir, *H. P. Lovecraft: A Pupil's View*, in 1953, sets forth an experience central to the majority of the writers represented in this collection, one shared by only a relatively few of Lovecraft's clients – 'The stories I sent him always came back so revised from their basic idea that I felt I was a complete failure as a writer.' The extent to which she felt herself indebted to Lovecraft was indicated in her insistence that half the fee paid by *Weird Tales* for *Medusa's Coil*†, published after Lovecraft's untimely death in 1937, be sent to Lovecraft's surviving aunt, Mrs Annie E. P. Gamwell. 'I had learned from him fundamental principles of writing technique and the appreciation of literature. . . . My debt to Lovecraft is great. I count myself fortunate that I was one of his epistolary friends and pupils.'

Lovecraft also encouraged his fiction clients to turn a hand to the macabre since, after all, this was his specialized field, in which he was far more at home than in the popular contemporary veins of romance or realism; fantasy was the one field in which he could be of the greatest service to his patrons. Any even casual reading of the revisions collected here offers patent evidence that with Hazel Heald's tale, *The Horror in the Museum**, Lovecraft saw himself rather more as a collaborator than a revisionist. The story is pure Lovecraft, even to the introduction of names from the Cthulhu Mythos. The same thing is true of *Out of the Eons*†.

And it is true, too, to some extent, of the stories that followed – William Lumley's *The Diary of Alonzo Typer**, Hazel Heald's *The Horror in the Burying Ground*†, Adolphe de Castro's *The Last Test*†, and *The Electric Executioner**, and the trio by Zealia (Brown Reed) Bishop – *The Curse of Yig*†, *Medusa's Coil*†, and the short novel, *The Mound**, one of the most impressive tales to result from Lovecraft's collaboration with writers who sought his professional help and one in which not only H. P. Lovecraft but also Frank Belknap Long had a hand.

One can well imagine the pleasure Lovecraft took in reworking some of these tales for, next to creating a new story of his own, he enjoyed nothing more than giving his vivid im-

†Included in this volume.

*Included in *The Horror in the Museum* (also published by Panther Books).

agination free rein in revising fiction that belonged to his favorite field. His letters are crowded with references to his revision work; he wrote about the drudgery of trying to advise amateur poets, of 'revising' their poems; he wrote about the difficulties of working with some writers who fancied themselves geniuses and had not a grain of ability – but he never once complained about rewriting a story in the domain of fantasy and the macabre, and there are frequent paragraphs listing stories in current issues of *Weird Tales* in which he 'had a hand'.

These 'revisions' which are either largely or totally Lovecraft, properly belong in the Lovecraft canon. They are uneven in manner and flavor, but Lovecraft's imagination and writing hand are not to be denied in these pages. The best of these tales are certainly good enough to stand among Lovecraft's stories – and why not? – since Lovecraft wrote most of what is memorable in them!

—AUGUST DERLETH

7 February 1970

THE HORROR IN THE MUSEUM

by Hazel Heald

It was languid curiosity which first brought Stephen Jones to Rogers' Museum. Someone had told him about the queer underground place in Southwark Street across the river, where waxen things so much more horrible than the worst effigies at Madame Tussaud's were shown, and he had strolled in one April day to see how disappointing he would find it. Oddly, he was not disappointed. There was something different and distinctive here, after all. Of course, the usual gory commonplaces were present – Landru, Doctor Crippen, Madame Demers, Rizzio, Lady Jane Grey, endless maimed victims of war and revolution, and monsters like Gilles de Rais and Marquis de Sade – but there were other things which had made him breathe faster and stay till the ringing of the closing bell. The man who had fashioned this collection could be no ordinary mountebank. There was imagination – even a kind of diseased genius – in some of this stuff.

Later he had learned about George Rogers. The man had been on the Tussaud staff, but some trouble had developed which led to his discharge. There were aspersions on his sanity and tales of his crazy forms of secret worship – though latterly his success with his own basement museum had dulled the edge of some criticisms while sharpening the insidious point of others. Teratology and the iconography of nightmare were his hobbies, and even he had had the prudence to screen off some of his worst effigies in a special alcove for adults only. It was this alcove which had fascinated Jones so much. There were lumpish hybrid things which only fantasy could spawn, molded with devilish skill, and colored in a horribly life-like fashion.

Some were the figures of well-known myth – gorgons, chimeras, dragons, cyclops, and all their shuddersome congeners. Others were drawn from darker and more furtively whispered cycles of subterranean legend – black, formless Tsathoggua, many-tentacled Cthulhu, proboscidian Chaugnar Faugn, and other rumored blasphemies from forbidden books like the *Necronomicon,* the *Book of Eibon,* or the *Unaussprechlichen Kulten* of von Junzt. But the worst were wholly original with Rogers, and represented shapes which no tale of antiquity had ever dared to suggest. Several were hideous parodies on forms of organic life we know, while others seemed taken from feverish dreams of other planets and other galaxies. The wilder paintings of Clark Ashton Smith might suggest a few – but nothing could suggest the effect of poignant, loathsome terror created by their great size and fiendishly cunning workmanship, and by the diabolically clever lighting conditions under which they were exhibited.

Stephen Jones, as a leisurely connoisseur of the bizarre in art, had sought out Rogers himself in the dingy office and workroom behind the vaulted museum chamber – an evil-looking crypt lighted dimly by dusty windows set slit-like and horizontal in the brick wall on a level with the ancient cobblestones of a hidden courtyard. It was here that the images were repaired – here, too, where some of them had been made. Waxen arms, legs, heads and torsos lay in grotesque array on various benches, while on high tiers of shelves matted wigs, ravenous-looking teeth, and glassy, staring eyes were indiscriminately scattered. Costumes of all sorts hung from hooks, and in one alcove were great piles of flesh-colored wax-cakes, and shelves filled with paint-cans and brushes of every description. In the center of the room was a large melting-furnace used to prepare the wax for molding, its fire-box topped by a huge iron container on hinges, with a spout which permitted the pouring of melted wax with the merest touch of a finger.

Other things in the dismal crypt were less describable – isolated parts of problematical entities whose assembled forms were the phantoms of delirium. At one end was a door of heavy plank, fastened by an unusually large padlock and with a very peculiar symbol painted over it. Jones, who had once had access to the dreaded *Necronomicon*, shivered involuntarily as he recognized that symbol. This showman, he reflected, must indeed be a person of disconcertingly wide scholarship in dark and dubious fields.

Nor did the conversation of Rogers disappoint him. The man was tall, lean, and rather unkempt, with large black eyes which gazed combustively from a pallid and usually stubble-covered face. He did not resent Jones's intrusion, but seemed to welcome the chance of unburdening himself to an interested person. His voice was of singular depth and resonance, and harbored a sort of repressed intensity bordering on the feverish. Jones did not wonder that many had thought him mad.

With every successive call – and such calls became a habit as the weeks went by – Jones had found Rogers more communicative and confidential. From the first there had been hints of strange faiths and practices on the showman's part, and later on these hints expanded into tales – despite a few odd corroborative photographs – whose extravagance was almost comic. It was some time in June, on a night when Jones had brought a bottle of good whisky and plied his host somewhat freely, that the really demented talk first appeared. Before that there had been wild enough stories – accounts of mysterious trips to Tibet, the African interior, the Arabian desert, the Amazon valley, Alaska, and certain little-known islands of the South Pacific, plus claims of having read such monstrous and half-fabulous books as the prehistoric Pnakotic fragments and the Dhol chants attributed to malign and non-human Leng – but nothing in all this had been so unmistakably insane as what had cropped out that June evening under the spell of the whisky.

To be plain, Rogers began making vague boasts of having found certain things in nature that no one had found before, and of having brought back tangible evidences of such discoveries. According to his bibulous harangue, he had gone farther than anyone else in interpreting the obscure and primal books he studied, and had been directed by them to certain remote places where strange survivals are hidden – survivals of eons and life-cycles earlier than mankind, and in some cases connected with other dimensions and other worlds, communication with which was frequent in the forgotten pre-human days. Jones marvelled at the fancy which could conjure up such notions, and wondered just what Rogers' mental history had been. Had his work amidst the morbid grotesqueries of Madame Tussaud's been the start of his imaginative flights, or was the tendency innate, so that his choice of occupation was merely one of its manifestations? At any rate, the man's work was merely very closely linked with his motions. Even now there was no mistaking the trend of his blackest hints about the nightmare monstrosities in the screened-off

'Adults only' alcove. Heedless of ridicule, he was trying to imply that not all of these demoniac abnormalities were artificial.

It was Jones's frank skepticism and amusement at these irresponsible claims which broke up the growing cordiality. Rogers, it was clear, took himself very seriously; for he now became morose and resentful, continuing to tolerate Jones only through a dogged urge to break down his wall of urbane and complacent incredulity. Wild tales and suggestions of rites and sacrifices to nameless elder gods continued, and now and then Rogers would lead his guest to one of the hideous blasphemies in the screened-off alcove and point out features difficult to reconcile with even the finest human craftsmanship. Jones continued his visits through sheer fascination, though he knew he had forfeited his host's regard. At times he would humor Rogers with pretended assent to some mad hint or assertion, but the gaunt showman was seldom to be deceived by such tactics.

The tension came to a head later in September. Jones had casually dropped into the museum one afternoon, and was wandering through the dim corridors whose horrors were now so familiar, when he heard a very peculiar sound from the general direction of Rogers' workroom. Others heard it too, and started nervously as the echoes reverberated through the great vaulted basement. The three attendants exchanged odd glances; and one of them, a dark, taciturn, foreign-looking fellow who always served Rogers as a repairer and assistant designer, smiled in a way which seemed to puzzle his colleagues and which grated very harshly on some facet of Jones's sensibilities. It was the yelp or scream of a dog, and was such a sound as could be made only under conditions of the utmost fright and agony combined. Its stark, anguished frenzy was appalling to hear, and in this setting of grotesque abnormality it held a double hideousness. Jones remembered that no dogs were allowed in the museum.

He was about to go to the door leading into the workroom, when the dark attendant stopped him with a word and a gesture. Mr Rogers, the man said in a soft, somewhat accented voice at once apologetic and vaguely sardonic, was out, and there were standing orders to admit no one to the workroom during his absence. As for that yelp, it was undoubtedly something out in the courtyard behind the museum. This neighborhood was full of stray mongrels, and their fights were sometimes shockingly noisy. There were no dogs in any part of the museum. But if Mr Jones wished to see Mr Rogers he might find him just before closing-time.

After this Jones climbed the old stone steps to the streets outside and examined the squalid neighborhood curiously. The leaning, decrepit buildings – once dwellings but now largely shops and warehouses – were very ancient indeed. Some of them were of a gabled type seeming to go back to Tudor times, and a faint miasmatic stench hung subtly about the whole region. Beside the dingy house whose basement held the museum was a low archway pierced by a dark cobbled alley, and this Jones entered in a vague wish to find the courtyard behind the workroom and settle the affair of the dog more comfortably in his mind. The courtyard was dim in the late afternoon light, hemmed in by rear walls even uglier and more intangibly menacing than the crumbling street facades of the evil old houses. Not a dog was in sight, and Jones wondered how the aftermath of such a frantic turmoil could have completely vanished so soon.

Despite the assistant's statement that no dog had been in the museum, Jones glanced nervously at the three small windows of the basement workroom – narrow, horizontal rectangles close to the grass-grown pavement, with grimy panes that stared repulsively and incuriously like the eyes of dead fish. To their left a worn flight of steps led to an opaque and heavily bolted door. Some impulse urged him to crouch low on the damp, broken cobblestones and peer in, on the chance that the thick green shades, worked by long cords that hung down to a reachable level, might not be drawn. The outer surfaces were thick with dirt, but as he rubbed them with his handkerchief he saw there was no obscuring curtain in the way of his vision.

So shadowed was the cellar from the inside that not much could be made out, but the grotesque working paraphernalia now and then loomed up spectrally as Jones tried each of the windows in turn. It seemed evident at first that no one was within; yet when he peered through the extreme right-hand window – the one nearest the entrance alley – he saw a glow of light at the farther end of the apartment which made him pause in bewilderment. There was no reason why any light should be there. It was an inner side of the room, and he could not recall any gas or electric fixture near that point. Another look defined the glow as a large vertical rectangle, and a thought occurred to him. It was in that direction that he had always noticed the heavy plank door with the abnormally large padlock – the door which was never opened, and above which was crudely smeared that hideous cryptic symbol from the fragmentary records of forbidden elder magic. It must be open now – and there was a light inside. All his former speculation as to where that door led, and as to what lay behind it, were now renewed with trebly disquieting force.

Jones wandered aimlessly around the dismal locality till close to six o'clock, when he returned to the museum to make the call on Rogers. He could hardly tell why he wished so especially to see the man just then, but there must have been some subconscious misgivings about that terribly unplaceable canine scream of the afternoon, and about the glow of light in that disturbing and usually unopened inner doorway with the heavy padlock. The attendants were leaving as he arrived, and he thought that Orabona – the dark foreign-looking assistant – eyed him with something like sly, repressed amusement. He did not relish that look – even though he had seen the fellow turn it on his employer many times.

The vaulted exhibition room was ghoulish in its desertion, but he strode quickly through it and rapped at the door of the office and workroom. Response was slow in coming, though there were footsteps inside. Finally, in response to a second knock, the lock rattled, and the ancient six-panelled portal creaked reluctantly open to reveal the slouching, feverish-eyed form of George Rogers. From the first it was clear that the showman was in an unusual mood. There was a curious mixture of reluctance and actual gloating in his welcome, and his talk at once veered to extravagances of the most hideous and incredible sort.

Surviving elder gods – nameless sacrifices – the other than artificial nature of some of the alcove horrors – all the usual boasts, but uttered in a tone of peculiarly increasing confidence. Obviously, Jones reflected, the poor fellow's madness was gaining on him. From time to time Rogers would send furtive glances toward the heavy, padlocked inner door at the end of the room, or toward a piece of coarse burlap on the floor not far from it, beneath which some small object appeared to be lying. Jones grew more nervous as the moments passed, and began to feel as hesitant about mentioning the afternoon's oddities as he had formerly been anxious to do so.

Rogers' sepulchrally resonant bass almost cracked under the excitement of his fevered rambling.

'Do you remember,' he shouted, 'what I told you about that ruined city in Indo-China where the Tcho-Tchos lived? You had to admit I'd been there when you saw the photographs, even if you did think I made that oblong swimmer in darkness out of wax. If you'd seen it writhing in the underground pools as I did. . . .

'Well, this is bigger still. I never told you about this, because I wanted to work out the later parts before making any claim. When you see the snapshots you'll know the geography couldn't have been faked, and I fancy I have another way of proving *It* isn't any waxed concoction of mine. You've never seen It, for the experiments wouldn't let me keep It on exhibition.'

The showman glanced queerly at the padlocked door.

'It all comes from that long ritual in the eighth Pnakotic fragment. When I got it figured out I saw it could have only one meaning. There were things in the north before the land of Lomar – before mankind existed – and this was one of them. It took us all the way to Alaska, and up the Nootak from Fort Morton, but the thing was there as we knew it would be. Great cyclopean ruins, acres of them. There was less left than we had hoped for, but after three million years what could one expect? And weren't the Eskimo legends all in the right direction? We couldn't get one of the beggars to go with us, and had to sledge all the way back to Nome for Americans. Orabona was no good up in that climate – it made him sullen and hateful.

'I'll tell you later how we found It. When we got the ice blasted out of the pylons of the central ruin the stairway was just as we knew it would be. Some carvings still there, and it was no trouble keeping the Yankees from following us in. Orabona shivered like a leaf – you'd never think it from the damned insolent way he struts around here. He knew enough of the Elder Lore to be properly afraid. The eternal light was gone, but our torches showed enough. We saw the bones of others who had been before us – eons ago, when the climate was warm. Some of these bones were of things you couldn't even imagine. At the third level down we found the ivory throne the fragments said so much about – and I may as well tell you it wasn't empty.

'The thing on that throne didn't move – and we knew then that It needed the nourishment of sacrifice. But we didn't want to wake It then. Better to get It to London first. Orabona and I went to the surface for the big box, but when we had packed it we couldn't get It up the three flights of steps. These steps weren't made for human beings, and their size bothered us. Anyway, it was devilish heavy. We had to have the Americans down to get It out. They weren't anxious to go into the place, but of course the worst thing was safely inside the box. We told them it was a batch of ivory carving – archeological stuff; and after seeing the carved throne they probably believed us. It's a wonder they didn't suspect hidden treasure and demand a share. They must have told queer tales around Nome later on; though I doubt if they ever went back to those ruins, even for the ivory throne.'

Rogers paused, felt around in his desk, and produced an envelope of good-sized photographic prints. Extracting one and laying it face down before him, he handed the rest to Jones. The set was certainly an odd one: ice-clad hills, dog sledges, men in furs, and vast tumbled ruins against a background of snow – ruins whose bizarre outlines and enormous stone blocks could hardly be accounted for. One flashlight view showed an incredible interior chamber with wild carvings and a curious throne whose proportion could not have been designed for a human occupant. The carvings of the gigantic masonry – high walls and peculiar vaulting overhead – were mainly symbolic, and involved both wholly unknown designs and certain hieroglyphs darkly cited in obscene legends. Over the throne loomed the same dreadful symbol which was now painted on the workroom wall above the padlocked plank door. Jones darted a nervous glance at the closed portal. Assuredly, Rogers had been to strange places and had seen strange things. Yet this mad interior picture might easily be a fraud – taken from a very clever stage setting. One must not be too credulous. But Rogers was continuing:

'Well, we shipped the box from Nome and got to London without any trouble. That was the first time we'd ever brought back anything that had a chance of coming alive. I didn't put It on display, because there were more important things to do for It. It needed the nourishment of sacrifice, for It was a god.

Of course I couldn't get It the sort of sacrifices which It used to have in Its day, for such things don't exist now. But there were other things which might do. The blood is the life, you know. Even the lemures and elementals that are older than the earth will come when the blood of men or beasts is offered under the right conditions.'

The expression on the narrator's face was growing very alarming and repulsive, so that Jones fidgeted involuntarily in his chair. Rogers seemed to notice his guest's nervousness, and continued with a distinctly evil smile.

'It was last year that I got It, and ever since then I've been trying rites and sacrifices. Orabona hasn't been much help, for he was always against the idea of waking It. He hates It – probably because he's afraid of what It will come to mean. He carries a pistol all the time to protect himself – fool, as if there were human protection against It! If I ever see him draw that pistol, I'll strangle him. He wanted me to kill It and make an effigy of It. But I've stuck by my plans, and I'm coming out on top in spite of all the cowards like Orabona and damned sniggering skeptics like you, Jones! I've chanted the rites and made certain sacrifices, *and last week the transition came.* The sacrifice was – received and enjoyed!'

Rogers actually licked his lips, while Jones held himself uneasily rigid. The showman paused and rose, crossing the room to the piece of burlap at which he had glanced so often. Bending down, he took hold of one corner as he spokc again.

'You've laughed enough at my work – now it's time for you to get some facts. Orabona tells me you heard a dog screaming around here this afternoon. *Do you know what that meant?*'

Jones started. For all his curiosity he would have been glad to get out without further light on the point which had so puzzled him. But Rogers was inexorable, and began to lift the square of burlap. Beneath it lay a crushed, almost shapeless mass which Jones was slow to classify. Was it a once-living thing which some agency had flattened, sucked dry of blood, punctured in a thousand places, and wrung into a limp, broken-boned heap of grotesqueness? After a moment Jones realized what it must be. It was what was left of a dog – a dog, perhaps of considerable size and whitish color. Its breed was past recognition, for distortion had come in nameless and hideous ways. Most of the hair was burned off as by some pungent acid, and the exposed, bloodless skin was riddled by innumerable circular wounds or incisions. The form of torture necessary to cause such results was past imagining.

Electrified with a pure loathing which conquered his mounting disgust, Jones sprang up with a cry.

'You damned sadist – you madman – you do a thing like this and dare to speak to a decent man!'

Rogers dropped the burlap with a malignant sneer and faced his oncoming guest. His words held an unnatural calm.

'Why, you fool, do you think *I* did this? What of it? It is not human and does not pretend to be. To sacrifice is merely to offer. I gave the dog to *It*. What happened is Its work, not mine. It needed the nourishment of the offering, and took it in Its own way. But let me show you what It looks like.'

As Jones stood hesitating, the speaker returned to his desk and took up the photograph he had laid face down without showing. Now he extended it with a curious look. Jones took it and glanced at it in an almost mechanical way. After a moment the visitor's glance became sharper and more absorbed, for the utterly satanic force of the object depicted had an almost hypnotic effect. Certainly, Rogers had outdone himself in modelling the eldritch nightmare which the camera had caught. The thing was a work of sheer, infernal genius, and Jones wondered how the public would react when it was placed on exhibition. So hideous a thing had no right to exist – probably the mere contemplation of it, after it was done, had completed the unhinging of its maker's mind and led him to worship it with brutal sacrifices. Only a stout sanity could resist the insidious suggestion that the blasphemy was – or had once been – some morbid and exotic form of actual life.

The thing in the picture squatted or was balanced on what appeared to be a clever reproduction of the monstrously carved throne in the other curious photograph. To describe it with any ordinary vocabulary would be impossible, for nothing even roughly corresponding to it has ever come within the imagination of sane mankind. It represented something meant perhaps to be roughly connected with the vertebrates of this planet – though one could not be too sure of that. Its bulk was cyclopean, for even squatted it towered to almost twice the height of Orabona, who was shown beside it. Looking sharply, one might trace its approximations toward the bodily features of the higher vertebrates.

There was an almost globular torso, with six long, sinuous limbs terminating in crab-like claws. From the upper end a subsidiary globe bulged forward bubble-like; its triangle of three staring, fishy eyes, its foot-long and evidently flexible proboscis, and a distended lateral system analogous to gills, suggesting that it was a head. Most of the body was covered with what at first appeared to be fur, but which on closer examination proved to be a dense growth of dark, slender tentacles or sucking filaments, each tipped with a mouth suggesting the head of an asp. On the head and below the proboscis the tentacles tended to be longer and thicker, and marked with spiral stripes – suggesting the traditional serpent-locks of Medusa. To say that such a thing could have an *expression* seems paradoxical; yet Jones felt that that triangle of bulging fish-eyes and that obliquely poised proboscis all bespoke a blend of hate, greed, and sheer cruelty incomprehensible to mankind because it was mixed with other emotions not of the world or this solar system. Into this bestial abnormality, he reflected, Rogers must have poured at once all his malignant insanity and all his uncanny sculptural genius. The thing was incredible – and yet the photograph proved that it existed.

Rogers interrupted his reveries.

'Well – what do you think of It? Now do you wonder what crushed the dog and sucked it dry with a million mouths? It needed nourishment – and It will need more. It is a god, and I am the first priest of Its latter-day hierarchy. Iä! Shub-Niggurath! The Goat with a Thousand Young!'

Jones lowered the photograph in disgust and pity.

'See here, Rogers, this won't do. There are limits, you know. It's a great piece of work, and all that, but it isn't good for you. Better not see it any more – let Orabona break it up, and try to forget about it. And let me tear this beastly picture up, too.'

With a snarl, Rogers snatched the photograph and returned it to the desk.

'Idiot – you – and you still think It's a fraud! You still think I made It, and you still think my figures are nothing but lifeless wax! Why, damn you, you're going to know! Not just now, for It is resting after the sacrifice – but later. Oh, yes – you will not doubt the power of It then.'

As Rogers glanced toward the padlocked inner door Jones retrieved his hat and stick from a near-by bench.

'Very well, Rogers, let it be later. I must be going now, but I'll call around tomorrow afternoon. Think my advice over and see if it doesn't sound sensible. Ask Orabona what he thinks, too.'

Rogers actually bared his teeth in wild-beast fashion.

'Must be going now, eh? Afraid, after all! Afraid, for all your bold talk! You say the effigies are only wax, and yet you run away when I begin to prove that they aren't. You're like the fellows who take my standing bet that they daren't spend the night in the museum – they come boldly enough, but after an hour they shriek and hammer to get out! Want me to ask Orabona, eh? You two – always against me! You want to break down the coming earthly reign of It!'

Jones preserved his calm.

'No, Rogers – there's nobody against you. And I'm not afraid of your figures, either, much as I admire your skill. But we're both a bit nervous tonight, and I fancy some rest will do us good.'

Again Rogers checked his guest's departure.

'Not afraid, eh? – then why are you so anxious to go? Look here – do you or don't you dare to stay alone here in the dark? What's your hurry if you don't believe in It?'

Some new idea seemed to have struck Rogers, and Jones eyed him closely.

'Why, I've no special hurry – but what would be gained by my staying here alone? What would it prove? My only objection is that it isn't very comfortable for sleeping. What good would it do either of us?'

This time it was Jones who was struck with an idea. He continued in a tone of conciliation.

'See here, Rogers – I've just asked you what it would prove if I stayed, when we both know. It would prove that your effigies are just effigies, and that you oughtn't to let your imagination go the way it's been going lately. Suppose I *do* stay. If I stick it out till morning, will you agree to take a new view of things – go on a vacation for three months or so and let Orabona destroy that new thing of yours? Come, now – isn't that fair?'

The expression on the showman's face was hard to read. It was obvious that he was thinking quickly, and that of sundry conflicting emotions, malign triumph was getting the upper hand. His voice held a choking quality as he replied.

'Fair enough! *If you do stick it out,* I'll take your advice. But stick you must. We'll go out for dinner and come back. I'll lock you in the display room and go home. In the morning I'll come down ahead of Orabona – he comes half an hour before the rest – and see how you are. But don't try it unless you are *very* sure of your skepticism. Others have backed out – you have that chance. And I suppose a pounding on the outer door would always bring a constable. You may not like it so well after a while – you'll be in the same building, though not in the same room with It.'

As they left the rear door into the dingy courtyard, Rogers took with him the piece of burlap – weighted with a gruesome burden. Near the center of the court was a manhole, whose cover the showman lifted quietly, and with a shuddersome suggestion of familiarity. Burlap and all, the burden went down to the oblivion of a cloacal labyrinth. Jones shuddered, and almost shrank from the gaunt figure at his side as they emerged into the street.

By unspoken mutual consent, they did not dine together, but agreed to meet in front of the museum at eleven.

Jones hailed a cab, and breathed more freely when he had crossed Waterloo Bridge and was approaching the brilliantly lighted Strand. He dined at a quiet cafe, and subsequently went to his home in Portland Place to bathe and get a few things. Idly he wondered what Rogers was doing. He had heard that the man had a vast, dismal house in the Walworth Road, full of obscure and forbidden books, occult paraphernalia, and wax images which he did not choose to place on exhibition. Orabona, he understood, lived in separate quarters in the same house.

At eleven Jones found Rogers waiting by the basement door in Southwark Street. Their words were few, but each seemed taut with a menacing tension. They agreed that the vaulted exhibition room alone should form the scene of the vigil, and Rogers did not insist that the watcher sit in the special adult alcove of supreme horrors. The showman, having extinguished all the lights with switches in the workroom, locked the door of that crypt with one of the keys on his crowded ring. Without shaking hands he passed out the street door, locked it after him, and stamped up the worn steps to the sidewalk outside. As his tread receded, Jones realized that the long, tedious vigil had commenced.

2

Later, in the utter blackness of the great arched cellar, Jones cursed the childish *näiveté* which had brought him there. For the first half-hour he had kept flashing on his pocket-light at intervals, but now just sitting in the dark on one of the visitors' benches had become a more nerve-wracking thing. Every time the beam shot out it lighted up some morbid, grotesque object – a guillotine, a nameless hybrid monster, a pasty-bearded face crafty with evil, a body with red torrents streaming from a severed throat. Jones knew that no sinister reality was attached to these things, but after that first half-hour he preferred not to see them.

Why he had bothered to humor that madman he could scarcely imagine. It would have been much simpler merely to have let him alone, or to have called in a mental specialist. Probably, he reflected, it was the fellow-feeling of one artist for another. There was so much genius in Rogers that he deserved every possible chance to be helped quietly out of his growing mania. Any man who could imagine and construct the incredibly life-like things that he had produced was surely not far from actual greatness. He had the fancy of a Sime or a Doré joined to the minute, scientific craftsmanship of a Blatschka. Indeed, he had done for the world of nightmare what the Blatschkas with their marvelously accurate plant models of finely wrought and colored glass had done for the world of botany.

At midnight the strokes of a distant clock filtered through the darkness, and Jones felt cheered by the message from a still-surviving outside world. The vaulted museum chamber was like a tomb – ghastly in its utter solitude. Even a mouse would be cheering company; yet Rogers had once boasted that – for 'certain reasons', as he said – no mice or even insects ever came near the place. That was very curious, yet it seemed to be true. The deadness and silence were virtually complete. If only something would make a sound! He shuffled his feet, and the echoes came spectrally out of the absolute stillness. He coughed, but there was something mocking in the staccato reverberations. He could not, he vowed, begin talking to himself. That meant nervous disintegration. Time seemed to pass with abnormal and disconcerting slowness. He could have sworn that hours had elapsed since he last flashed the light on his watch, yet here was only the stroke of midnight.

He wished that his senses were not so preternaturally keen. Something in the darkness and stillness seemed to have sharpened them, so that they responded to faint intimations hardly strong enough to be called true impressions. His ears seemed at times to catch a faint, elusive susurrus which could not *quite* be identified with the nocturnal hum of the squalid streets outside, and he thought of vague, irrelevant things like the music of the spheres and the unknown, inaccessible life of alien dimensions pressing on our own. Rogers often speculated about such things.

The floating specks of light in his blackness-drowned eyes seemed inclined to take on curious symmetries of pattern and motion. He had often wondered about those strange rays from the unplumbed abyss which scintillate before us in the absence of all earthly illumination, but he had never known any that behaved just as these were behaving. They lacked the restful aimlessness of ordinary light-specks – suggesting some will and purpose remote from any terrestrial conception.

Then there was that suggestion of odd stirrings. Nothing was open, yet in spite of the general draftlessness Jones felt that the air was not uniformly quiet. There were intangible variations in pressure – not quite decided enough to suggest the loathsome pawings of unseen elementals. It was abnormally chilly, too. He did not like any of this. The air tasted salty, as if it were mixed with the brine of dark subterrene waters, and there was a bare hint of some odor of ineffable mustiness. In the daytime he had never noticed that the waxen figures had an odor. Even now that half-received hint was not the way wax figures ought to smell. It was more like the faint smell of specimens in a natural-history museum. Curious, in view of Rogers' claims that his figures were not all artificial – indeed, it was probably that claim which made one's imagination conjure up the olfactory suspicion. One must guard against excesses of imagination – had not such things driven poor Rogers mad?

But the utter loneliness of this place was frightful. Even the distant chimes seemed to come from across cosmic gulfs. It made Jones think of that insane picture which Rogers had showed him – the wildly carved chamber with the cryptic throne which the fellow had claimed was part of a three-million-year-old ruin in the shunned and inaccessible solitudes of the Arctic. Perhaps Rogers had been to Alaska, but that picture was certainly nothing but stage scenery. It couldn't normally be otherwise, with all that carving and those terrible symbols. And that monstrous shape supposed to have been found on that throne – what a flight of diseased fancy! Jones wondered just how far he actually was from the insane masterpiece in wax – probably it was kept behind that heavy, padlocked plank door leading somewhere out of the workroom. But it would never do to brood about a waxen image. Was not the present room full of such things, some of them scarcely less horrible than the dreadful 'IT'? And beyond a thin canvas screen on the left was the 'Adults only' alcove with its nameless phantoms of delirium.

The proximity of the numberless waxen shapes began to get on Jones's nerves more and more as the quarter-hours wore on. He knew the museum so well that he could not get rid of their usual images even in the total darkness. Indeed, the darkness had the effect of adding to the remembered images certain very disturbing imaginative overtones. The guillotine seemed to creak, and the bearded face of Landru – slayer of his fifty wives – twisted itself into expressions of monstrous menace. From the severed throat of Madame Demers a hideous bubbling sound seemed to emanate, while the headless, legless victim of a trunk murder tried to edge closer and closer on its gory stumps. Jones began shutting his eyes to see if that would dim the images, but found it was useless. Besides, when he shut his eyes the strange, purposeful patterns of light-specks became more disturbingly pronounced.

Then suddenly he began trying to keep the hideous images he had formerly been trying to banish. He tried to keep them because they were giving place to still more hideous ones. In spite of himself his memory began reconstructing the utterly non-human blasphemies that lurked in the obscurer corners, and these lumpish hybrid growths oozed and wriggled toward him as though hunting him down in a circle. Black Tsathoggua molded itself from a toad-like gargoyle to a long, sinuous line with hundreds of rudimentary feet, and a lean, rubbery night-gaunt spread its wings as if to advance and smother the watcher. Jones braced himself to keep from screaming. He knew he was reverting to the traditional terrors of his childhood, and resolved to use his adult reason to keep the phantoms at bay. It helped a bit, he found, to flash the light again. Frightful as were the images it showed, these were not as bad as what his fancy called out of the utter blackness.

But there were drawbacks. Even in the light of his torch he could not help suspecting a slight, furtive trembling on the part of the canvas partition screening off the terrible 'Adults only' alcove. He knew what lay beyond, and shivered. Imagination called up the shocking forms of fabulous Yog-Sothoth – only a congeries of iridescent globes, yet stupendous in its malign suggestiveness. What was this accursed mass slowly floating toward him and bumping on the partition that stood in the way? A small bulge in the canvas far to the right suggested the sharp horn of Gnoph-keh, the hairy myth-thing of the Greenland ice, that walked sometimes on two legs, sometimes on four, and sometimes on six. To get this stuff out of his head Jones walked boldly toward the hellish alcove with torch burning steadily. Of course, none of his fears was true. Yet were not the long, facial tentacles of great Cthulhu actually swaying, slowly and insidiously? He knew they were flexible, but he had not realized that the draft caused by his advance was enough to set them in motion.

Returning to his former seat outside the alcove, he shut his eyes and let the symmetrical light-specks do their worst. The distant clock boomed a single stroke. Could it be only one? He flashed the light on his watch and saw that it was precisely that hour. It would be hard indeed waiting for morning. Rogers would be down at about eight o'clock, ahead of even Orabona. It would be light outside in the main basement long before that, but none of it could penetrate here. All the windows in this basement had been bricked up but the three small ones facing the court. A pretty bad wait, all told.

His ears were getting most of the hallucinations now – for he could swear he heard stealthy, plodding footsteps in the workroom beyond the closed and locked door. He had no business thinking of that unexhibited horror which Rogers called 'It.' The thing was a contamination – it had driven its maker mad, and now even its picture was calling up imaginative terrors. It was very obviously beyond that padlocked door of heavy planking. Those steps were certainly pure imagination.

Then he thought he heard the key turn in the workroom door. Flashing on his torch, he saw nothing but the ancient six-panelled portal in its proper position. Again he tried darkness and closed his eyes, but there followed a harrowing illusion of creaking – not the guillotine this time, but the slow, furtive opening of the workroom door. He would not scream. Once he screamed, he would be lost. There was a sort of padding or shuffling audible now, and it was slowly advancing toward him. He must retain command of himself. Had he not done so when the nameless brain-shapes tried to close in on him? The shuffling crept nearer, and his resolution failed. He did not scream but merely gulped out a challenge.

'Who goes there? Who are you? What do you want?'

There was no answer, but the shuffling kept on. Jones did not know which he feared most to do – turn on his flashlight or stay in the dark while the thing crept upon him. This thing was different, he felt profoundly, from the other terrors of the evening. His fingers and throat worked spasmodically. Silence was impossible, and the suspense of utter blackness was beginning to be the most intolerable of all conditions. Again he cried out hysterically – 'Halt! Who goes there?' – as he switched on the revealing beam of his torch. Then, paralyzed by what he saw, he dropped the flashlight and screamed – not once but many times.

Shuffling toward him in the darkness was the gigantic, blasphemous form of a black thing not wholly ape and not wholly insect. Its hide hung loosely upon its frame, and its rugose, dead-eyed rudiment of a head swayed drunkenly from side to side. Its forepaws were extended, with talons spread wide, and its whole body was taut with murderous malignity despite its utter lack of facial expression. After the screams and the final coming of darkness it leaped, and in a moment had Jones pinned to the floor. There was no struggle for the watcher had fainted.

Jones's fainting spell could not have lasted more than a moment, for the nameless thing was apishly dragging him through the darkness when he began recovering consciousness. What started him fully awake were the sounds which the thing was making – or rather, the voice with which it was making them. That voice was human, and it was familiar.

Only one living being could be behind the hoarse, feverish accents which were chanting to an unknown horror.

'Iä! Iä!' it was howling. 'I am coming, O Rhan-Tegoth, coming with the nourishment. You have waited long and fed ill, but now you shall have what was promised. That and more, for instead of Orabona it will be one of the high degree who had doubted you. You shall crush and drain him, with all his doubts, and grow strong thereby. And ever after among men he shall be shown as a monument to your glory. Rhan-Tegoth, infinite and invincible, I am your slave and high-priest. You are hungry, and I shall provide. I read the sign and have led you forth. I shall feed you with blood, and you shall feed me with power. Iä! Shub-Niggurath! The Goat with a Thousand Young!'

In an instant all the terrors of the night dropped from Jones like a discarded cloak. He was again master of his mind, for he knew the very earthly and material peril he had to deal with. This was no monster of fable, but a dangerous madman. It was Rogers, dressed in some nightmare covering of his own insane designing, and about to make a frightful sacrifice to the devil-god he had fashioned out of wax. Clearly, he must have entered the workroom from the rear courtyard, donned his disguise, and then advanced to seize his neatly-trapped and fear-broken victim. His strength was prodigious, and if he was to be thwarted, one must act quickly. Counting on the madman's confidence in his unconsciousness he determined to take him by surprise, while his grasp was relatively lax. The feel of a threshold told him he was crossing into the pitch-black workroom.

With the strength of mortal fear Jones made a sudden spring from the half-recumbent posture in which he was being dragged. For an instant he was free of the astonished maniac's hands, and in another instant a lucky lunge in the dark had put his own hands at his captor's weirdly concealed throat. Simultaneously Rogers gripped him again, and without further preliminaries the two were locked in a desperate struggle of life and death. Jones's athletic training, without doubt, was his sole salvation; for his mad assailant, freed from every inhibition of fair play, decency, or even self-preservation, was an engine of savage destruction as formidable as a wolf or panther.

Guttural cries sometimes punctured the hideous tussle in the dark. Blood spurted, clothing ripped, and Jones at last felt the actual throat of the maniac, shorn of its spectral mask. He spoke not a word, but put every ounce of energy into the defense of his life. Rogers kicked, gouged, butted, bit, clawed, and spat – yet found strength to yelp out actual sentences at times. Most of his speech was in a ritualistic jargon full of references to 'It' or 'Rhan-Tegoth,' and to Jones's overwrought nerves it seemed as if the cries echoed from an infinite distance of demoniac snortings and bayings. Toward the last they were rolling on the floor, overturning benches or striking against the walls and the brick foundations of the central melting-furnace. Up to the very end Jones could not be certain of saving himself, but chance finally intervened in his favor. A jab of his knee against Rogers' chest produced a general relaxation, and a moment later he knew he had won.

Though hardly able to hold himself up, Jones rose and stumbled about the walls seeking the light-switch – for his flashlight was gone, together with most of his clothing. As he lurched along he dragged his limp opponent with him, fearing a sudden attack when the madman came to. Finding the switch-box, he fumbled till he had the right handle. Then, as the wildly disordered workroom burst into sudden radiance, he set about binding Rogers with such cords and belts as he could easily find. The fellow's disguise – or what was left of it – seemed to be made of a puzzling queer sort of leather. For some reason it made Jones's flesh crawl to touch it, and there seemed to be an alien, rusty odor about it. In the normal clothes beneath it was Rogers' key-ring, and this the exhausted victor seized as his final passport to freedom. The shades at the small, slit-like windows were all securely drawn, and he let them remain so.

Washing off the blood of battle at a convenient sink, Jones donned the most ordinary-looking and least ill-fitting clothes he could find on the costume hooks. Testing the door to the courtyard, he found it fastened with a spring-lock which did not require a key from the inside. He kept the key-ring, however, to admit him on his return with aid – for plainly, the thing to do was to call in an alienist. There was no telephone in the museum, but it would not take long to find an all-night restaurant or chemist's shop where one could be had. He had almost opened the door to go when a torrent of hideous abuse from across the room told him that Rogers – whose visible injuries were confined to a long, deep scratch down the left cheek – had regained consciousness.

'Fool! Spawn of North-Yidik and effluvium of K'thun! Son of the dogs that howl in the maelstrom of Azathoth! You would have been sacred and immortal, and now you are betraying It and Its priest! Beware – for It is hungry! It would have been Orabona – that damned treacherous dog ready to turn against me and It – but I give you the honor instead. Now you must both beware, for It is not gentle without Its priest.

'Iä! Iä! Vengeance is at hand! Do you know you would have been immortal? Look at the furnace! There is a fire ready to light, and there is wax in the kettle. I would have done with you as I have done with other once-living forms. Hei! You, who have vowed all my effigies are waxen, would have become a waxen effigy yourself! The furnace was all ready! When It had had its fill, and you were like that dog I showed you, I would have made your flattened, punctured fragments immortal! Wax would have done it. Haven't you said I'm a great artist? Wax in every pore – wax over every square inch of you – Iä! Iä! And ever after the world would have looked at your mangled carcass and wondered how I ever imagined and made such a thing! Hei! and Orabona would have come next, and others after him – and thus would my waxen family have grown!

'Dog – do you still think I *made* all my effigies? Why not say *preserved*? You know by this time the strange places I've been to, and the strange things I've brought back. Coward – you could never face the dimensional shambler whose hide I put on to scare you – the mere sight of it alive, or even the full-fledged thought of it, would kill you instantly with fright! Iä! Iä! It waits hungry for the blood that is the life!'

Rogers, propped against the wall, swayed to and fro in his bonds.

'See here, Jones – if I let you go will you let me go? It must be taken care of by Its high priest. Orabona will be enough to keep It alive – and when he is finished I will make his fragments immortal in wax for the world to see. It could have been you, but you have rejected the honor. I won't bother you again. Let me go, and I will share with you the power that It will bring me. Iä! Iä! Great is Rhan-Tegoth! Let me go! Let me go! It is starving down there beyond that door, and if It dies the Old Ones can never come back. Hei! Hei! Let me go!'

Jones merely shook his head, though the hideousness of the showman's imaginings revolted him. Rogers, now staring wildly at the padlocked plank door, thumped his head again and again against the brick wall and kicked with his tightly bound ankles. Jones was afraid he would injure himself, and advanced to bind him more firmly to some stationary object. Writhing, Rogers edged away from him and set up a series of frenetic ululations whose utter, monstrous unhumanness was appalling, and whose sheer volume was almost incredible. It seemed impossible that any human throat could produce noises so loud and piercing, and Jones felt that if this continued there would be no need to telephone for aid. It could not be long before a constable would investigate, even granting that there were no listening neighbors in this deserted warehouse district.

'Wza-y'ei! Wza-y'ei!' howled the madman. *'Y'kaa haa bho – ii, Rhan-Tegoth – Cthulhu fthagn – Ei! Ei! Ei! Ei! – Rhan-Tegoth. Rhan-Tegoth, Rhan-Tegoth!'*

The tautly trussed creature, who had started squirming his way across the littered floor, now reached the padlocked plank door and commenced knocking his head thunderously against it. Jones dreaded the task of binding him further, and wished he were not so exhausted from the previous struggle. This violent aftermath was getting hideously on his nerves, and he began to feel a return of the nameless qualms he had felt in the dark. Everything about Rogers and his museum was so hellishly morbid and suggestive of black vistas beyond life! It was loathsome to think of the waxen masterpiece of abnormal genius which must at this very moment be lurking close at hand in the blackness beyond the heavy, padlocked door.

And now something happened which sent an additional chill down Jones's spine, and caused every hair – even the tiny growth on the backs of his hands – to bristle with a vague fright beyond classification. Rogers had suddenly stopped screaming and beating his head against the stout plank door, and was straining up to a sitting posture, head cocked on one side as if listening intently for something. All at once a smile of devilish triumph overspread his face, and he began speaking intelligibly again – this time in a hoarse whisper contrasting oddly with his former stentorian howling.

'Listen, fool! Listen hard! *It* has heard me, and is coming. Can't you hear It splashing out of Its tank down there at the end of the runway? I dug it deep, because there was nothing too good for It. It is amphibious, you know – you saw the gills in the picture. It came to the earth from lead-gray Yuggoth, where the cities are under the warm deep sea. It can't stand up in there – too tall – has to sit or crouch. Let me get my keys – we must let It out and kneel down before It. Then we will go out and find a dog or cat – or perhaps a drunken man – to give It the nourishment It needs.'

It was not what the madman said, but the way he said it, that disorganized Jones so badly. The utter, insane confidence and sincerity in that crazed whisper were damnably contagious. Imagination, with such a stimulus, could find an active menace in the devilish wax figure that lurked unseen just beyond the heavy planking. Eyeing the door in unholy fascination, Jones noticed that it bore several distinct cracks, though no marks of violent treatment were visible on this side. He wondered how large a room or closet lay behind it, and how the waxen figure was arranged. The maniac's idea of a tank and runway was as clever as all his other imaginings.

Then, in one terrible instant, Jones completely lost the power to draw breath. The leather belt he had seized for Rogers' further strapping fell from his limp hands, and a spasm of shivering convulsed him from head to foot. He might have known the place would drive him mad as it had driven Rogers – and now he *was* mad. He was mad, for he now harbored hallucinations more weird than any which had assailed him earlier that night. The madman was bidding him hear the splashing of a mythical monster in a tank beyond the door – and now, God help him, *he did hear it!*

Rogers saw the spasm of horror reach Jones's face and transform it to a staring mask of fear. He cackled.

'At last, fool, you believe! At last you know! You hear It and It comes! Get me my keys, fool – we must do homage and serve It!'

But Jones was past paying attention to any human words, mad or sane. Phobic paralysis held him immobile and half conscious, with wild images racing phantasmagorically through his helpless imagination. There *was* a splashing. There *was* padding or shuffling, as of great wet paws on a solid surface. Something *was* approaching. Into his nostrils, from the cracks in that nightmare plank door, poured a noisome animal stench like and yet unlike that of the mammal cages at the zoological gardens in Regent's Park.

He did not know now whether Rogers was talking or not. Everything real had faded away, and he was a statue obsessed with dreams and hallucinations so unnatural that they became almost objective and remote from him. He thought he heard a sniffing or snorting from the unknown gulf beyond the door, and when a sudden baying, trumpeting noise assailed his ears he could not feel sure that it came from the tightly bound maniac whose image swam uncertainly in his shaken vision. The photograph of that accursed, unseen wax thing persisted in floating through his consciousness. Such a thing had no right to exist. Had it not driven him mad?

Even as he reflected, a fresh evidence of madness beset him. Something, he thought, was fumbling with the latch of the heavy padlocked door. It was patting and pawing and pushing at the planks. There was a thudding on the stout wood, which grew louder and louder. The stench was horrible. And now the assault on that door from the inside was a malign, determined pounding like the strokes of a battering-ram. There was an ominous cracking – a splintering – a welling fetor – a falling plank – *a black paw ending in a crab-like claw. . . .*

'Help! Help! God help me! . . . Aaaaaaa! . . .'

With intense effort Jones is today able to recall a sudden bursting of his fear-paralysis into the liberation of frenzied automatic flight. What he evidently did must have paralleled curiously the wild, plunging flights of maddest nightmares; for he seems to have leaped across the disordered crypt at almost a single bound, yanked open the outside door, which closed and locked itself after him with a clatter, sprung up the worn stone steps three at a time, and raced frantically and aimlessly out of that dark cobblestoned court and through the squalid streets of Southwark.

Here the memory ends. Jones does not know how he got home, and there is no evidence of his having hired a cab. Probably he raced all the way by blind instinct – over Waterloo Bridge, along the Strand and Charing Cross, and up Haymarket and Regent Street to his own neighborhood. He still had on the queer melange of museum costumes when he grew conscious enough to call the doctor.

A week later the nerve specialists allowed him to leave his bed and walk in the open air.

But he had not told the specialists much. Over his whole experience hung a pall of madness and nightmare, and he felt that silence was the only course. When he was up, he scanned intently all the papers which had accumulated since that hideous night, but found no reference to anything queer at the museum. How much, after all, had been reality? Where did reality end and morbid dream begin? Had his mind gone wholly to pieces in that dark exhibition chamber, and had the whole fight with Rogers been a fantasm of fever? It would help to put him on his feet if he could settle some of these maddening points. He *must* have seen that damnable photograph of the wax image called 'It,' for no brain but Rogers' could ever have conceived such a blasphemy.

It was a fortnight before he dared to enter Southwark Street again. He went in the middle of the morning, when there was the greatest amount of sane, wholesome activity around the ancient, crumbling shops and warehouses. The museum's sign was still there, and as he approached he saw that the place was open. The gateman nodded in pleasant recognition as he summoned up the courage to enter, and in the vaulted chamber below an attendant touched his cap cheerfully. Perhaps everything had been a dream. Would he dare to knock at the door of the workroom and look for Rogers?

Then Orabona advanced to greet him. His dark, sleek face was a trifle sardonic, but Jones felt that he was not unfriendly. He spoke with a trace of accent.

'Good morning, Mr Jones. It is some time since we have seen you here. Did you wish Mr Rogers? I'm sorry, but he is away. He had word of business in America, and had to go. Yes, it was very sudden. I am in charge now – here, and at the house. I try to maintain Mr Rogers' high standard – till he is back.'

The foreigner smiled – perhaps from affability alone. Jones scarcely knew how to reply, but managed to mumble out a few inquiries about the day after his last visit. Orabona seemed greatly amused by the questions, and took considerable care in framing his replies.

'Oh, yes, Mr Jones – the 28th of last month. I remember it for many reasons. In the morning – before Mr Rogers got here, you understand – I found the workroom in quite a mess. There was a great deal of – cleaning up –to do. There had been – late work, you see. Important new specimen given its secondary baking process. I took complete charge when I came.

'It was a hard specimen to prepare – but of course Mr Rogers had taught me a great deal. He is, as you know, a very great artist. When he came he helped me complete the specimen – helped very materially, I assure you – but he left soon without even greeting the men. As I tell you, he was called away suddenly. There were important chemical reactions involved. They made loud noises – in fact, some teamsters in the court outside fancy they heard several pistol shots – very amusing idea!

'As for the new specimen – that matter is very unfortunate. It is a great masterpiece – designed and made, you understand, by Mr Rogers. He will see about it when he gets back.'

Again Orabona smiled.

'The police, you know. We put it on display a week ago, and there were two or three faintings. One poor fellow had an epileptic fit in front of it. You see, it is a trifle – stronger – than the rest. Larger, for one thing. Of course, it was in the adult alcove. The next day a couple of men from Scotland Yard looked it over and said it was too morbid to be shown. Said we'd have to remove it. It was a tremendous shame – such a masterpiece of art – but I didn't feel justified in appealing to the courts in Mr Rogers' absence. He would not like so much publicity with the police now – but when he gets back – when he gets back—'

For some reason or other Jones felt a mounting tide of uneasiness and repulsion. But Orabona was continuing.

'You are a connoisseur, Mr Jones. I am sure I violate no law in offering you a private view. It may be – subject, of course, to Mr Rogers' wishes – that we shall destroy the specimen some day – but that would be a crime.'

Jones had a powerful impulse to refuse the sight and flee precipitately, but Orabona was leading him forward by the arm with an artist's enthusiasm. The adult alcove, crowded with nameless horrors, held no visitors. In the farther corner a large niche had been curtained off, and to this the smiling assistant advanced.

'You must know, Mr Jones, that the title of this specimen is "The Sacrifice to Rhan-Tegoth."'

Jones started violently, but Orabona appeared not to notice.

'The shapeless, colossal god is a feature in certain obscure legends which Mr Rogers had studied. All nonsense, of course, as you've so often assured Mr Rogers. It is supposed to have come from outer space, and to have lived in the Arctic three million years ago. It treated its sacrifices rather peculiarly and horribly, as you shall see. Mr Rogers had made it fiendishly life-like – even to the face of the victim.'

Now trembling violently, Jones clung to the brass railing in front of the curtained niche. He almost reached out to stop Orabona when he saw the curtain beginning to swing aside, but some conflicting impulse held him back. The foreigner smiled triumphantly.

'Behold!'

Jones reeled in spite of his grip on the railing.

'God! – great God!'

Fully ten feet high despite a shambling, crouching attitude expressive of infinite cosmic malignancy, a monstrosity of unbelievable horror was shown starting forward from a cyclopean ivory throne covered with grotesque carvings. In the central pair of its six legs it bore a crushed, flattened, distorted, bloodless thing, riddled with a million punctures, and in places seared as with some pungent acid. Only the mangled head of the victim, lolling upside down at one side, revealed that it represented something once human.

The monster itself needed no title for one who had seen a certain hellish photograph. That damnable print had been all too faithful; yet it could not carry the full horror which lay in the gigantic actuality. The globular torso – the bubble-like suggestion of a head – the three fishy eyes – the foot-long proboscis – the bulging gills – the monstrous capillation of asp-like suckers – the six sinuous limbs with their black paws and crab-like claws – God! the familiarity of that black paw ending in a crab-like claw! . . .

Orabona's smile was utterly damnable. Jones choked, and stared at the hideous exhibit with a mounting fascination which perplexed and disturbed him. What half-revealed horror was holding and forcing him to look longer and search out details? This had driven Rogers mad . . . Rogers, supreme artist . . . said they weren't artificial. . . .

Then he localized the thing that held him. It was the crushed waxen victim's lolling head, and something that it implied. This head was not entirely devoid of a face, and that face was familiar. It was like the mad face of poor Rogers. Jones peered closer, hardly knowing why he was driven to do so. Wasn't it natural for a mad egotist to mold his own features into his masterpiece? Was there anything more that subconscious vision had seized on and suppressed in sheer terror?

The wax of the mangled face had been handled with boundless dexterity. Those punctures – how perfectly they reproduced the myriad wounds somehow inflicted on that poor dog! But there was something more. On the left cheek one could trace an irregularity which seemed outside the general scheme – as if the sculptor had sought to cover up a defect of his first modelling. The more Jones looked at it, the more mysteriously it horrified him – and then, suddenly, he remembered a circumstance which brought his horror to a head. That night of hideousness – the tussle – the bound madman – *and the long, deep scratch down the left cheek of the actual living Rogers. . . .*

Jones, releasing his desperate clutch on the railing, sank in a total faint.

Orabona continued to smile.

THE CRAWLING CHAOS

by H. P. Lovecraft and Elizabeth Berkeley

Of the pleasures and pains of opium much has been written. The ecstasies and horrors of De Quincey and the *paradis artificiels* of Baudelaire are preserved and interpreted with an art which makes them immortal, and the world knows well the beauty, the terror and the mystery of those obscure realms into which the inspired dreamer is transported. But much as has been told, no man has yet dared intimate the *nature* of the phantasms thus unfolded to the mind, or hint at the *direction* of the unheard-of roads along whose ornate and exotic course the partaker of the drug is so irresistibly borne. De Quincey was drawn back into Asia, that teeming land of nebulous shadows whose hideous antiquity is so impressive that 'the vast age of the race and name overpowers the sense of youth in the individual,' but farther than that he dared not go. Those who *have* gone farther seldom returned; and even when they have, they have been either silent or quite mad. I took opium but once – in the year of the plague, when doctors sought to deaden the agonies they could not cure. There was an overdose – my physician was worn out with horror and exertion – and I travelled very far indeed. In the end I returned and lived, but my nights are filled with strange memories, nor have I ever permitted a doctor to give me opium again.

The pain and pounding in my head had been quite unendurable when the drug was administered. Of the future I had no heed; to escape, whether by cure, unconsciousness, or death, was all that concerned me. I was partly delirious, so that it is hard to place the exact moment of transition, but I think the effect must have begun shortly before the pounding ceased to be painful. As I have said, there was an overdose; so my reactions were probably far from normal. The sensation of falling, curiously dissociated from the idea of gravity or direction, was paramount; though there was a subsidiary impression of unseen throngs in incalculable profusion, throngs of infinitely diverse nature, but all more or less related to me.

Sometimes it seemed less as though I were falling, than as though the universe or the ages were falling past me. Suddenly my pain ceased, and I began to associate the pounding with an external rather than internal force. The falling had ceased also, giving place to a sensation of uneasy, temporary rest; and when I listened closely, I fancied the pounding was that of the vast, inscrutable sea as its sinister, colossal breakers lacerated some desolate shore after a storm of titanic magnitude. Then I opened my eyes.

For a moment my surroundings seemed confused, like a projected image hopelessly out of focus, but gradually I realized my solitary presence in a strange and beautiful room lighted by many windows. Of the exact nature of the apartment I could form no idea, for my thoughts were still far from settled, but I noticed vari-coloured rugs and draperies, elaborately fashioned tables, chairs, ottomans, and divans, and delicate vases and ornaments which conveyed a suggestion of the exotic without being actually alien. These things I noticed, yet they were not long uppermost in my mind. Slowly but inexorably crawling upon my consciousness and rising above every other impression, came a dizzying fear of the unknown; a fear all the greater because I could not analyse it, and seeming to concern a stealthily approaching menace; not death, but some nameless, unheard-of thing inexpressibly more ghastly and abhorrent.

Presently I realized that the direct symbol and excitant of my fear was the hideous pounding whose incessant reverberations throbbed maddeningly against my exhausted brain. It seemed to come from a point outside and below the edifice in which I stood, and to associate itself with the most terrifying mental images. I felt that some horrible scene or object lurked beyond the silk-hung walls, and shrank from glancing through the arched, latticed windows that opened so bewilderingly on every hand. Perceiving shutters attached to these windows, I closed them all, averting my eyes from the exterior as I did so. Then, employing a flint and steel which I found on one of the small tables, I lit the many candles reposing about the walls in arabesque sconces. The added sense of security brought by closed shutters and artificial light calmed my nerves to some degree, but I could not shut out the monotonous pounding. Now that I was calmer, the sound became as fascinating as it was fearful, and I felt a contradictory desire to seek out its source despite my still powerful shrinking. Opening a portiere at the side of the room nearest the pounding, I beheld a small and richly draped corridor ending in a carven door and large oriel window. To this window I was irresistibly drawn, though my ill-defined apprehensions seemed almost equally bent on holding me back. As I approached it I could see a chaotic whirl of waters in the distance. Then, as I attained it and glanced out on all sides, the stupendous picture of my surroundings burst upon me with full and devastating force.

I beheld such a sight as I have never beheld before, and which no living person can have seen save in the delirium of fever or the inferno of opium. The building stood on a narrow point of land – or what was *now* a narrow point of land – fully three hundred feet above what must lately have been a seething vortex of mad waters. On either side of the house there fell a newly washed-out precipice of red earth, whilst ahead of me the hideous waves were still rolling in frightfully, eating away the land with ghastly monotony and deliberation. Out a mile or more there rose and fell menacing breakers at least fifty feet in height, and on the far horizon ghoulish black clouds of grotesque contour were resting and brooding like unwholesome vultures. The waves were dark and purplish, almost black, and clutched at the yielding red mud of the bank as if with uncouth, greedy hands. I could not but feel that some noxious marine mind had declared a war of extermination upon all the solid ground, perhaps abetted by the angry sky.

Recovering at length from the stupor into which this unnatural spectacle had thrown me, I realized that my actual physical danger was acute. Even whilst I gazed, the bank had lost many feet, and it could not be long before the house would fall undermined into the awful pit of lashing waves. Accordingly I hastened to the opposite side of the edifice, and finding a door, emerged at once, locking it after me with a curious key which had hung inside. I now beheld more of the strange region about me, and marked a singular division which seemed to exist in the hostile ocean and firmament. On each side of the jutting promontory different conditions held sway. At my left as I faced inland was a gently heaving sea with great green waves rolling peacefully in under a brightly shining sun. Something about that sun's nature and position made me shudder, but I could not then tell, and cannot tell now, what it was. At my right also was the sea, but it was blue, calm, and only gently undulating, while the sky above it was darker and the washed-out bank more nearly white than reddish.

I now turned my attention to the land, and found occasion for fresh surprise; for the vegetation resembled nothing I had ever seen or read about. It was apparently tropical or at least sub-tropical – a conclusion borne out by the intense heat of the air. Sometimes I thought I could trace strange analogies with the flora of my native land, fancying that the well-known plants and shrubs might assume such forms under a radical change of climate; but the gigantic and omnipresent palm trees were plainly foreign. The house I had just left was very small – hardly more than a cottage – but its material was evidently marble, and its architecture was weird and composite, involving a quaint fusion of Western and Eastern forms. At the corners were Corinthian columns, but the red tile roof was like that of a Chinese pagoda. From the door inland there stretched a path of singularly white sand, about four feet wide, and lined on either side with stately palms and unidentifiable flowering shrubs and plants. It lay toward the side of the promontory where the sea was blue and the bank rather whitish. Down this path I felt impelled to flee, as if pursued by some malignant spirit from the pounding ocean. At first it was slightly uphill, then I reached a gentle crest. Behind me I saw the scene I had left; the entire point with the cottage and the black water, with the green sea on one side and the blue sea on the other, and a curse unnamed and unnameable lowering over all. I never saw it again, and often wonder. . . . After this last look I strode ahead and surveyed the inland panorama before me.

The path, as I have intimated, ran along the right-hand shore as one went inland. Ahead and to the left I now viewed a magnificent valley comprising thousands of acres, and covered with a swaying growth of tropical grass higher than my head. Almost at the limit of vision was a colossal palm tree which seemed to fascinate and beckon me. By this time wonder and escape from the imperilled peninsula had largely dissipated my fear, but as I paused and sank fatigued to the path, idly digging with my hands into the warm, whitish-golden sand, a new and acute sense of danger seized me.

Some terror in the swishing tall grass seemed added to that of the diabolically pounding sea, and I started up crying aloud and disjointedly, 'Tiger? Tiger? Is it Tiger? Beast? Beast? Is it a Beast that I am afraid of?' My mind wandered back to an ancient and classical story of tigers which I had read; I strove to recall the author, but had difficulty. Then in the midst of my fear I remembered that the tale was by Rudyard Kipling; nor did the grotesqueness of deeming him an ancient author occur to me. I wished for the volume containing this story, and had almost started back toward the doomed cottage to procure it when my better sense and the lure of the palm prevented me.

Whether or not I could have resisted the backward beckoning without the counter-fascination of the vast palm tree, I do not know. This attraction was now dominant, and I left the path and crawled on hands and knees down the valley's slope despite my fear of the grass and the serpents it might contain. I resolved to fight for life and reason as long as possible against all menaces of sea or land, though I sometimes feared defeat as the maddening swish of the uncanny grass joined the still audible and irritating pounding of the distant breakers. I would frequently pause and put my hands to my ears for relief, but could never quite shut out the detestable sound. It was, as it seemed to me, only after ages that I finally dragged myself to the beckoning palm tree and lay quiet beneath its protecting shade.

There now ensued a series of incidents which transported me to the opposite extremes of ecstasy and horror; incidents which I tremble to recall and dare not seek to interpret. No sooner had I crawled beneath the overhanging foliage of the palm, than there dropped from its branches a young child of such beauty as I never beheld before. Though ragged and dusty, this being bore the features of a faun or demigod, and seemed almost to diffuse a radiance in the dense shadow of the tree. It smiled and extended its hand, but before I could arise and speak I heard in the upper air the exquisite melody of singing; notes high and low blent with a sublime and ethereal harmoniousness. The sun had by this time sunk below the horizon, and in the twilight I saw an aureole of lambent light encircled the child's head. Then in a tone of silver it addressed me: 'It is the end. They have come down through the gloaming from the stars. Now all is over, and beyond the

Arinurian streams we shall dwell blissfully in Teloe.' As the child spoke, I beheld a soft radiance through the leaves of the palm tree, and rising greeted a pair whom I knew to be the chief singers among those I had heard. A god and goddess they must have been, for such beauty is not mortal; and they took my hands, saying, 'Come, child, you have heard the voices, and all is well. In Teloe beyond the Milky Way and the Arinurian streams are cities all of amber and chalcedony. And upon their domes of many facets glisten the images of strange and beautiful stars. Under the ivory bridges of Teloe flow rivers of liquid gold bearing pleasure-barges bound for blossomy Cytharion of the Seven Suns. And in Teloe and Cytharion abide only youth, beauty, and pleasure, nor are any sounds heard, save of laughter, song, and the lute. Only the gods dwell in Teloe of the golden rivers, but among them shalt thou dwell.'

As I listened, enchanted, I suddenly became aware of a change in my surroundings. The palm tree, so lately overshadowing my exhausted form, was now some distance to my left and considerably below me. I was obviously floating in the atmosphere; companioned not only by the strange child and the radiant pair, but by a constantly increasing throng of half-luminous, vine-crowned youths and maidens with windblown hair and joyful countenance. We slowly ascended together, as if borne on a fragrant breeze which blew not from the earth but from the golden nebulae, and the child whispered in my ear that I must look always upward to the pathways of light, and never backward to the sphere I had just left. The youths and maidens now chanted mellifluous choriambics to the accompaniment of lutes, and I felt enveloped in a peace and happiness more profound than any I had in life imagined, when the intrusion of a single sound altered my destiny and shattered my soul. Through the ravishing strains of the singers and the lutanists, as if in mocking, daemoniac concord, throbbed from gulfs below the damnable, the detestable pounding of that hideous ocean. And as those black breakers beat their message into my ears I forgot the words of the child and looked back, down upon the doomed scene from which I thought I had escaped.

Down through the aether I saw the accursed earth turning, ever turning, with angry and tempestuous seas gnawing at wild desolate shores and dashing foam against the tottering towers of deserted cities. And under a ghastly moon there gleamed sights I can never describe, sights I can never forget; deserts of corpselike clay and jungles of ruin and decadence where once stretched the populous plains and villages of my native land, and maelstroms of frothing ocean where once rose the mighty temples of my forefathers. Around the northern pole steamed a morass of noisome growths and miasmal vapours, hissing before the onslaught of the ever-mounting waves that curled and fretted from the shuddering deep. Then a rending report clave the night, and athwart the desert of deserts appeared a smoking rift. Still the black ocean foamed and gnawed, eating away the desert on either side as the rift in the centre widened and widened.

There was now no land left but the desert, and still the fuming ocean ate and ate. All at once I thought even the pounding sea seemed afraid of something, afraid of dark gods of the inner earth that are greater than the evil god of waters, but even if it was it could not turn back; and the desert had suffered too much from those nightmare waves to help them now. So the ocean ate the last of the land and poured into the smoking gulf, thereby giving up all it had ever conquered. From the new-flooded lands it flowed again, uncovering death and decay; and from its ancient and immemorial bed it trickled loathsomely, uncovering nighted secrets of the years when Time was young and the gods unborn. Above the waves rose weedy remembered spires. The moon laid pale lilies of light on dead London, and Paris stood up from its damp grave to be sanctified with star-dust. Then rose spires and monoliths that were weedy but not remembered; terrible spires and monoliths of lands that men never knew were lands.

There was not any pounding now, but only the unearthly roaring and hissing of waters tumbling into the rift. The smoke of that rift had changed to steam, and almost hid the world as it grew denser and denser. It seared my face and hands, and when I looked to see how it affected my companions I found they had all disappeared. Then very suddenly it ended, and I knew no more till I awaked upon a bed of convalescence. As the cloud of steam from the Plutonic gulf finally concealed the entire surface from my sight, all the firmament shrieked at a sudden agony of mad reverberations which shook the trembling aether. In one delirious flash and burst it happened; one blinding, deafening holocaust of fire, smoke, and thunder that dissolved the wan moon as it sped outward to the void.

And when the smoke cleared away, and I sought to look upon the earth, I beheld against the background of cold, humorous stars only the dying sun and the pale mournful planets searching for their sister.

FOUR O'CLOCK

by Sonia Greene

About two in the morning I knew it was coming. The great black silences of night's depth told me, and a monstrous cricket, chirping with a persistence too hideous to be unmeaning, made it certain. It is to be at four o'clock – at four in the dusk before dawn, just as he said it would be. I had not fully believed it previously, because the prophecies of vindictive madmen are seldom to be taken with seriousness. Besides, I was not justly to be blamed for what had befallen him at four o'clock on that other morning; that terrible morning whose memory will never leave me. And when, at length, he had died and was buried in the ancient cemetery just across the road from my east windows, I was certain that his curse could not harm me. Had I not seen his lifeless clay securely pinned down by huge shovelfuls of mould? Might I not feel assured that his crumbling bones would be powerless to bring me the doom at a day and an hour so precisely stated? Such, indeed, had been my thoughts until this shocking night itself; this night of incredible chaos, of shattered certainties, and of nameless portents.

I had retired early, hoping fatuously to snatch a few hours of sleep despite the prophecy which haunted me. Now that the time was so close at hand, I found it harder and harder to dismiss the vague fears which had always lain beneath my conscious thoughts. As the cooling sheets soothed my fevered body, I could find nothing to soothe my still more fevered mind; but lay tossing and uneasily awake, trying first one position and then another in a desperate effort to banish with slumber that one damnable insistent notion – *that it is to occur at four o'clock.*

Was this frightful unrest due to my surroundings; to the fateful locality in which I was sojourning after so many years? Why, I now asked myself bitterly, had I permitted circumstance to place me on this night of all nights, in that well-remembered house and that well-remembered room whose east windows overlook the lonely road and the ancient country cemetery beyond? In my mind's eye every detaid of that unpretentious necropolis rose before me – its white fence, its ghost-like granite shafts, and the hovering auras of those on whom the worms fed. Finally the force of the conception led my vision to depths more remote and more forbidden, and I saw under the neglected grass the silent shapes of the things from which the auras came – the calm sleepers, the rotting things, the things which had twisted frantically in their coffins before sleep came, and the peaceful bones in every stage of disintegration from the complete and coherent skeleton to the huddled handful of dust. Most of all I envied the dust. Then new terror came as my fancy encountered *his* grave. Into that sepulchre I dared not let my thought stray, and I should have screamed had not something forestalled the malign power that pulled my mental sight. That something was a sudden gust of wind, sprung from nowhere amidst the calm night, which unfastened the shutter of the nearest window, throwing it back with a shivery slam and uncovering to my actual waking glance the antique cemetery itself, brooding spectrally beneath an early morning moon.

I speak of this gust as something merciful, yet know now that it was only transiently and mockingly so. For no sooner had my eyes compassed the moonlight scene than I became aware of a fresh omen, this time too unmistakable to be classed as an empty phantasm, which arose from among the gleaming tombs across the road. Having glanced with instinctive apprehension toward the spot where *he* lay mouldering – a spot cut off from my gaze by the window-frame – I perceived with trepidation the approach of an indescribable something which flowed menacingly from that very direction; a vague, vaporous, formless mass of greyish-white substance of spirit, dull and tenuous as yet, but every moment increasing in awesome and cataclysmic potentiality. Try as I might to dismiss it as a natural meteorological phenomenon, its fearsomely portentous and *deliberate* character grew upon me amidst new thrills of horror and apprehension; so that I was scarcely unprepared for the definitely purposeful and malevolent culmination which soon occurred. That culmination, bringing with it a hideous symbolic foreshadowing of the end, was equally simple and threatening. The vapor each moment thickened and piled up, assuming at last a half tangible aspect; while the surface toward me gradually became circular in outline, and markedly concave; as it slowly ceased its advance and stood spectrally at the end of the road. And as it stood there, faintly quivering in the damp night air under that unwholesome moon, I saw that its aspect was that of the pallid and gigantic dial of a distorted *clock*.

Hideous events now followed in demoniac succession. There took shape in the lower right-hand part of the vaporous dial a black and formidable creature, shapeless and only half seen, yet having four prominent claws which reached out greedily at me – claws redolent of noxious fatality in their very contour and location; since they formed too plainly the dreaded outlines, and filled too unmistakably the exact position, of the numeral IV on the quivering dial of doom. Presently the monstrosity stepped or wriggled out of the concave surface of the dial, and began to approach me by some unexplained kind of locomotion. The four talons, long, thin, and straight, were now seen to be tipped by disgusting, thread-like tentacles, each with a vile intelligence of its own, which groped about incessantly, slowly at first, but gradually increasing in velocity until I was nearly driven mad by the sheer dizziness of their motion. And as a crowning horror I began to hear all the subtle and cryptical noises that pierced the intensified night silence; a thousand-fold magnified, and in one voice reminding me of the abhorred hour of *four*. In vain I tried to pull up the coverlet to shut them out; in vain I tried to drown them with my screams. I was mute and paralyzed, yet agonizingly aware of every unnatural sight and sound in that devastating, moon-cursed stillness. Once I managed to get my head beneath the covers – once when the cricket's shrieking of that hideous phrase, *four-o'clock*, seemed about to shatter my brain – but that only aggravated the terror, making the roars of that detestable creature strike me like the blows of a titanic sledgehammer.

And now, as I withdrew my tortured head from its fruitless protection, I found augmented diabolism to harass my eyes. Upon the newly painted wall of my apartment, as if called forth by the tentacled monster from the tomb, there danced mockingly before me a myriad company of beings, black, grey, and white, such as only the fancy of the god-stricken might visualize. Some were of infinitesimal smallness; others covered vast areas. In minor details each had a grotesque and horrible individuality; in general outlines they all conformed to the same nightmare pattern despite their vastly varied size. Again I tried to shut out the abnormalities of the night, but vainly as before. The dancing things on the wall waxed and waned in magnitude, approaching and receding as they trod their morbid and menacing measure. And the aspect of each was that of some demon clock-face with one sinister hour always figured thereon – the dreaded, the doom-delivering hour of *four.*

Baffled in every attempt to shake off the circling and relentless delirium, I glanced once more toward the unshuttered window and beheld again the monster which had come from the grave. Horrible it had been before; indescribable it had now become. The creature, formerly of indeterminate substance, was now formed of red and malignant fire; and waved repulsively its four tentacled claws – unspeakable tongues of living flame. It stared and stared at me out of the blackness; sneeringly, mockingly; now advancing, now retiring. Then, in the tenebrous silence, those four writhing talons of fire beckoned invitingly to their demoniacally dancing counterparts on the walls, and seemed to beat time rhythmically to the shocking saraband till the world was one ghoulishly gyrating vortex of leaping, prancing, gliding, leering, taunting, threatening *four o'clocks.*

Somewhere, beginning afar off and advancing over the sphinx-like sea and the febrile marshes, I heard the early morning wind come soughing; faintly at first, then louder and louder until its unceasing burden flowed as a deluge of whirring, buzzing cacophony bringing always the hideous threat, '*four o'clock, four o'clock,* FOUR O'CLOCK.' Monotonously it grew from a whimper to a deafening roar, as of a giant cataract, but finally reached a climax and began to subside. As it receded into the distance it left upon my sensitive ears such a vibration as is left by the passing of a swift and ponderous railway train; this, and a stark dread whose intensity gave it something of the tranquility of resignation.

The end is near. All sound and vision have become one vast chaotic maelstrom of lethal, clamorous menace, wherein are fused all the ghastly and unhallowed four o'clocks which have existed since immemorial time began, and all which will exist in eternities to come. The flaming monster is advancing closely now, its charnel tentacles brushing my face and its talons curving hungrily as they grope toward my throat. At last I can see its face through the churning and phosphorescent vapors of the graveyard air, and with devastating pangs I realize that it is in essence an awful, colossal, gargoyle-like caricature of *his* face – the face of him from whose uneasy grave it has issued. Now I know that my doom is indeed sealed; that the wild threats of the madman were in truth the demon maledictions of a potent fiend, and that my innocence will prove no protection against the malign volition which craves a causeless vengeance. He is determined to pay me with interest for what he suffered at that spectral hour; determined to drag me out of the world into realms which only the mad and the devil-ridden know.

And as amidst the seething of hell's flames and the tumult of the damned those fiery claws point murderously at my throat, I hear upon the mantel the faint whirring sound of a timepiece; the whirring which tells me that it is about to strike the hour whose name now flows incessantly from the death-like and cavernous throat of the rattling, jeering, croaking grave-monster before me – the accursed, the infernal hour of *four o'clock.*

WINGED DEATH

by Hazel Heald

The Orange Hotel stands in High Street near the railway station in Bloemfontein, South Africa. On Sunday, January 24, 1932, four men sat shivering from terror in a room on its third floor. One was George C. Titteridge, proprietor of the hotel; another was police constable Ian De Witt of the Central Station; a third was Johannes Bogaert, the local coroner; the fourth, and apparently the least disorganized of the group, was Doctor Cornelius Van Keulen, the coroner's physician.

On the floor, uncomfortably evident amid the stifling summer heat, was the body of a dead man – but this was not what the four were afraid of. Their glances wandered from the table, on which lay a curious assortment of things, to the ceiling overhead, across whose smooth whiteness a series of huge, faltering alphabetical characters had somehow been scrawled in ink; and every now and then Doctor Van Keulen would glance half furtively at a worn leather blank-book which he held in his left hand. The horror of the four seemed about equally divided among the blank-book, the scrawled words on the ceiling, and a dead fly of peculiar aspect which floated in a bottle of ammonia on the table. Also on the table were an open inkwell, a pen and writing-pad, a physician's medical case, a bottle of hydrochloric acid, and a tumbler about a quarter full of black oxide of manganese.

The worn leather book was the journal of the dead man on the floor, and had at once made it clear that the name Frederick N. Mason, Mining Properties, Toronto, Canada, signed in the hotel register, was a false one. There were other things – terrible things – which it likewise made clear; and still other things of far greater terror at which it hinted hideously without making them clear or even fully believable. It was the half-belief of the four men, fostered by lives spent close to the black, settled secrets of brooding Africa, which made them shiver so violently in spite of the searing January heat.

The blank-book was not a large one, and the entries were in a fine handwriting, which, however, grew careless and nervous-looking toward the last. It consisted of a series of jottings at first rather irregularly spaced, but finally becoming daily. To call it a diary would not be quite correct, for it chronicled only one set of its writer's activities. Doctor Van Keulen recognized the name of the dead man the moment he opened the cover, for it was that of an eminent member of his own profession who had been largely connected with African matters. In another moment he was horrified to find his name linked with a dastardly crime officially unsolved, which had filled the newspapers some four months before. And the farther he read, the deeper grew his horror, awe, and sense of loathing and panic.

Here, in essence, is the text which the doctor read aloud in that sinister and increasingly noisome room while the three men around him breathed hard, fidgeted in their chairs, and darted frightened glances at the ceiling, the table, the thing on the floor, and one another:

JOURNAL OF
THOMAS SLAUENWITE, M.D.

Touching punishment of Henry Sargent Moore, Ph.D., of Brooklyn, New York, Professor of Invertebrate Biology in Columbia University, New York, N.Y. Prepared to be read after my death, for the satisfaction of making public the accomplishment of my revenge, which may otherwise never be imputed to me even if it succeeds.

January 5, 1929 – I have now fully resolved to kill Doctor Henry Moore, and a recent incident has shown me how I shall do it. From now on, I shall follow a consistent line of action; hence the beginning of this journal.

It is hardly necessary to repeat the circumstances which have driven me to this course, for the informed part of the public is familiar with all the salient facts. I was born in Trenton, New Jersey, on April 12, 1885, the son of Doctor Paul Slauenwite, formerly of Pretoria, Transvaal, South Africa. Studying medicine as part of my family tradition, I was led by my father (who died in 1916, while I was serving in France in a South African regiment) to specialize in African fevers; and after my graduation from Columbia spent much time in researches which took me from Durban, in Natal, up to the equator itself.

In Mombasa I worked out my new theory of the transmission and development of remittent fever, aided only slightly by the papers of the late government physician, Sir Norman Sloane, which I found in the house I occupied. When I published my results I became at a single stroke a famous authority. I was told of the probability of an almost supreme position in the South African health service, and even a probable knighthood, in the event of my becoming a naturalized citizen, and accordingly I took the necessary steps.

Then occurred the incident for which I am about to kill Henry Moore. This man, my classmate and friend of years in America and Africa, chose deliberately to undermine my claim to my own theory; alleging that Sir Norman Sloane had anticipated me in every essential detail, and implying that I had probably found more of his papers than I had stated in my account of the matter. To buttress this absurd accusation he produced certain personal letters from Sir Norman which indeed showed that the older man had been over my ground, and that he would have published his results very soon but for his sudden death. This much I could only admit with regret. What I could not excuse was the jealous suspicion that I had stolen the theory from Sir Norman's papers. The British government, sensibly enough, ignored these aspersions, but withheld the half-promised appointment and knighthood on the ground that my theory, while original with me, was not in fact new.

I could soon see that my career in Africa was perceptibly checked: though I had placed all my hopes on such a career, even to the point of resigning American citizenship. A distinct coolness toward me had arisen among the Government set in Mombasa, especially among those who had known Sir Norman. It was then that I resolved to be even with Moore sooner or later, though I did not know how. He had been jealous of my early celebrity, and had taken advantage of his old correspondence with Sir Norman to ruin me. This from the friend whom I had myself led to take an interest in Africa – whom I had coached and inspired till he achieved his present moderate fame as an authority on African entomology. Even now, though, I will not deny that his attainments are profound. I made him, and in return he has ruined me. Now – some day – I shall destroy him.

When I saw myself losing ground in Mombasa, I applied for my present situation in the interior – at M'gonga, only fifty miles from the Uganda line. It is a cotton and ivory trading-post, with only eight white men besides myself. A beastly hole, almost on the equator, and full of every sort of fever known to mankind. Poisonous snakes and insects everywhere, and niggers with diseases nobody ever hear of outside medical college. But my work is not hard, and I have always had plenty of time to plan things to do to Henry Moore. It amuses me to give his *Diptera of Central and Southern Africa* a prominent place on my shelf. I suppose it actually is a standard manual – they use it at Columbia, Harvard, and Wisconsin – but my own suggestions are really responsible for half its strong points.

Last week I encountered the thing which decided me how to kill Moore. A party from Uganda brought in a black with a queer illness which I can't yet diagnose. He was lethargic, with a very low temperature, and shuffled in a peculiar way. Most of the others were afraid of him and said he was under some kind of witch-doctor spell; but Gobo, the interpreter, said he had been bitten by an insect. What it was, I can't imagine – for there is only a slight puncture on the arm. It is bright red, though, with a purple ring around it. Spectral-looking – I don't wonder the boys lay it to black magic. They seem to have seen cases like it before, and say there's really nothing to do about it.

Old N'Kuru, one of the Galla boys at the post, says it must be the bite of a devil-fly, which makes its victim waste away gradually and die, and then takes hold of his soul and personality if it is still alive itself – flying around with all his likes, dislikes, and consciousness. A queer legend – and I don't know of any local insect deadly enough to account for it. I gave this sick black – his name is Mevana – a good shot of quinine and took a sample of his blood for testing, but haven't made much progress. There is certainly a strange germ present, but I can't even remotely identify it. The nearest thing to it is the bacillus one finds in oxen, horses, and dogs that the tsetse-fly has bitten; but tsetse-flies don't infect human beings, and this is too far north for them anyway.

However – the important thing is that I've decided how to kill Moore. If this interior region has insects as poisonous as the natives say, I'll see that he gets a shipment of them from a source he won't suspect, and with plenty of assurances that they are harmless. Trust him to throw overboard all caution when it comes to studying an unknown species – and then we'll see how nature takes its course! It ought not to be hard to find an insect that scares the blacks so much. First to see how poor Mevana turns out – and then to find my envoy of death.

Jan. 7 – Mevana is no better, though I have injected all the antitoxins I know of. He has fits of trembling, in which he rants affrightedly about the way his soul will pass when he dies into the insect that bit him, but between them he remains in a kind of half-stupor. Heart action still strong, so I may pull him through. I shall try to, for he can probably guide me better than anyone to the region where he was bitten.

Meanwhile I'll write to Doctor Lincoln, my predecessor here, for Allen, the head factor, says he had a profound knowledge of the local sicknesses. He ought to know about the death-fly if any white man does. He's at Nairobi now, and a black runner ought to get me a reply in a week – using the railway for half the trip.

Jan. 10 – Patient unchanged, but I have found what I want! It was in an old volume of the local health records, which I've been going over diligently while waiting to hear from Lincoln. Thirty years ago there was an epidemic that killed off thousands of natives in Uganda, and it was definitely traced to a rare fly called *glossina palpalis* – a sort of cousin of the *glossina marsitans,* or tsetse. It lives in the bushes on the shores of lakes and rivers, and feeds on the blood of crocodiles, antelopes, and large mammals. When these food animals have the germ of trypanosomiasis, or sleeping-sickness, it picks it up and develops acute infectivity after an incubation period of thirty-one days. Then for seventy-five days it is sure death to anyone or anything it bites.

Without doubt, this must be the 'devil-fly' the niggers talk about. Now I know what I'm heading for. Hope Mevana pulls through. Ought to hear from Lincoln in four or five days – he has a great reputation for success in things like this. My worst problem will be to get the flies to Moore without his recognizing them. With his cursed plodding scholarship it would be just like him to know all about them since they're actually on record.

2

Jan. 15 – Just heard from Lincoln, who confirms all that the records say about *glossina palpalis.* He has a remedy for sleeping-sickness which has succeeded in a great number of cases when not given too late. Inter-muscular injections of tryparsamide. Since Mevana was bitten about two months ago, I don't know how it will work – but Lincoln says that cases have been known to drag on eighteen months, so possibly I'm not too late. Lincoln sent over some of his stuff, so I've just given Mevana a stiff shot. In a stupor now. They've brought his principal wife from the village, but he doesn't even recognize her. If he recovers, he can certainly show me where the flies are. He's a great crocodile hunter, according to report, and knows all Uganda like a book. I'll give him another shot tomorrow.

Jan. 16 – Mevana seems a little brighter today, but his heart action is slowing up a bit. I'll keep up the injections, but not overdo them.

Jan. 17 – Recovery really pronounced today. Mevana opened his eyes and showed signs of actual consciousness, though dazed, after the injection. Hope Moore doesn't know about tryparsamide. There's a good chance he won't, since he never leaned much toward medicine. Mevana's tongue seemed paralyzed, but I fancy that will pass off if I can only wake him up. Wouldn't mind a good sleep myself, but not of this kind!

Jan. 25 – Mevana nearly cured! In another week I can let him take me into the jungle. He was frightened when he first came to – about having the fly take his personality after he died – but brightened up finally when I told him he was going to get well. His wife, Ugowe, takes good care of him now, and I can rest a bit. Then for the envoys of death!

Feb. 3 – Mevana is well now, and I have talked with him about a hunt for flies. He dreads to go near the place where they got him, but I am playing on his gratitude. Besides, he has an idea that I can ward off disease as well as cure it. His pluck would shame a white man – there's no doubt that he'll go. I can get off by telling the head factor the trip is in the interest of local health work.

March 12 – In Uganda at last! Have five boys besides Mevana, but they are all Gallas. The local blacks couldn't be hired to come near the region after the talk of what had happened to Mevana. This jungle is a pestilential place – steaming with miasmal vapors. All the lakes look stagnant. In one spot we came upon a trace of cyclopean ruins which made even the Gallas run past in a wide circle. They say these megaliths are older than man, and that they used to be a haunt or outpost of 'The Fishers from Outside' – whatever that means – and of the evil gods Tsadogwa and Clulu. To this day they are said to have a malign influence, and to be connected somehow with the devil-flies.

March 15 – Struck Lake Mlolo this morning – where Mevana was bitten. A hellish, green-scummed affair, full of crocodiles, Mevana has fixed up a flytrap of fine wire netting baited with crocodile meat. It has a small entrance, and once the quarry get in, they don't know enough to get out. As stupid as they are deadly, and ravenous for fresh meat or a bowl of blood. Hope we can get a good supply. I've decided that I must experiment with them – finding a way to change their appearance so that Moore won't recognize them. Possibly I can cross them with some other species, producing a strange hybrid whose infection-carrying capacity will be undiminished. We'll see. I must wait, but am in no hurry now. When I get ready I'll have Mevana get me some infected meat to feed my envoys of death – and then for the post-office. Ought to be no trouble getting infection, for this country is a veritable pest-hole.

March 16 – Good luck. Two cages full. Five vigorous specimens with wings glistening like diamonds. Mevana is emptying them into a large can with a tightly meshed top, and I think we caught them in the nick of time. We can get them to M'gonga without trouble. Taking plenty of crocodile meat for their food. Undoubtedly all or most of it is infected.

April 20 – Back at M'gonga and busy in the laboratory. Have sent to Doctor Joost in Pretoria for some tsetse flies for hybridization experiments. Such a crossing, if it will work at all, ought to produce something pretty hard to recognize yet at the same time just as deadly as the *palpalis*. If this doesn't work, I shall try certain other diptera from the interior, and I have sent to Doctor Vandervelde at Nyangwe for some of the Congo types. I shan't have to send Mevana for more tainted meat after all; for I find I can keep cultures of the germ *trypanosoma gambiense*, taken from the meat we got last month, almost indefinitely in tubes. When the time comes, I'll taint some fresh meat and feed my winged envoys a good dose – then *bon voyage* to them!

June 18 – My tsetse flies from Joost came today. Cages for breeding were all ready long ago, and I am now making selections. Intend to use ultra-violet rays to speed up the life-cycle. Fortunately I have the needed apparatus in my regular equipment. Naturally I tell no one what I'm doing. The ignorance of the few men here makes it easy for me to conceal my aims and pretend to be merely studying existing species for medical reasons.

June 29 – The crossing is fertile! Good deposits of eggs last Wednesday, and now I have some excellent larvae. If the mature insects look as strange as these do, I need do nothing more. Am preparing separate numbered cages for the different specimens.

July 7 – New hybrids are out! Disguise is excellent as to shape, but sheen of wings still suggests *palpalis.* Thorax has faint suggestions of the stripes of the tsetse. Slight variation in individuals. Am feeding them all on tainted crocodile meat, and after infectivity develops will try them on some of the blacks – apparently, of course, by accident. There are so many mildly venomous flies around here that it can easily be done without exciting suspicion. I shall loose an insect in my tightly screened dining-room when Batta, my house-boy, brings in breakfast – keeping well on guard myself. When it has done its work I'll capture or swat it – an easy thing because of its stupidity – or asphyxiate it by filling the room with chlorine gas. If it doesn't work the first time, I'll try again until it does. Of course, I'll have the tryparsamide handy in case I get bitten myself – but I shall be careful to avoid a bite, for no antidote is really certain.

Aug. 10 – Infectivity mature, and managed to get Batta stung in fine shape. Caught the fly on him, returning it to its cage. Eased up the pain with iodine, and the poor devil is quite grateful for the service. Shall try a variant specimen on Gamba, the factor's messenger tomorrow. That will be all the tests I shall dare to make here, but if I need more I shall take some specimens to Ukala and get additional data.

Aug. 11 – Failed to get Gamba, but recaptured the fly alive.

Batta still seems as well as usual, and has no pain in the back where he was stung. Shall wait before trying to get Gamba again.

Aug. 14 – Shipment of insects from Vandervelde at last. Fully seven distinct species, some more or less poisonous. Am keeping them well fed in case the tsetse crossing doesn't work. Some of these fellows look very unlike the *palpalis*, but the trouble is that they may not make a fertile cross with it.

Aug. 17 – Got Gamba this afternoon, but had to kill the fly on him. It nipped him in the left shoulder. I dressed the bite, and Gamba is as grateful as Batta was. No change in Batta.

Aug. 20 – Gamba unchanged so far – Batta too. Am experimenting with a new form of disguise to supplement the hybridization – some sort of dye to change the telltale glitter of the *palpalis'* wings. A bluish tint would be best – something I could spray on a whole batch of insects. Shall begin by investigating things like Prussian and Turnbull's blue – iron and cyanogen salts.

Aug. 25 – Batta complained of a pain in his back today – things may be developing.

Sept. 3 – Have made fair progress in my experiments. Batta shows signs of lethargy, and says his back aches all the time. Gamba beginning to feel uneasy in his bitten shoulder.

Sept. 24 – Batta worse and worse, and beginning to get frightened about his bite. Thinks it must be a devil-fly, and entreated me to kill it – for he saw me cage it – until I pretended to him that it had died long ago. Said he didn't want his soul to pass into it upon his death. I give him shots of plain water with a hypodermic to keep his morale up. Evidently the fly retains all the properties of the *palpalis*. Gamba down, too, and repeating all of Batta's symptoms. I may decide to give him a chance with tryparsamide, for the effect of the fly is proved well enough. I shall let Batta go on, however, for I want a rough idea of how long it takes to finish a case.

Dye experiments coming along finely. An isomeric form of ferrous ferro-cyanide, with some admixture of potassium salts, can be dissolved in alcohol and sprayed on the insects with splendid effect. It stains the wings blue without affecting the dark thorax much, and doesn't wear off when I sprinkle the specimens with water. With this disguise, I think I can use the present tsetse hybrids and avoid bothering with any more experiments. Sharp as he is, Moore couldn't recognize a blue-winged fly with a half-tsetse thorax. Of course, I keep all this dye business strictly under cover. Nothing must ever connect me with the blue flies later on.

Oct. 9 – Batta is lethargic and has taken to his bed. Have been giving Gamba tryparsamide for two weeks, and fancy he'll recover.

Oct. 25 – Batta very low, but Gamba nearly well.

Nov. 18 – Batta died yesterday, and a curious thing happened which gave me a real shiver in view of the native legends and Batta's own fears. When I returned to the laboratory after the death I heard the most singular buzzing and thrashing in cage 12, which contained the fly that bit Batta. The creature seemed frantic, but stopped still when I appeared – lighting on the wire netting and looking at me in the oddest way. It reached its legs through the wires as if it were bewildered. When I came back from dining with Allen, the thing was dead. Evidently it had gone wild and beaten its life out on the sides of the cage.

It certainly is peculiar that this should happen just as Batta died. If any black had seen it, he'd have laid it at once to the absorption of the poor devil's soul. I shall start my blue-stained hybrids on their way before long now. The hybrids' rate of killing seems a little ahead of the pure *palpalis'* rate, if anything. Batta died three months and eight days after infection – but of course there is always a wide margin of uncertainty. I almost wish I had let Gamba's case run on.

Dec. 5 – Busy planning how to get my envoys to Moore. I must have them appear to come from some disinterested entomologist who has read his *Diptera of Central and Southern Africa* and believes he would like to study this 'new and unidentifiable species.' There must also be ample assurances that the blue-winged fly is harmless, as proved by the natives' long experience. Moore will be off his guard, and one of the flies will surely get him sooner or later – though one can't tell just when.

I'll have to rely on the letters of New York friends – they still speak of Moore from time to time – to keep me informed of early results, though I dare say the papers will announce his death. Above all, I must show no interest in his case. I shall mail the flies while on a trip, but must not be recognized when I do it. The best plan will be to take a long vacation in the interior, grow a beard, mail the package at Ukala while passing as a visiting entomologist, and return here after shaving off the beard.

April 12, 1930 – Back in M'gonga after my long trip. Everything has come off finely – with clockwork precision. Have sent the flies to Moore without leaving a trace. Got a Christmas vacation Dec. 15th, and set out at once with the proper stuff. Made a very good mailing container with room to include some germ-tainted crocodile meat as food for the envoys. By the end of February I had beard enough to shape into a close Vandyke.

Showed up at Ukala March 9th and typed a letter to Moore on the trading-post machine. Signed it 'Nevil Wayland-Hall' – supposed to be an entomologist from London. Think I took just the right tone – interest of a brother-scientist, and all that. Was artistically casual in emphasizing the 'complete harmlessness' of the specimens. Nobody suspected anything. Shaved the beard as soon as I hit the bush, so that there wouldn't be any uneven tanning by the time I got back here. Dispensed with native bearers except for one small stretch of swamp – I can do wonders with one knapsack, and my sense of direction is good. Lucky I'm used to such travelling. Explained my protracted absence by pleading a touch of fever and some mistakes in direction when going through the bush.

But now comes the hardest part psychologically – waiting for news of Moore without showing the strain. Of course, he may possibly escape a bite until the venom is played out – but with his recklessness the chances are one hundred to one against him. I have no regrets; after what he did to me, he deserves this and more.

June 30, 1930 – Hurrah! The first step worked! Just heard casually from Dyson of Columbia that Moore had received some new blue-winged flies from Africa, and he is badly puzzled over them! No word of any bite – but if I know Moore's slipshod ways as I think I do there'll be one before long!

August 27, 1930 – Letter from Morton in Cambridge. He says Moore writes of feeling very run-down, and tells of an insect bite on the back of his neck – from a curious new specimen that he received about the middle of June. Have I succeeded? Apparently Moore doesn't connect the bite with his weakness. If this is the real stuff, then Moore was bitten well within the insect's period of infectivity.

Sept. 12, 1930 – Victory! Another line from Dyson says that Moore is really in an alarming shape. He now traces his illness to the bite, which he received around noon on June 19, and is quite bewildered about the identity of the insect. Is trying to get in touch with the 'Nevil Wayland-Hall' who sent him the shipment. Of the hundred-odd that I sent, about twenty-five seem to have reached him alive. Some escaped at the time of the bite, but several larvae have appeared from eggs laid since the time of mailing. He is, Dyson says, carefully incubating these larvae. When they mature I suppose he'll identify the tsetse-*palpalis* hybridization – but that won't do him much good now. He'll wonder, though, why the blue wings aren't transmitted by heredity!

Nov. 8, 1930 – Letters from half a dozen friends tell of Moore's serious illness. Dyson's came today. He says Moore is utterly at sea about the hybrids that came from the larvae and is beginning to think that the parents got their blue wings in some artificial way. Has to stay in bed most of the time now. No mention of using tryparsamide.

Feb. 13, 1931 – Not so good! Moore is sinking, and seems to know no remedy, but I think he suspects one. Had a very chilly letter from Morton last month, which told nothing of Moore; and now Dyson writes – also rather constrainedly – that Moore is forming theories about the whole matter. He's been making a search for 'Wayland Hall' by telegraph – at London, Ukala, Nairobi, Mombasa, and other places – and of course finds nothing. I judge that he's told Dyson whom he suspects, but that Dyson doesn't believe it yet. Fear Morton does believe it.

I see that I'd better lay plans for getting out of here and effacing my identity for good. What an end to a career that started out so well! More of Moore's work – but this time he's paying for it in advance! Believe I'll go back to South Africa – and meanwhile will quietly deposit funds there to the credit of my new self – 'Frederick Nasmyth Mason of Toronto, Canada, broker in mining properties.' Will establish a new signature for identification. If I never have to take the step, I can easily re-transfer the funds to my present self.

Aug. 15, 1931 – Half a year gone, and still suspense. Dyson and Morton – as well as several other friends – seem to have stopped writing me. Doctor James of San Francisco hears from Moore's friends now and then, and says Moore is in an almost continuous coma. He hasn't been able to walk since May. As long as he could talk he complained of being cold. Now he can't talk, though it is thought he still has glimmers of consciousness. His breathing is short and quick, and can be heard some distance away. No question but the *trypanosoma gambiense* is feeding on him – but he holds out better than the niggers around here. Three months and eight days finished Batta and here Moore is alive over a year after his biting. Heard rumors last month of an intensive search around Ukala for 'Wayland-Hall.' Don't think I need to worry yet, though, for there's absolutely nothing in existence to link me with this business.

Oct. 7, 1931 – It's over at last! News in the *Mombasa Gazette.* Moore died September 20 after a series of trembling fits and with a temperature vastly below normal. So much for that! I said I'd get him, and I did! The paper has a three-column report of his long illness and death, and of the futile search for 'Wayland-Hall.' Obviously, Moore was a bigger character in Africa than I had realized. The insect that bit him has now been fully identified from the surviving specimens and developed larvae, and the wing-staining is also detected. It is universally realized that the flies were prepared and shipped with intent to kill. Moore, it appears, communicated certain suspicions to Dyson, but the latter – and the police – are maintaining secrecy because of absence of proof. All of Moore's enemies are being looked up, and the Associated Press hints that 'an investigation, possibly involving an eminent physician now abroad, will follow.'

One thing at the very end of the report – undoubtedly, the cheap romancing of a yellow journalist – gives me a curious shudder in view of the legends of the blacks and the way the fly happened to go wild when Batta died. It seems that an odd incident occurred on the night of Moore's death; Dyson having been aroused by the buzzing of a blue-winged fly – which immediately flew out the window – just before the nurse telephoned the death news from Moore's home, miles away in Brooklyn.

But what concerns me most is the African end of the matter. People at Ukala remember the bearded stranger who typed the letter and sent the package, and the constabulary are combing the country for any blacks who may have carried him. I didn't use many, but if officers question the Ubandes who took me through the N'Kini jungle belt I'll have more to explain than I like. It looks as if the time has come for me to vanish; so tomorrow I believe I'll resign and prepare to start for parts unknown.

Nov. 9, 1931 – Hard work getting my resignation acted on, but release came today. I didn't want to aggravate suspicion by decamping outright. Last week I heard from James about Moore's death – but nothing more than is in the papers. Those around him in New York seem rather reticent about details, though they all talk about a searching investigation. No word from any of my friends in the east. Moore must have spread some dangerous suspicions around before he lost consciousness – but there isn't an iota of proof he could have adduced.

Still, I am taking no chances. On Thursday I shall start for Mombasa, and when there will take a steamer down the coast to Durban. After that I shall drop from sight – but soon afterward the mining properties' broker Frederick Nasmyth Mason, from Toronto, will turn up in Johannesburg.

Let this be the end of my journal. If in the end I am not suspected, it will serve its original purpose after my death and reveal what would otherwise not be known. If, on the other hand, these suspicions do materialize and persist, it will confirm and clarify the vague charges, and fill in many important and puzzling gaps. Of course, if danger comes my way I shall have to destroy it.

Well, Moore is dead – as he amply deserves to be. Now Doctor Thomas Slauenwite is dead, too. And when the body formerly belonging to Thomas Slauenwite is dead, the public may have this record.

3

Jan. 15, 1932 – A new year – and a reluctant reopening of this journal. This time I am writing solely to relieve my mind, for it would be absurd to fancy that the case is not definitely closed. I am settled in the Vaal Hotel, Johannesburg, under my new name, and no one has so far challenged my identity. Have had some inconclusive business talks to keep up my part as a mine broker, and believe I may actually work myself into that business. Later I shall go to Toronto and plant a few evidences for my fictitious past.

But what is bothering me is an insect that invaded my room around noon today. Of course I have had all sorts of nightmares about blue flies of late, but those were only to be expected in view of my prevailing nervous strain. This thing, however, was a waking actuality, and I am utterly at a loss to account for it. It buzzed around my bookshelf for fully a quarter of an hour, and eluded every attempt to catch or kill it. The queerest thing was its color and aspect – for it had blue wings and was in every way a duplicate of my hybrid envoys of death. How it could possibly be one of these in fact, I certainly don't know. I disposed of all the hybrids – stained and unstained – that I didn't send to Moore, and can't recall any instance of escape.

Can this be wholly an hallucination? Or could any of the specimens that escaped in Brooklyn when Moore was bitten have found their way back to Africa? There was that absurd story of the blue fly that waked Dyson when Moore died – but after all, the survival and return of some of the things is not impossible. It is perfectly plausible that the blue should stick to their wings, too, for the pigment I devised was almost as good as tattooing for permanence. By elimination, that would seem to be the only rational explanation for this thing; though it is very curious that the fellow has come as far south as this. Possibly it's some hereditary homing instinct inherent in the tsetse strain. After all, that side of him belongs to South Africa.

I must be on my guard against a bite. Of course the original venom – if this is actually one of the flies that escaped from Moore – was worn out ages ago; but the fellow must have fed as he flew back from America, and he may well have come through Central Africa and picked up a fresh infectivity. Indeed, that's more probable than not; for the *palpalis* half of his heredity would naturally take him back to Uganda, and all the *trypanosomiasis* germs. I still have some of the tryparsamide left – I couldn't bear to destroy my medicine case, incriminating though it may be – but since reading up on the subject I am not so sure about the drug's action as I was. It gives one a fighting chance – certainly it saved Gamba – but there's always a large probability of failure.

It's devilish queer that this fly should have happened to come into my room – of all places in the wide expanse of Africa! Seems to strain coincidence to the breaking-point. I suppose that if it comes again, I shall certainly kill it. I'm surprised that it escaped me today, for ordinarily these fellows are extremely stupid and easy to catch. Can it be a pure illusion after all? Certainly the heat is getting me of late as it never did before – even up around Uganda.

Jan. 16 – Am I going insane? The fly came again this noon, and acted so anomalously that I can't make head or tail of it. Only delusion on my part could account for what that buzzing pest seemed to do. It appeared from nowhere, and went straight to my bookshelf – circling again and again to front a copy of Moore's *Diptera of Central and Southern Africa*. Now and then it would light on top or back of the volume, and occasionally it would dart forward toward me and retreat before I could strike at it with a folded paper. Such cunning is unheard of among the notoriously stupid African diptera. For nearly half an hour I tried to get the cursed thing, but at last it darted out the window through a hole in the screen that I hadn't noticed. At times I fancied it deliberately mocked me by coming within reach of my weapon and then skilfully sidestepping as I struck out. I must keep a tight hold of my consciousness.

Jan. 17 – Either I am mad or the world is in the grip of some sudden suspension of the laws of probability as we know them. That damnable fly came in from somewhere just before noon and commenced buzzing around the copy of Moore's *Diptera* on my shelf. Again I tried to catch it, and again yesterday's experience was repeated. Finally the pest made for the open inkwell on my table and dipped itself in – just the legs and thorax, keeping its wings clear. Then it sailed up to the ceiling and lit – beginning to crawl around in a curved patch and leaving a trail of ink. After a time it hopped a bit and made a single ink spot unconnected with the trail – then it dropped squarely in front of my face, and buzzed out of my sight before I could get it.

Something about this whole business struck me as monstrously sinister and abnormal – more so than I could explain to myself. When I looked at the ink-trail on the ceiling from different angles, it seemed more and more familiar to me, and it dawned on me suddenly that it formed an absolutely perfect question mark. What device could be more malignly appropriate? It is a wonder that I did not faint. So far the hotel attendants have not noticed it. Have not seen the fly this afternoon and evening, but am keeping my inkwell securely closed. I think my extermination of Moore must be preying on me, and giving me morbid hallucinations. Perhaps there is no fly at all.

Jan. 18 – Into what strange hell of living nightmare am I plunged? What occurred today is something which could not normally happen – *and yet an hotel attendant has seen the marks on the ceiling and concedes their reality.* About 11 o'clock this morning, as I was writing on a manuscript, something darted down to the inkwell for a second and flashed aloft again before I could see what it was. Looking up, I saw that hellish fly on the ceiling as it had been before – crawling along and tracing another trail of curves and turns. There was nothing I could do, but I folded a newspaper in readiness to get the creature if it should fly near enough. When it had made several turns on the ceiling it flew into a dark corner and disappeared, and as I looked upward at the doubly defaced plastering I saw that the new ink-trail was that of a huge unmistakable figure 5!

For a time I was almost unconscious from a wave of nameless menace for which I could not fully account. Then I summoned up my resolution and took an active step. Going out to a chemist's shop I purchased some gum and other things necessary for preparing a sticky trap – also a duplicate inkwell. Returning to my room, I filled the new inkwell with the sticky mixture and set it where the old one had been, leaving it open. Then I tried to concentrate my mind on some reading. About 3 o'clock I heard the accursed insect again, and saw it circling around the new inkwell. It descended to the sticky surface but did not touch it, and afterward sailed straight toward me – retreating before I could hit it. Then it went to the bookshelf and circled around Moore's treatise. There is something profound and diabolic about the way the intruder hovers near that book.

The worst part was the last. Leaving Moore's book, the insect flew over to the open window and began beating itself rhythmically against the wire screen. There would be a series of beats and then a series of equal length and another pause, and so on. Something about this performance held me motionless for a couple of moments, but after that I went over to the window and tried to kill the noxious thing. As usual, no use. It merely flew across the room to a lamp and began beating the same tattoo on the stiff cardboard shade. I felt a vague desperation, and proceeded to shut all the doors as well as the window whose screen had the imperceptible hole. It seemed very necessary to kill this persistent being, whose hounding was rapidly unseating my mind. Then, unconsciously counting, I began to notice that each of its series of beatings contained just *five* strokes.

Five – the same number that the thing had traced in ink on the ceiling in the morning! Could there be any conceivable connection? The notion was maniacal, for that would argue a human intellect and a knowledge of written figures in the hybrid fly. A human intellect – did not that take one back to the most primitive legends of the Uganda blacks? And yet there was that infernal cleverness in eluding me as contrasted with the normal stupidity of the breed. As I laid aside my folded paper and sat down in growing horror, the insect buzzed aloft and disappeared through a hole in the ceiling where the radiator pipe went to the room above.

The departure did not soothe me, for my mind had started on a train of wild and terrible reflections. If this fly had a human intelligence, where did that intelligence come from? Was there any truth in the native notion that these creatures acquire the personality of their victims after the latters' death? If so, whose personality did this fly bear? I had reasoned out that it must be one of those which escaped from Moore at the time he was bitten. *Was this the envoy of death which had bitten Moore? If so, what did it want with me?* What did it want with me anyway? In a cold perspiration I remembered the actions of the fly that had bitten Batta when Batta died. Had its own personality been displaced by that of its dead victim? Then there was that sensational news account of the fly that waked Dyson when Moore died. As for the fly that was hounding me – could it be that a vindictive human personality drove it on? How it hovered around Moore's book! – I refused to think any farther than that. All at once I began to feel sure that the creature was indeed infected, and in the most virulent way. With a malign deliberation so evident in every act, it must surely have charged itself on purpose with the deadliest bacilli in all Africa. My mind, thoroughly shaken, was not taking the thing's human qualities for granted.

I now telephoned the clerk and asked for a man to stop up the radiator pipehole and other possible chinks in my room. I spoke of being tormented by flies, and he seemed to be quite sympathetic. When the man came, I showed him the inkmarks on the ceiling, which he recognized without difficulty. So they are real! The resemblance to a question mark and a figure five puzzled and fascinated him. In the end he stopped up all the holes he could find, and mended the window-screen, so that I can now keep both windows open. He evidently thought me a bit eccentric, especially since no insects were in sight while he was here. But I am past minding that. So far the fly has not appeared this evening. God knows what it is, what it wants, or what will become of me!

Jan. 19 – I am utterly engulfed in horror. *The thing has touched me.* Something monstrous and demoniac is at work around me, and I am a helpless victim. In the morning, when I returned from breakfast, that winged fiend from hell brushed into the room over my head, and began beating itself against the window-screen as it did yesterday. This time, though, each series of beats contained only *four* strokes. I rushed to the window and tried to catch it, but it escaped as usual and flew over to Moore's treatise, where it buzzed around mockingly. Its vocal equipment is limited, but I noticed that its spells of buzzing came in groups of four.

By this time I was certainly mad, for I called out to it *'Moore, Moore, for God's sake, what do you want?'* When I did so, the creature suddenly ceased its circling, flew toward me, and made a low, graceful dip in the air, somehow suggestive of a bow. Then it flew back to the book. At least, I seemed to see it do all this – though I am trusting my senses no longer.

And then the worst thing happened. I had left my door open, hoping the monster would leave if I could not catch it; but about 11:30 I shut the door, concluding it had gone. Then I settled down to read. Just at noon I felt a tickling on the back of my neck, but when I put my hand up nothing was there. In a moment I felt the tickling again – and before I could move, that nameless spawn of hell sailed into view from behind, did another of those mocking, graceful dips in the air, and flew out through the keyhole – which I had never dreamed was large enough to allow its passage.

That the thing had touched me, I could not doubt. It had touched me without injuring me – and then I remembered in a sudden cold fright that Moore had been bitten *on the back of the neck at noon.* No invasion since then – but I have stuffed all the keyholes with paper and shall have a folded paper ready for use whenever I open the door to leave or enter.

Jan. 20 – I cannot yet believe fully in the supernatural, yet I fear none the less that I am lost. The business is too much for me. Just before noon today that devil appeared *outside* the window and repeated its beating operations; but this time in series of *three.* When I went to the window it flew off out of sight. I still have resolution enough to take one more defensive step. Removing both windowscreens, I coated them with my sticky preparation – the one I used in the inkwell – outside and inside, and set them back in place. If that creature attempts another tattoo, it will be its last!

Rest of the day in peace. Can I weather this experience without becoming a maniac?

Jan. 21 – On board train for Bloemfontein.

I am routed. The thing is winning. It has a diabolic intelligence against which all my devices are powerless. It appeared outside the window this morning, *but did not touch the sticky screen.* Instead it sheered off without lighting and began buzzing around in circles – *two at a time*, followed by a pause in the air. After several of these performances it flew off out of sight over the roofs of the city. My nerves are just about at the breaking-point, for these *suggestions of numbers* are capable of a hideous interpretation. Monday the thing dwelt on the figure *five*; Tuesday it was *four*; Wednesday it was *three*; and now today it is *two. Five, four, three, two* – what can this be save some monstrous and unthinkable *counting-off of days*? For what purpose, only the evil powers of the universe can know. I spent all the afternoon packing and arranging about my trunks, and now I have taken the night express for Bloemfontein. Flight may be useless, but what else can one do?

Jan. 22 – Settled at the Orange Hotel, Bloemfontein – a comfortable and excellent place – but the horror followed me. I had shut all the doors and windows, stopped all the keyholes, looked for any possible chinks, and pulled down all the shades

– but just before noon I heard a dull tap on one of the windowscreens. I waited – and after a long pause another tap came. A second pause, and still another single tap. Raising the shade, I saw that accursed fly, as I had expected. It described one large, slow circle in the air, and then flew out of sight. I was left as weak as a rag, and had to rest on the couch. *One*! This was clearly the burden of the monster's present message. *One* tap, *one* circle. Did this mean *one* more day for me before some unthinkable doom? Ought I to flee again, or entrench myself here by sealing up the room?

After an hour's rest I felt able to act, and ordered a large reserve supply of canned and packaged food – also linen and towels – sent in. Tomorrow I shall not under any circumstances open any crevice of door or window. When the food and linen came the black looked at me queerly, but I no longer care how eccentric – or insane – I may appear. I am hounded by powers worse than the ridicule of mankind. Having received my supplies, I went over every square millimeter of the walls, and stopped up every microscopic opening I could find. At last I feel able to get real sleep.

(Handwriting here becomes irregular, nervous, and very difficult to decipher.)

Jan. 23 – It is just before noon, and I feel that something very terrible is about to happen. Didn't sleep as late as I expected, even though I got almost no sleep on the train the night before. Up early, and have had trouble getting concentrated on anything – reading or writing. That slow, deliberate counting-off of days is too much for me. I don't know which has gone wild – nature or my head. Until about eleven I did very little except walk up and down the room.

Then I heard a rustle among the food packages brought in yesterday, and that demoniac fly crawled out before my eyes. I grabbed something flat and made passes at the thing despite my panic fear, but with no more effect than usual. As I advanced, that blue-winged horror retreated as usual to the table where I had piled my books, and lit for a second on Moore's *Diptera of Central and Southern Africa*. Then as I followed, it flew over to the mantel clock and lit on the dial near the figure 12. Before I could think up another move it had begun to crawl around the dial very slowly and deliberately – in the direction of the hands. It passed under the minute hand, curved down and up, passed under the hour hand, and finally came to a stop exactly at the figure 12. As it hovered there it fluttered its wings with a buzzing noise.

Is this a portent of some sort? I am getting as superstitious as the blacks. The hour is now a little after eleven. Is twelve the end? I have just one last resort, brought to my mind through utter desperation. Wish I had thought of it before. Recalling that my medicine case contains both of the substances necessary to generate chlorine gas, I have resolved to fill the room with that lethal vapor – asphyxiating the fly while protecting myself with an ammonia-sealed handkerchief tied over my face. Fortunately I have a good supply of ammonia. This crude mask will probably neutralize the acrid chlorine fumes till the insect is dead – or at least helpless enough to crush. But I must be quick. How can I be sure that the thing will not suddenly dart for me before my preparations are complete? I ought not to be stopping to write in this journal.

Later – Both chemicals – hydrochloric acid and manganese dioxide – on the table all ready to mix. I've tied the handkerchief over my nose and mouth, and have a bottle of ammonia ready to keep it soaked until the chlorine is gone. Have battened down both windows. But I don't like the actions of that hybrid demon. It stays on the clock, but is very slowly crawling around backward from the 12 mark to meet the gradually advancing minute hand.

Is this to be my last entry in this journal? It would be useless to try to deny what I suspect. Too often a grain of incredible truth lurks behind the wildest and most fantastic of legends. Is the personality of Henry Moore trying to get at me through this blue-winged devil? Is this the fly that bit him, and that in consequence absorbed his consciousness when he died? If so, and if it bites me, will my own personality displace Moore's and enter that buzzing body when I die of the bite later on? Perhaps, though, I need not die even if it gets me. There is always a chance with tryparsamide. And I regret nothing. Moore had to die, be the outcome what it will.

Slightly later.

The fly has paused on the clock-dial near the 45-minute mark. It is now 11:30. I am saturating the handkerchief over my face with ammonia and keeping the bottle handy for further applications. This will be the final entry before I mix the acid and manganese and liberate the chlorine. I ought not to be losing time, but it steadies me to get things down on paper.

But for this record, I'd have lost all my reason long ago. The fly seems to be getting restless, and the minute hand is approaching it. Now for the chlorine. . . .

(End of the journal)

On Sunday, Jan. 24, 1932, after repeated knocking had failed to gain any response from the eccentric man in Room 303 of the Orange Hotel, a black attendant entered with a pass key and at once fled shrieking downstairs to tell the clerk what he had found. The clerk, after notifying the police, summoned the manager; and the latter accompanied Constable De Witt, Coroner Bogaert, and Doctor Van Keulen to the fatal room.

The occupant lay dead on the floor – his face upward, and bound with a handkerchief which smelled strongly of ammonia. Under this covering the features showed an expression of stark, utter fear which transmitted itself to the observers. On the back of the neck Doctor Van Keulen found a virulent insect bite – dark red, with a purple ring around it – which suggested a tsetse fly or something less innocuous. An examination indicated that death must be due to heart-failure induced by sheer fright rather than to the bite – though a subsequent autopsy indicated that the germ of *trypanosomiasis* had been introduced into the system.

On the table were several objects – a worn leather blank-book containing the journal just described, a pen, writing-pad, and open inkwell, a doctor's medicine case with the initials 'T. S.' marked in gold, bottles of ammonia and hydrochloric acid, and a tumbler about a quarter full of black manganese dioxide. The ammonia bottle demanded a second look because something besides the fluid seemed to be in it. Looking closer, Coroner Bogaert saw that the alien occupant was a fly.

It seemed to be some sort of hybrid with vague tsetse affiliations, but its wings – showing faintly blue despite the action of the strong ammonia – were a complete puzzle. Something about it waked a faint memory of newspaper reading in Doctor Van Keulen – a memory which the journal was soon to confirm. Its lower parts seemed to have been stained with ink, so thoroughly that even the ammonia had not bleached them. Possibly it had fallen at one time into the inkwell, though the wings were untouched. But how had it managed to fall into the narrow-necked ammonia bottle? It was as if the creature had deliberately crawled in and committed suicide!

But the strangest thing of all was what Constable De Witt noticed on the smooth white ceiling overhead as his eyes roved about curiously. At his cry the other three followed his gaze – even Doctor Van Keulen, who had for some time been thumbing through the worn leather book with an expression of mixed horror, fascination, and incredulity. The thing on the ceiling was a series of shaky, straggling ink-tracks such as might have been made by the crawling of some ink-drenched insect. At once everyone thought of the stains on the fly so oddly found in the ammonia bottle.

But these were no ordinary ink-tracks. Even a first glance revealed something hauntingly familiar about them, and closer inspection brought gasps of startled wonder from all four observers. Coroner Bogaert instinctively looked around the room to see if there were any conceivable instrument or arrangement of piled-up furniture which could make it possible for those straggling marks to have been drawn by human agency. Finding nothing of the sort, he resumed his curious and almost awestruck upward glance.

For beyond a doubt these inky smudges formed definite letters of the alphabet – letters coherently arranged in English words. The doctor was the first to make them out clearly, and the others listened breathlessly as he recited the insane-sounding message so incredibly scrawled in a place no human hand could reach:

'SEE MY JOURNAL – *IT* GOT ME FIRST – I DIED – THEN I SAW I WAS IN *IT* – THE BLACKS ARE RIGHT – STRANGE POWERS IN NATURE – NOW I WILL DROWN WHAT IS LEFT—'

Presently, amid the puzzled hush that followed, Doctor Van Keulen commenced reading aloud from the worn leather journal.

THE LOVED DEAD

by C. M. Eddy, Jr.

It's midnight. Before dawn they will find me and take me to a black cell where I shall languish interminably, while insatiable desires gnaw at my vitals and wither up my heart, till at last I become one with the dead that I love.

My seat is the fetid hollow of an aged grave; my desk is the back of a fallen tombstone worn smooth by devastating centuries; my only light is that of the stars and a thin-edged moon, yet I can see as clearly as though it were midday. Around me on every side, sepulchral sentinels guarding unkempt graves, the tilting, decrepit headstones lie half-hidden in masses of nauseous, rotting vegetation. Above the rest, silhouetted against the living sky, an august monument lifts its austere, tapering spire like the spectral chieftain of a lemurian horde. The air is heavy with the noxious odors of fungi and the scent of damp, mouldy earth, but to me it is the aroma of Elysium. It is still – terrifyingly still – with a silence whose very profundity bespeaks the solemn and the hideous. Could I choose my habitation it would be in the heart of some such city of putrefying flesh and crumbling bones; for their nearness sends ecstatic thrills through my soul, causing the stagnant blood to race through my veins and my torpid heart to pound with delirious joy – for the presence of death is life to me!

My early childhood was one long, prosaic and monotonous apathy. Strictly ascetic, wan, pallid, undersized, and subject to protracted spells of morbid moroseness, I was ostracized by the healthy, normal youngsters of my own age. They dubbed me a spoil-sport, and 'old woman', because I had no interest in the rough, childish games they played, or any stamina to participate in them, had I so desired.

Like all rural villages, Fenham had its quota of poison-tongued gossips. Their prying imaginations hailed my lethargic temperament as some abhorrent abnormality; they compared me with my parents and shook their heads in ominous doubt at the vast difference. Some of the more superstitious openly pronounced me a changeling while others who knew something of my ancestry called attention to the vague mysterious rumors concerning a great-great-grand uncle who had been burned at the stake as a necromancer.

Had I lived in some larger town, with greater opportunities for congenial companionship, perhaps I could have overcome this early tendency to be a recluse. As I reached my teens I grew even more sullen, morbid, and apathetic. My life lacked motivation. I seemed in the grip of something that dulled my senses, stunted my development, retarded my activities, and left me unaccountably dissatisfied.

I was sixteen when I attended my first funeral. A funeral in Fenham was a pre-eminent social event, for our town was noted for the longevity of its inhabitants. When, moreover, the funeral was that of such a well-known character as my grandfather, it was safe to assume that the townspeople would turn out *en masse* to pay due homage to his memory. Yet I did not view the approaching ceremony with even latent interest. Anything that tended to lift me out of my habitual inertia held for me only the promise of physical and mental disquietude. In deference to my parents' importunings, mainly to give myself relief from their caustic condemnations of what they chose to call my unfilial attitude, I agreed to accompany them.

There was nothing out of the ordinary about my grandfather's funeral unless it was the voluminous array of floral tributes; but this, remember, was my first initiation to the solemn rites of such an occasion. Something about the darkened room, the oblong coffin with its somber drapings, the banked masses of fragrant blooms, the dolorous manifestations of the assembled villagers, stirred me from my normal listlessness and arrested my attention. Roused from my momentary reverie by a nudge from my mother's sharp elbow, I followed her across the room to the casket where the body of my grandparent lay.

For the first time I was face to face with Death. I looked down upon the calm placid face lined with its multitudinous wrinkles, and saw nothing to cause so much of sorrow. Instead, it seemed to me that my grandfather was immeasurably content, blandly satisfied. I felt swayed by some strange discordant sense of elation. So slowly, so stealthily had it crept over me, that I could scarcely define its coming. As I mentally review that portentous hour it seems that it must have originated with my first glimpse of that funeral scene, silently strengthening its grip with subtle insidiousness. A baleful malignant influence that seemed to emanate from the corpse itself held me with magnetic fascination. My whole being seemed charged with some ecstatic electrifying force, and I felt my form straighten without conscious volition. My eyes were trying to burn beneath the closed lids of the dead man's and read some secret message they concealed. My heart gave a sudden leap of unholy glee, and pounded against my ribs with demoniacal force as if to free itself from the confining walls of my frail frame. Wild, wanton, soul-satisfying sensuality engulfed me. Once more the vigorous prod of a maternal elbow jarred me into activity. I had made my way to the sable-shrouded coffin with leaden tread; I walked away with new-found animation.

I accompanied the cortege to the cemetery, my whole physical being permeated with this mystic enlivening influence. It was as if I had quaffed deep draughts of some exotic elixir – some abominable concoction brewed from blasphemous formulae in the archives of Belial.

The townsfolk were so intent upon the ceremony that the radical change in my demeanor passed unnoticed by all save my father and my mother, but in the fortnight that followed, the village busybodies found fresh material for their vitriolic tongues in my altered bearing. At the end of the fortnight, however, the potency of the stimulus began to lose its effectiveness. Another day or two and I had completely reverted to my old-time languor, though not to the complete and engulfing insipidity of the past. Before, there had been an utter lack of desire to emerge from the enervation; now vague and indefinable unrest disturbed me. Outwardly I had become myself again, and the scandal-mongers turned to some more engrossing subject. Had they even so much as dreamed the true cause of my exhilaration they would have shunned me as if I were a filthy, leprous thing. Had I visioned the execrable power behind my brief period of elation I would have locked myself forever from the rest of the world and spent my remaining years in penitent solitude.

Tragedy often runs in trilogies, hence despite the proverbial longevity of our townspeople, the next five years brought the death of both my parents. My mother went first, in an accident of the most unexpected nature; and so genuine was my grief that

I was honestly surprised to find its poignancy mocked and contradicted by that almost forgotten feeling of supreme and diabolical ecstasy. Once more my heart leaped wildly within me, once more it pounded at trip-hammer speed and sent the hot blood coursing through my veins with meteoric fervor. I shook from my shoulders the harassing cloak of stagnation only to replace it with the infinitely more horrible burden of loathsome, unhallowed desire. I haunted the deathchamber where the body of my mother lay, my soul athirst for the devilish nectar that seemed to saturate the air of the darkened room. Every breath strengthened me, lifted me to towering heights of seraphic satisfaction. I knew, now, that it was but a sort of drugged delirium which must soon pass and leave me correspondingly weakened by its malign power, yet I could no more control my longing than I could untwist the Gordian knots in the already tangled skein of my destiny.

I knew, too, that through some strange satanic curse my life depended upon the dead for its motive force; that there was a singularity in my makeup which responded only to the awesome presence of some lifeless clod. A few days later, frantic for the bestial intoxicant on which the fullness of my existence depended, I interviewed Fenham's sole undertaker and talked him into taking me on as a sort of apprentice.

The shock of my mother's demise had visibly affected my father. I think that if I had broached the idea of such *outré* employment at any other time he would have been emphatic in his refusal. As it was he nodded acquiescence after a moment's sober thought. How little did I dream that he would be the object of my first practical lesson!

He, too, died suddenly; developing some hitherto unsuspected heart affliction. My octogenarian employer tried his best to dissuade me from the unthinkable task of embalming his body, nor did he detect the rapturous glint in my eyes as I finally won him over to my damnable point of view. I cannot hope to express the reprehensible, the unutterable thoughts that swept in tumultuous waves of passion through my racing heart as I labored over the lifeless clay. Unsurpassed love was the keynote of these concepts, a love greater – far greater – than any I had ever borne him while he was alive.

My father was not a rich man, but he had possessed enough of worldly goods to make him comfortably independent. As his sole heir I found myself in rather a paradoxical position.

My early youth had totally failed to fit me for contact with the modern world, yet the primitive life of Fenham with its attendant isolation palled upon me. Indeed, the longevity of the inhabitants defeated my sole motive in arranging my indenture.

After settling the estate it proved an easy matter to secure my release and I headed for Bayboro, a city some fifty miles away. Here my year of apprenticeship stood me in good stead. I had no trouble in establishing a favorable connection as an assistant with the Gresham Corporation, a concern that maintained the largest funeral parlors in the city. I even prevailed upon them to let me sleep upon the premises – for already the proximity of the dead was becoming an obsession.

I applied myself to my task with unwonted zeal. No case was too gruesome for my impious sensibilities, and I soon became master at my chosen vocation. Every fresh corpse brought into the establishment meant a fulfilled promise of ungodly gladness, of irreverent gratification; a return of that rapturous tumult of the arteries which transformed my grisly task into one of beloved devotion – yet every carnal satiation exacted its toll. I came to dread the days that brought no dead for me to gloat over, and prayed to all the obscene gods of the nethermost abysses to bring swift, sure death upon the residents of the city.

Then came the nights when a skulking figure stole surreptitiously through the shadowy streets of the suburbs; pitchdark nights when the midnight moon was obscured by heavy lowering clouds. It was a furtive figure that blended with the trees and cast fugitive glances over its shoulder; a figure bent on some malignant mission. After one of these prowlings the morning papers would scream to their sensation-mad clientele the details of some nightmare crime; column on column of lurid gloating over abominable atrocities; paragraph on paragraph of impossible solutions and extravagant, conflicting suspicions. Through it all I felt a supreme sense of security, for who would for a moment suspect an employee in an undertaking establishment, where Death was supposedly an everyday affair, of seeking surcease from unnameable urgings in the cold-blooded slaughter of his fellow-beings? I planned each crime with maniacal cunning, varying the manner of my murders so that no one would even dream that all were the work of one blood-stained pair of hands. The aftermath of each nocturnal venture was an ecstatic hour of pleasure, pernicious and unalloyed; a pleasure always heightened by the chance that its delicious source might later be assigned to my gloating administrations in the course of my regular occupation. Sometimes that double and ultimate pleasure did occur – O rare and delicious memory!

During long nights when I clung to the shelter of my sanctuary, I was prompted by the mausoleum silence to devise new and unspeakable ways of lavishing my affections upon the dead that I loved – the dead that gave me life!

One morning Mr Gresham came much earlier than usual – came to find me stretched out upon a cold slab deep in ghoulish slumber, my arms wrapped about the stark, stiff, naked body of a fetid corpse! He roused me from my salacious dreams, his eyes filled with mingled detestation and pity. Gently but firmly he told me that I must go, that my nerves were unstrung, that I needed a long rest from the repellent tasks my vocation required, that my impressionable youth was too deeply affected by the dismal atmosphere of my environment. How little did he know of the demoniacal desires that spurred me on in my disgusting infirmities! I was wise enough to see that argument would only strengthen his belief in my potential madness – it was far better to leave than to invite discovery of the motive underlying my action.

After this I dared not stay long in one place for fear some overt act would bare my secret to an unsympathetic world. I drifted from city to city, from town to town. I worked in morgues, around cemeteries, once in a crematory – anywhere that afforded me an opportunity to be near the dead that I so craved.

Then came the World War. I was one of the first to go across, one of the last to return. Four years of blood-red charnel Hell . . . sickening slime of rain and rotten trenches . . . deafening bursting of hysterical shells . . . monotonous droning of sardonic bullets . . . smoking frenzies of Phlegethon's fountains . . . stifling fumes of murderous gases . . . grotesque remnants of smashed and shredded bodies . . . four years of transcendent satisfaction.

In every wanderer there is a latent urge to return to the scenes of his childhood. A few months later found me making my way through the familiar byways of Fenham. Vacant dilapidated farm houses lined the adjacent roadsides, while the years had brought equal retrogression to the town itself. A mere handful of the houses were occupied, but among those was the one I had once called home. The tangled, weed-choked driveway, the broken window panes, the uncared-for acres that stretched behind, all bore mute confirmation of the tales that guarded inquiries had elicited – that it now sheltered a dissolute drunkard who eked out a meager existence from the chores his few neighbors gave him out of sympathy for the mistreated wife and undernourished child who shared his lot. All in all, the glamour surrounding my youthful environment was entirely dispelled; so, prompted by some errant foolhardy thought, I next turned my step toward Bayboro.

Here, too, the years had brought changes, but in reverse order. The small city I remembered had almost doubled in size despite its wartime depopulation. Instinctively I sought my former place of employment, finding it still there but with an unfamiliar name and 'Successor to' above the door, for the influenza epidemic had claimed Mr Gresham, while the boys were overseas. Some fateful mood impelled me to ask for work. I referred to my tutelage under Mr Gresham with some trepidation, but my fears were groundless – my late employer had carried the secret of my unethical conduct with him to the grave. An opportune vacancy ensured my immediate re-installation.

Then came vagrant haunting memories of scarlet nights of impious pilgrimages, and an uncontrollable desire to renew those illicit joys. I cast caution to the winds and launched upon another series of damnable debaucheries. Once more the yellow sheets found welcome material in the devilish details of my crimes, comparing them to the red weeks of horror that had appalled the city years before. Once more the police sent out their dragnet and drew into its enmeshing folds – nothing!

My thirst for the noxious nectar of the dead grew to a consuming fire, and I began to shorten the periods between my odious exploits. I realized that I was treading on dangerous ground, but demoniac desire gripped me in its torturing tentacles and urged me on.

All this time my mind was becoming more and more benumbed to any influence except the satiation of my insane longings. Little details vitally important to one bent on such evil escapades escaped me. Somehow, somewhere, I left a vague trace, an elusive clue, behind – not enough to warrant my arrest, but sufficient to turn the tide of suspicion in my direction. I sensed this espionage, yet was helpless to stem the surging demand for more dead to quicken my enervated soul.

Then came the night when the shrill whistle of the police roused me from my fiendish gloating over the body of my latest victim, a gory razor still clutched tightly in my hand. With one dexterous motion I closed the blade and thrust it into the pocket of the coat I wore. Nightsticks beat a lusty tattoo upon the door. I crashed the window with a chair, thanking Fate I had chosen one of the cheaper tenement districts for my locale. I dropped into a dingy alley as blue-coated forms burst through the shattered door. Over shaky fences, through filthy back yards, past squalid ramshackle houses, down dimly-lighted narrow streets I fled. I thought at once of the wooded marshes that lay beyond the city and stretched for half a hundred miles till they touched the outskirts of Fenham. If I could reach this goal I would be temporarily safe. Before dawn I was plunging headlong through the foreboding wasteland, stumbling over the rotting roots of half-dead trees whose naked branches stretched out like grotesque arms striving to encumber me with mocking embraces.

The imps of the nefarious gods to whom I offered my idolatrous prayers must have guided my footsteps through that menacing morass. A week later – wan, bedraggled, and emaciated – I lurked in the woods a mile from Fenham. So far I had eluded my pursuers, yet I dared not show myself, for I knew that the alarm must have been sent broadcast. I vaguely hoped I had thrown them off the trail. After that first frenetic night I had heard no sound of alien voices, no crashing of heavy bodies through the underbrush. Perhaps they had concluded that my body lay hidden in some stagnant pool or had vanished forever in the tenacious quagmire.

Hunger gnawed at my vitals with poignant pangs, thirst left my throat parched and dry. Yet far worse was the unbearable hunger of my starving soul for the stimulus I found only in the nearness of the dead. My nostrils quivered in sweet recollection. No longer could I delude myself with the thought that this desire was a mere whim of the heated imagination. I knew now that it was an integral part of life itself; that without it I should burn out like an empty lamp. I summoned all my remaining energy to fit me for the task of satisfying my accursed appetite. Despite the peril attending my move I set out to reconnoiter, skirting the sheltering shadows like an obscene wraith. Once more I felt that strange sensation of being led by some unseen satellite of Satan. Yet even my sin-steeped soul revolted for a moment when I found myself before my native abode, the scene of my youthful hermitage.

Then these disquieting memories faded. In their place came overwhelming lustful desire. Behind the rotting walls of this old house lay my prey. A moment later I had raised one of the shattered windows and climbed over the sill. I listened for a moment, every sense alert, every muscle tensed for action. The silence reassured me. With cat-like tread I stole through the familiar rooms until stertorous snores indicated the place where I was to find surcease from my sufferings. I allowed myself a sigh of anticipated ecstasy as I pushed open the door of the bedchamber. Panther-like I made my way to the supine form stretched out in a drunken stupor. The wife and child – where were they? – well, they could wait. My clutching fingers groped for his throat.

Hours later I was again the fugitive, but a new-found stolen strength was mine. Three silent forms slept to wake no more. It was not until the garish light of day penetrated my hiding-place that I visualized the certain consequences of my rashly purchased relief. By this time the bodies must have been discovered. Even the most obtuse of the rural police must surely link the tragedy with my flight from the nearby city. Besides, for the first time I had been careless enough to leave some tangible proof of my identity – my fingerprints on the throats of the newly dead. All day I shivered in nervous apprehension. The mere crackling of a dry twig beneath my feet conjured mental images that appalled me. That night, under cover of the protecting darkness, I skirted Fenham and made for the woods that lay beyond. Before dawn came the first definite hint of renewed pursuit – the distant baying of hounds.

Through the long night I pressed on, but by morning I could feel my artificial strength ebbing. Noon brought once more the insistent call of the contaminating curse, and I knew I must fall by the way unless I could once more experience that exotic intoxication that came only with the proximity of the loved dead. I had traveled in a wide semicircle. If I pushed steadily ahead, midnight would bring me to the cemetery where I had laid my parents years before. My only hope, I felt certain, lay in reaching this goal before I was overtaken. With silent prayer to the devils that dominated my destiny I turned leaden feet in the direction of my last stronghold.

God! Can it be that a scant twelve hours have passed since I started for my ghostly sanctuary? I have lived an eternity in each leaden hour. But I have reached a rich reward. The noxious odors of this neglected spot are frankincense to my suffering soul!

The first streaks of dawn are graying the horizon. They are coming! My sharp ears catch the far-off howling of the dogs! It is but a matter of minutes before they find me and shut me away forever from the rest of the world, to spend my days in ravaging yearnings till at last I join the dead I love!

They shall not take me! A way of escape is open! A coward's choice, perhaps, but better – far better – than endless months of nameless misery. I will leave this record behind me that some soul may perhaps understand why I make this choice.

The razor! It has nestled forgotten in my pocket since my flight from Bayboro. Its blood-stained blade gleams oddly in the waning light of the thin-edged moon. One slashing stroke across my left wrist and deliverance is assured. . . .

Warm, fresh blood spatters grotesque patterns on dingy, decrepit slabs . . . phantasmal hordes swarm over the rotting graves . . . spectral fingers beckon me . . . ethereal fragments of unwritten melodies rise in celestial crescendo . . . distant stars dance drunkenly in demoniac accompaniment . . . a thousand tiny hammers beat hideous dissonances on anvils inside my chaotic brain . . . gray ghosts of slaughtered spirits parade in mocking silence before me . . . scorched tongues of invisible flame sear the brand of Hell upon my sickened soul . . . I can – write – no – more. . . .

THE GHOST-EATER

by C. M. Eddy, Jr.

Moon-Madness? A touch of fever? I wish I could think so! But when I am alone after dark in the waste places where my wanderings take me, and hear across infinite voids the demon echoes of those screams and snarls, and that detestable crunching of bones, I shudder again at the memory of that eldritch night.

I knew less of woodcraft in those days, though the wilderness called just as strongly to me as it does now. Up to that night I had always been careful to employ a guide, but circumstances now suddenly forced me to a trial of my own skill. It was midsummer in Maine, and, despite my great need to get from Mayfair to Glendale by the next noon, I could find no person willing to pilot me. Unless I took the long route through Petewisset, which would not bring me to my goal in time, there would be dense forests to penetrate; yet whenever I asked for a guide I was met with refusal and evasion.

Stranger that I was, it seemed odd that everyone should have glib excuses. There was too much 'important business' on hand for such a sleepy village, and I knew that the natives were lying. But they all had 'imperative duties,' or said that they had; and would do no more than assure me that the trail through the woods was very plain, running due north, and not in the least difficult for a vigorous young fellow. If I started while the morning was still early, they averred, I could get to Glendale by sundown and avoid a night in the open. Even then I suspected nothing. The prospect seemed good, and I resolved to try it alone, let the lazy villagers hang back as they might. Probably I would have tried it even if I had suspected; for youth is stubborn, and from childhood I had only laughed at superstition and old wives' tales.

So before the sun was high I had started off through the trees at a swinging stride, lunch in my hand, guardian automatic in my pocket, and belt filled with crisp bills of large denominations. From the distances given me and a knowledge of my own speed, I had figured on making Glendale a little after sunset; but I knew that even if detained overnight through some miscalculation, I had plenty of camping experience to fall back on. Besides, my presence at my destination was not really necessary till the following noon.

It was the weather that set my plans awry. As the sun rose higher, it scorched through even the thickets of the foliage, and burned up my energy at every step. By noon my clothes were soaking with perspiration, and I felt myself faltering in spite of all my resolution. As I pushed deeper into the woods I found the trail greatly obstructed with underbrush, and at many points nearly effaced. It must have been weeks – perhaps months – since anyone had broken his way through; and I began to wonder if I could, after all, live up to my schedule.

At length, having grown very hungry, I looked for the deepest patch of shade I could find, and proceeded to eat the lunch which the hotel had prepared for me. There were some indifferent sandwiches, a piece of stale pie, and a bottle of very light wine; by no means sumptuous fare, but welcome enough to one in my state of overheated exhaustion.

It was too hot for smoking to be of any solace, so I did not take out my pipe. Instead I stretched myself at full length under the trees when my meal was done, intent on stealing a few moments' rest before commencing the last lap of my journey. I suppose I was a fool to drink that wine; for, light though it was, it proved just enough to finish the work the sultry, oppressive day had begun. My plan called for the merest momentary relaxation, yet, with scarcely a warning yawn, I dropped off into a sound slumber.

When I opened my eyes twilight was closing in about me. A wind fanned my cheeks, restoring me quickly to full perception; and as I glanced up at the sky I saw with apprehension that black racing clouds were leading on a solid wall of darkness prophetic of violent thunderstorm. I knew now that I could not reach Glendale before morning, but the prospect of a night in the woods – my first night of lone forest camping – became very repugnant under these trying conditions. In a moment I decided to push along for a while at least, in the hope of finding some shelter before the tempest should break.

Darkness spread over the woods like a heavy blanket. The lowering clouds grew more threatening, and the wind increased to a veritable gale. A flash of distant lightning illuminated the sky, followed by an ominous rumble that seemed to hint of malign pursuit. Then I felt a drop of rain on my outstretched hand; and though still walking on automatically, resigned myself to the inevitable. Another moment and I had seen the light; the light of a window through the trees and the darkness. Eager only for shelter, I hastened toward it – would to God I had turned and fled!

There was a sort of imperfect clearing on the farther side of which, with its back against the primeval wood, stood a building. I had expected a shanty or log-cabin, but stopped short in surprise when I beheld a neat and tasteful little house of two stories; some seventy years old by its architecture, yet still in a state of repair betokening the closest and most civilized attention. Through the small panes of one of the lower windows a bright light shone, and toward this – spurred by the impact of another raindrop – I presently hurried across the clearing, rapping loudly on the doors as soon as I gained the steps.

With startling promptness my knock was answered by a deep, pleasant voice which uttered the single syllable, 'Come!'

Pushing open the unlocked door, I entered a shadowy hall lighted by an open doorway at the right, beyond which was a book-lined room with the gleaming window. As I closed the outer door behind me I could not help noticing a peculiar odor about the house; a faint, elusive, scarcely definable odor which somehow suggested animals. My host, I surmised, must be a hunter or trapper, with his business conducted on the premises.

The man who had spoken sat in a capacious easy-chair beside a marble-topped center table, a long lounging-robe of gray swathing his lean form. The light from a powerful argand lamp threw his features into prominence, and as he eyed me curiously I studied him in no less detail. He was strikingly handsome, with thin, clean-shaven face, glossy, flaxen hair neatly brushed, long, regular eyebrows that met in a slanting angle above the nose, shapely ears set low and well back on the head, and large expressive gray eyes almost luminous in their animation. When he smiled a welcome he showed a magnificently even set of firm white teeth, and as he waved me to a chair I was struck by the fineness of his slender hands, with their long, tapering fingers whose ruddy, almond-shaped nails were slightly curved and exquisitely manicured. I could not help wondering why a man of such engaging personality should choose the life of a recluse.

'Sorry to intrude,' I ventured, 'but I've given up the hope of making Glendale before morning, and there's a storm coming on which sent me looking for cover.' As if to corroborate my words, there came at this point a vivid flash, a crashing reverberation, and the first breaking of a torrential downpour that beat maniacally against the windows.

My host seemed oblivious to the elements, and flashed me another smile when he answered. His voice was soothing and well modulated, and his eyes held a calmness almost hypnotic.

'You're welcome to whatever hospitality I can offer, but I'm afraid it won't be much. I've a game leg, so you'll have to do most of the waiting on yourself. If you're hungry you'll find plenty in the kitchen – plenty of food, if not of ceremony!' It seemed to me that I could detect the slightest trace of a foreign accent in his tone, though his language was fluently correct and idiomatic.

Rising to an impressive height, he headed for the door with long, limping steps, and I noticed the huge hairy arms that hung at his side in such curious contrast with his delicate hands.

'Come,' he suggested. 'Bring the lamp along with you. I might as well sit in the kitchen as here.'

I followed him into the hall and the room across it, and at his direction ransacked the woodpile in the corner and the cupboard on the wall. A few moments later, when the fire was going nicely, I asked him if I might not prepare food for both; but he courteously declined.

'It's too hot to eat,' he told me. 'Besides, I had a bite before you came.'

After washing the dishes left from my lone meal, I sat down for a while, smoking my pipe contentedly. My host asked a few questions about the neighboring villages, but lapsed into sullen taciturnity when he learned I was an outsider. As he brooded there silently I could not help feeling a quality of strangeness in him; some subtle alienage that could hardly be analyzed. I was quite certain, for one thing, that he was tolerating me because of the storm rather than welcoming me with genuine hospitality.

As for the storm, it seemed almost to have spent itself. Outside, it was already growing lighter – for there was a full moon behind the clouds – and the rain had dwindled to a trivial drizzle. Perhaps, I thought, I could now resume my journey after all; an idea which I suggested to my host.

'Better wait till morning,' he remarked. 'You say you're afoot, and it's a good three hours to Glendale. I've two bedrooms upstairs, and you're welcome to one of them if you care to stay.'

There was a sincerity in his invitation which dispelled any doubts I had held regarding his hospitality, and I now concluded that his silences must be the result of long isolation from his fellows in this wilderness. After sitting without a word through three fillings of my pipe, I finally began to yawn.

'It's been rather a strenuous day for me,' I admitted, 'and I guess I'd better be making tracks for bed. I want to be up at sunrise, you know, and on my way.'

My host waved his arm toward the door, through which I could see the hall and the staircase.

'Take the lamp with you,' he instructed. 'It's the only one I have, but I don't mind sitting in the dark, really. Half the time I don't light it at all when I'm alone. Oil is so hard to get out here, and I go to the village so seldom. Your room is the one on the right, at the head of the stairs.'

Taking the lamp and turning in the hall to say good-night, I could see his eyes glowing almost phosphorescently in the darkened room I had left; and I was half reminded for a moment of the jungle, and the circles of eyes that sometimes glow just beyond the radius of the campfire. Then I started upstairs.

As I reached the second floor I could hear my host limping across the hall to the other room below, and perceived that he moved with owlish sureness despite the darkness. Truly, he had but little need of the lamp. The storm was over, and as I entered the room assigned me I found it bright with the rays of a full moon that streamed on to the bed from an uncurtained south window. Blowing out the lamp and leaving the house in darkness but for the moonbeams, I sniffed at the pungent odor that rose above the scent of the kerosene – the quasi-animal odor I had noticed on first entering the place. I crossed to the window and threw it wide, breathing deep of the cool, fresh night air.

When I started to undress I paused almost instantly, recalling my money belt, still in its place about my waist. Possibly, I reflected, it would be well not to be too hasty or unguarded;

for I had read of men who seized just such an opportunity to rob and even to murder the stranger within their dwellings. So, arranging the bedclothes to look as if they covered a sleeping figure, I drew the room's only chair into the concealing shadows, filled and lighted my pipe again, and sat down to rest or watch, as the occasion might demand.

I could not have been sitting there long when my sensitive ears caught the sound of footsteps ascending the stairs. All the old lore of robber landlords rushed on me afresh, when another moment revealed that the steps were plain, loud, and careless, with no attempt at concealment; while my host's tread, as I had heard it from the head of the staircase, was a soft limping stride. Shaking the ashes from my pipe, I slipped it into my pocket. Then, seizing and drawing my automatic, I rose from the chair, tiptoed across the room, and crouched tensely in a spot which the opening door would cover.

The door opened, and into the shaft of moonlight stepped a man I had never seen before. Tall, broad-shouldered, and distinguished, his face half hidden by a heavy square-cut beard and his neck buried in a high black stock of a pattern long obsolete in America, he was indubitably a foreigner. How he could have entered the house without my knowledge was quite beyond me, nor could I believe for an instant that he had been concealed in either of the two rooms or the hall below me. As I gazed intently at him in the insidious moonbeams it seemed to me that I could see directly through his sturdy form; but perhaps this was only an illusion that came from my shock of surprise.

Noticing the disarray of the bed, but evidently missing the intended effect of occupancy, the stranger muttered something to himself in a foreign tongue and proceeded to disrobe. Flinging his clothes into the chair I had vacated, he crept into bed, pulled the covers over him, and in a moment or two was breathing with the regular respiration of a sound sleeper.

My first thought was to seek out my host and demand an explanation, but a second later I deemed it better to make sure that the whole incident was not a mere delusive aftereffect of my wine-drugged sleep in the woods. I still felt weak and faint, and despite my recent supper was as hungry as if I had not eaten since that noonday lunch.

I crossed to the bed, reached out, and grasped at the shoulder of the sleeping man. Then, barely checking a cry of mad fright and dizzy astonishment, I fell back with pounding pulses and dilated eyes. *For my clutching fingers had passed directly through the sleeping form, and seized only the sheet below!*

A complete analysis of my jarred and jumbled sensations would be futile. The man was intangible, yet I could still see him there, hear his regular breathing, and watch his figure as it half-turned beneath the clothes. And then, as I was quite certain of my own madness or hypnosis, I heard other footsteps on the stairs; soft, padding, doglike, limping footsteps, pattering up, up, up. . . . And again that pungent animal smell, this time in redoubled volume. Dazed and dream-drowsed, I crept once more behind the protecting opened door, shaken to the marrow, but now resigned to any fate known or nameless.

Then into that shaft of eery moonlight stepped the gaunt form of a great gray wolf. Limped, I should have said, for one hind foot was held in the air, as though wounded by some stray shot. The beast turned its head in my direction, and as it did so the pistol dropped from my twitching fingers and clattered unheeded to the floor. The ascending succession of horrors was fast paralyzing my will and consciousness, *for the eyes that now glared toward me from that hellish head were the gray phosphorescent eyes of my host as they had peered at me through the darkness of the kitchen.*

I do not yet know whether it saw me. The eyes turned from my direction to the bed, and gazed gluttonously on the spectral sleeping form there. Then the head tilted back, and from that demon throat came the most shocking ululation I have ever heard; a thick, nauseous, lupine howl that made my heart stand still. The form on the bed stirred, opened his eyes, and shrank from what he saw. The animal crouched quivering, and then – as the ethereal figure uttered a shriek of mortal human anguish and terror that no ghost of legend could counterfeit – sprang straight for its victim's throat, its white, firm, even teeth flashing in the moonlight as they closed on the jugular vein of the screaming phantasm. The scream ended in a blood-choked gurgle, and the frightened human eyes turned glassy.

That scream had roused me to action, and in a second I had retrieved my automatic and emptied its entire contents into the wolfish monstrosity before me. *But I heard the un-*

hindered thud of each bullet as it imbedded itself in the opposite wall.

My nerves gave way. Blind fear hurled me toward the door, and blind fear prompted the one backward glance in which I saw that the wolf had sunk its teeth into the body of its quarry. Then came that culminating sensory impression and the devastating thought to which it gave birth. This was the same body I had thrust my hand *through* a few moments before . . . and yet as I plunged down that black nightmare staircase *I could hear the crunching of bones.*

How I found the trail to Glendale, or how I managed to traverse it, I suppose I shall never know. I only know that sunrise found me on the hill at the edge of the woods, with the steepled village outspread below me, and the blue thread of the Cataqua sparkling in the distance. Hatless, coatless, ashen-faced, and as soaked with perspiration as if I had spent the night abroad in the storm, I hesitated to enter the village till I had recovered at least some outward semblance of composure. At last I picked my way down hill and through the narrow streets with their flagstone sidewalks and Colonial doorways till I reached the Lafayette House, whose proprietor eyed me askance.

'Where from so early, son? And why the wild look?'

'I've just come through the woods from Mayfair.'

'You – came – through – the Devil's Woods – *last night* – and – *alone*?' The old man stared with a queer look of alternate horror and incredulity.

'Why not?' I countered, 'I couldn't have made it in time through Petowisset, and I had to be here not later than this noon.'

'And last night was *full moon!* . . . My Gawd!' He eyed me curiously. 'See anything of Vasili Oukranikov or the Count?'

'Say, do I look that simple? What are you trying to do – jolly me?'

But his tone was as grave as a priest's as he replied. 'You must be new to these parts, sonny. If you weren't you'd know all about Devil's Woods and the full moon and Vasili and the rest.'

I felt anything but flippant, yet knew I must not seem serious after my earlier remarks. 'Go on – I know you're dying to tell me. I'm like a donkey – all ears.'

Then he told the legend in his dry way, stripping it of vitality and convincingness through lack of coloring, detail, and atmosphere. But for me it needed no vitality or convincingness that any poet could have given. Remember what I had witnessed, and remember that I had never heard of the tale until *after* I had had the experience and fled from the terror of those crunched phantom bones.

'There used to be quite a few Russians scattered betwixt here and Mayfair – they came after one of their nihilist troubles back in Russia. Vasili Oukranikov was one of 'em – a tall, thin, handsome chap with shiny yellow hair and a wonderful manner. They said, though, that he was a servant of the devil – a werewolf and eater of men.

'He built him a house in the woods about a third of the way from here to Mayfair and lived all alone. Every once in a while a traveler would come out of the woods with some pretty strange tale about being chased by a big wolf with shining human eyes – like Oukranikov's. One night somebody took a pot shot at the wolf, and the next time the Russian came into Glendale he walked with a limp. That settled it. There wasn't any mere suspicion now, but hard facts.

'Then he sent to Mayfair for the Count – his name was Feodar Tchernevsky and he had bought the old gambrel-roofed Fowler place up State Street – to come out and see him. They all warned the Count, for he was a fine man and a splendid neighbor, but he said he could take care of himself all right. It was the night of the full moon. He was brave as they make 'em, and all he did was to tell some men he had around the place to follow him to Vasili's if he didn't show up in decent time. They did – and you tell me, sonny, that you've been through those woods at night?'

'Sure I tell you' – I tried to appear nonchalant – 'I'm no Count, and here I am to tell the tale! . . . But what did the men find at Oukranikov's house?'

'They found the Count's mangled body, sonny, and a gaunt gray wolf hovering over it with blood-slavering jaws. You can guess who the wolf was. And folks do say that at every full moon – but sonny, didn't you see or hear anything?'

'Not a thing, pop! And say, what became of the wolf – or Vasili Oukranikov?'

'Why, son, they killed it – filled it full of lead and buried it in the house, and then burned the place down – you know, all this was sixty years ago when I was a little shaver, but I remember it as if 'twas yesterday.'

I turned away with a shrug of my shoulders. It was all so quaint and silly and artificial in the full light of day. But sometimes when I am alone after dark in waste places, and hear the demon echoes of those screams and snarls, and that detestable crunching of bones, I shudder again at the memory of that eldritch night.

THE DIARY OF ALONZO TYPER

by William Lumley

Editor's Note: Alonzo Hasbrouch Typer of Kingston, New York, was last seen and recognized on April 17, 1908, around noon, at the Hotel Richmond in Batavia. He was the only survivor of an ancient Ulster County family, and was fifty-three years old at the time of his disappearance.

Mr Typer was educated privately and at Columbia and Heidelberg universities. All his life was spent as a student, the field of his researches including many obscure and generally feared borderlands of human knowledge. His papers on vampirism, ghouls, and poltergeist phenomena were privately printed after rejection by many publishers. He resigned from the Society for Psychical Research in 1900 after a series of peculiarly bitter controversies.

At various times Mr Typer traveled extensively, sometimes dropping out of sight for long periods. He is known to have visited obscure spots in Nepal, India, Tibet, and Indo-China, and passed most of the year 1899 on mysterious Easter Island. The extensive search for Mr Typer after his disappearance yielded no results, and his estate was divided among distant cousins in New York City.

The diary herewith presented was allegedly found in the ruins of a large country house near Attica, N.Y., which had borne a curiously sinister reputation for generations before its collapse. The edifice was very old, antedating the general white settlement of the region, and had formed the home of a strange and secretive family named van der Heyl, which had migrated from Albany in 1746 under a curious cloud of witchcraft suspicion. The structure probably dated from about 1760.

Of the history of the van der Heyls very little is known. They remained entirely aloof from their normal neighbors, employed negro servants brought directly from Africa and speaking little English, and educated their children privately and at European colleges. Those of them who went out into the world were soon lost to sight though not before gaining evil repute for association with Black Mass groups and cults of even darker significance.

Around the dreaded house a straggling village arose, populated by Indians and later by renegades from the surrounding country, which bore the dubious name of Chorazin. Of the singular hereditary strains which afterward appeared in the mixed Chorazin villagers, several monographs have been written by ethnologists. Just behind the village, and in sight of the van der Heyl house, is a steep hill crowned with a peculiar ring of ancient standing stones which the Iroquois always regarded with fear and loathing. The origin and nature of the stones, whose date, according to archeological and climatological evidence, must be fabulously early, is a problem still unsolved.

From about 1795 onward, the legends of the incoming pioneers and later population have much to say about strange cries and chants proceeding at certain seasons from Chorazin and from the great house and hill of standing stones; though there is reason to suppose that the noises ceased about 1872, when the entire van der Heyl household – servants and all – suddenly and simultaneously disappeared.

Thenceforward the house was deserted; for other disastrous events – including three unexplained deaths, five disappearances, and four cases of sudden insanity – occurred when later owners and interested visitors attempted to stay in it. The house, village, and extensive rural areas on all sides reverted to the state and were auctioned off in the absence of discoverable van der Heyl heirs. Since about 1890 the owners (successively the late Charles A. Shields and his son Oscar S. Shields, of Buffalo) have left the entire property in a state of absolute neglect, and have warned all inquirers not to visit the region.

Of those known to have approached the house during the last forty years, most were occult students, police officers, newspaper men, and odd characters from abroad. Among the latter was a mysterious Eurasian, probably from Cochin-China, whose later appearance with blank mind and bizarre mutilations excited wide press notice in 1903.

Mr Typer's diary – a book about $6 \times 3\frac{1}{2}$ inches in size, with tough paper and an oddly durable binding of thin sheet metal – was discovered in the possession of one of the decadent Chorazin villagers on November 16, 1935, by a state policeman sent to investigate the rumored collapse of the deserted van der Heyl mansion. The house had indeed fallen, obviously from sheer age and decrepitude, in the severe gale of November 12. Disintegration was peculiarly complete, and no thorough search of the ruins could be made for several weeks. John Eagle, the swarthy, simian-faced, Indian-like villager who had the diary, said that he found the book quite near the surface of the debris, in what must have been an upper front room.

Very little of the contents of the house could be identified, though an enormous and astonishingly solid brick vault in the cellar (whose ancient iron door had to be blasted open because of the strangely figured and perversely tenacious lock) remained intact and presented several puzzling features. For one thing, the walls were covered with still undeciphered hieroglyphs roughly incised in the brickwork. Another peculiarity was a huge circular aperture in the rear of the vault, blocked by a cave-in evidently caused by the collapse of the house.

But strangest of all was the apparently *recent* deposit of some fetid, slimy, pitch-black substance on the flagstoned floor, extending in a yard-broad, irregular line with one end at the blocked circular aperture. Those who first opened the vault declared that the place smelled like the snake-house at a zoo.

The diary, which was apparently designed solely to cover an investigation of the dreaded van der Heyl house by the vanished Mr Typer, has been proved by handwriting experts to be genuine. The script shows signs of increasing nervous strain as it progresses toward the end, in places becoming almost illegible. Chorazin villagers – whose stupidity and taciturnity baffle all students of the region and its secrets – admit no recollection of Mr Typer as distinguished from other rash visitors to the dreaded house.

The text of the diary is here given verbatim and without comment. How to interpret it, and what, other than the writer's madness, to infer from it, the reader must decide for himself. Only the future can tell what its value may be in solving a generation-old mystery. It may be remarked that genealogists confirm Mr Typer's belated memory in the matter of *Adriaen Sleght*.

THE DIARY

Arrived here about 6 P.M. Had to walk all the way from Attica in the teeth of an oncoming storm, for no one would rent me a horse or rig, and I can't run an automobile. This place is even worse than I had expected, and I dread what is coming, even though I long at the same time to learn the secret. All too soon will come the night – the old Walpurgis sabbat horror – and after that time in Wales I know what to look for. Whatever comes, I shall not flinch. Prodded by some unfathomable urge, I have given my whole life to the quest of unholy mysteries. I came here for nothing else, and will not quarrel with fate.

It was very dark when I got here, though the sun had by no means set. The stormclouds were the densest I had ever seen, and I could not have found my way but for the lightning-flashes. The village is a hateful little back-water, and its few inhabitants no better than idiots. One of them saluted me in a queer way, as if he knew me. I could see very little of the landscape – just a small, swamp valley of strange brown weed-stalks and dead fungi surrounded by scraggly, evilly twisted trees with bare boughs. But behind the village is a dismal-looking hill on whose summit is a circle of great stones with another stone at the center. That, without question, is the vile primordial thing V——— told me about the N———estbat.

The great house lies in the midst of a park all overgrown with curious-looking briars. I could scarcely break through, and when I did the vast age and decrepitude of the building almost stopped me from entering. The place looked filthy and diseased, and I wondered how so leprous a bulk could hang together. It is wooden; and though its original lines are hidden by a bewildering tangle of wings added at various dates, I think it was first built in the square colonial fashion of New England. Probably that was easier to build than a Dutch stone house – and then, too, I recall that Dirck van der Heyl's wife was from Salem, a daughter of the unmentionable Abaddon Corey. There was a small pillared porch, and I got under it just as the storm burst. It was a fiendish tempest – black as midnight, with rain in sheets, thunder and lightning like the day of general dissolution, and a wind that actually clawed at me.

The door was unlocked, so I took out my electric torch and went inside. Dust was inches thick on the floor and furniture, and the place smelled like a mold-caked tomb. There was a hall reaching all the way through, and a curving staircase on the right.

I plowed my way upstairs and selected this front room to camp out in. The whole place seems fully furnished, though most of the furniture is breaking down. This is written at 8 o'clock, after a cold meal from my traveling-case. After this the village people will bring me supplies; though they won't agree to come any closer than the ruins of the park gate until (as they say) later. I wish I could get rid of an unpleasant feeling of familiarity with this place.

Later

I am conscious of several presences in this house. One in particular is decidedly hostile toward me – a malevolent will which is seeking to break down my own and overcome me. I must not countenance this for an instant, but must use all my forces to resist it. It is appallingly evil, and definitely non-human. I think it must be allied to powers outside Earth – powers in the spaces behind time and beyond the universe. It towers like a colossus, bearing out what is said in the Aklo writings. There is such a feeling of vast size connected with it that I wonder these chambers can contain its bulk – and yet it has no visible bulk. Its age must be unutterably vast – shockingly, indescribably so.

April 18

Slept very little last night. At 3 A.M. a strange, creeping wind began to pervade the whole region, ever rising until the house rocked as if in a typhoon. As I went down the staircase to see to the rattling front door the darkness took half-visible forms in my imagination. Just below the landing I was pushed violently from behind – by the wind, I suppose, though I could have sworn I saw the dissolving outlines of a gigantic black paw as I turned quickly about. I did not lose my footing, but safely finished the descent and shot the heavy bolt of the dangerously shaking door.

I had not meant to explore the house before dawn; yet now,

unable to sleep again and fired with mixed terror and curiosity, I felt reluctant to postpone my search. With my powerful torch I plowed through the dust to the great south parlor, where I knew the portraits would be. There they were, just as V——— had said, and as I seemed to know from some obscurer source as well. Some were so blackened and dust-clouded that I could make little or nothing of them, but from those I could trace I recognized that they were indeed of the hateful line of the van der Heyls. Some of the paintings seemed to suggest faces I had known; but just what faces, I could not recall.

The outlines of that frightful hybrid Joris – spawned in 1773 by old Dirck's youngest daughter – were clearest of all, and I could trace the green eyes and the serpent look in his face. Every time I shut off the flashlight that face would seem to glow in the dark until I half fancied it shone with a faint, greenish light of its own. The more I looked, the more evil it seemed, and I turned away to avoid hallucinations of changing expression.

But that to which I turned was even worse. The long, dour face, small, closely set eyes and swine-like features identified it at once, even though the artist had striven to make the snout look as human as possible. This was what V——— had whispered about. As I stared in horror, I thought the eyes took on a reddish glow, and for a moment the background seemed replaced by an alien and seemingly irrelevant scene – a lone, bleak moor beneath a dirty yellow sky, whereon grew a wretched-looking blackthorn bush. Fearing for my sanity, I rushed from that accursed gallery to the dust-cleared corner upstairs where I have my 'camp.'

Later

Decided to explore some of the labyrinthine wings of the house by daylight. I cannot get lost, for my footprints are distinct in the ankle-deep dust, and I can trace other identifying marks when necessary. It is curious how easily I learn the intricate windings of the corridors. Followed a long, outflung northerly 'ell' to its extremity, and came to a locked door, which I forced. Beyond was a very small room quite crowded with furniture, and with the paneling badly worm-eaten. On the outer wall I spied a black space behind the rotting woodwork, and discovered a narrow secret passage leading downward to unknown inky depths. It was a steeply inclined chute or tunnel without steps or hand-holds, and I wondered what its use could have been.

Above the fireplace was a moldy painting, which I found on close inspection to be that of a young woman in the dress of the late Eighteenth Century. The face is of classic beauty, yet with the most fiendishly evil expression which I have ever known the human countenance to bear. Not merely callousness, greed, and cruelty, but some quality hideous beyond human comprehension seems to sit upon those finely carved features. And as I looked it seemed to me that the artist – or the slow processes of mold and decay – had imparted to that pallid complexion a sickly greenish cast, and the least suggestion of an almost imperceptibly scaly texture. Later I ascended to the attic, where I found several chests of strange books – many of utterly alien aspects in letters and in physical form alike. One contained variants of the Aklo formulae which I had never known to exist. I have not yet examined the books on the dusty shelves downstairs.

April 19

There are certainly unseen presences here, even though the dust bears no footprints but my own. Cut a path through the briars yesterday to the park gate where my supplies are left, but this morning I found it closed. Very odd, since the bushes are barely stirring with spring sap. Again I had that feeling of something at hand so colossal that the chambers can scarcely contain it. This time I feel more than one of the presences is of such a size, and I know now that the third Aklo ritual – which I found in that book in the attic yesterday – would make such being solid and visible. Whether I shall dare to try this materialization remains to be seen. The perils are great.

Last night I began to glimpse evanescent shadow-faces and forms in the dim corners of the halls and chambers – faces and forms so hideous and loathsome that I dare not describe them. They seem allied in substance to that titanic paw which tried to push me down the stairs the night before last, and must of course be phantoms of my disturbed imagination. What I am seeking would not be quite like these things. I have seen the paw again, sometimes alone and sometimes with its mate, but I have resolved to ignore all such phenomena.

Early this afternoon I explored the cellar for the first time, descending by a ladder found in a store-room, since the wooden steps had rotted away. The whole place is a mass of nitrous encrustations, with amorphous mounds marking the spots where various objects have disintegrated. At the farther end is a narrow passage which seems to extend under the northerly 'ell' where I found the little locked room, and at the end of this is a heavy brick wall with a locked iron door. Apparently belonging to a vault of some sort, this wall and door bear evidences of Eighteenth-Century workmanship and must be contemporary with the oldest additions to the house – clearly pre-Revolutionary. On the lock, which is obviously older than the rest of the ironwork, are engraved certain symbols which I cannot decipher.

V——— had not told me about this vault. It fills me with a greater disquiet than anything else I have seen, for every time I approach it I have an almost irresistible impulse to *listen* for something. Hitherto no untoward *sounds* have marked my stay in this malign place. As I left the cellar I wished devoutly that the steps were still there; for my progress up the ladder seemed maddeningly slow. I do not want to go down there again – and yet some evil genius urges me to try it *at night* if I would learn what is to be learned.

April 20

I have sounded the depths of horror – only to be made aware of still lower depths. Last night the temptation was too strong, and in the black small hours I descended once more into that nitrous, hellish cellar with my flashlight, tiptoeing among the amorphous heaps to that terrible brick wall and locked door. I made no sound, and refrained from whispering any of the incantations I knew, but I listened with mad intentness.

At last I heard the sounds from beyond those barred plates of sheet iron, the menacing padding and muttering, as of gigantic night-things within. Then, too, there was a damnable slithering, as of a vast serpent or sea-beast dragging its monstrous folds over a paved floor. Nearly paralyzed with fright, I glanced at the huge rusty lock, and at the alien, cryptic hieroglyphs graven upon it. They were signs I could not recognize, and something in their vaguely Mongoloid technique hinted at a blasphemous and indescribable antiquity. At times I fancied I could see them glowing with a greenish light.

I turned to flee, but found that vision of the titan paws before me, the great talons seeming to swell and become more tangible as I gazed. Out of the cellar's evil blackness they stretched, with shadowy hints of scaly wrists beyond them, and with a waxing, malignant will guiding their horrible gropings. Then I heard from behind me – within that abominable vault – a fresh burst of muffled reverberations which seemed to echo from far horizons like distant thunder. Impelled by this greater fear, I advanced toward the shadowy paws with my flashlight and saw them vanish before the full force of the electric beam. Then up the ladder I raced, torch between my teeth, nor did I rest till I had regained my upstairs 'camp.'

What is to be my ultimate end, I dare not imagine. I came as a seeker, but now I know that something is seeking me. I could not leave if I wished. This morning I tried to go to the gate for my supplies, but found the briars twisted tightly in my path. It was the same in every direction – behind and on all sides of the house. In places the brown, barbed vines had uncurled to astonishing heights, forming a steel-like hedge against my egress. The villagers are connected with all this. When I went indoors I found my supplies in the great front hall, though without any clue to how they came there. I am sorry now that I swept the dust away. I shall scatter some more and see what prints are left.

This afternoon I read some of the books in the great shadowy library at the rear of the ground floor, and formed certain suspicions which I cannot bear to mention. I had never seen the text of *Pnakotic Manuscrips* or of the *Eltdown Shards* before, and would not have come here had I known what they contain. I believe it is too late now – for the awful Sabbat is only ten days away. It is for that night of horror that *they* are saving me.

April 21

I have been studying the portraits again. Some have names attached, and I noticed one – of an evil-faced woman, painted some two centuries ago – which puzzled me. It bore the name of Trintje van der Heyl Sleght, and I have a distinct impression that I once met the name of Sleght before, in some significant connection. It was not horrible then, though it becomes so now. I must rack my brain for the clue.

The eyes of these pictures haunt me. Is it possible that some of them are emerging more distinctly from their shrouds of dust and decay and mold? The serpent-faced and swine-faced warlocks stare horribly at me from their blackened frames, and a score of other hybrid faces are beginning to peer out of shadowy backgrounds. There is a hideous look of family resemblance in them all, and that which is human is more horrible than that which is non-human. I wish they reminded me less of other faces – faces I have known in the past. They were an accursed line, and Cornelis of Leyden was the worst of them. It was *he* who broke down the barrier after his father had found that other key. I am sure that V——— knows only a fragment of the horrible truth, so that I am indeed unprepared and defenseless. What of the line before old Claes? What he did in 1591 could never have been done without generations of evil heritage, or some link with the outside. And what of the branches this monstrous line has sent forth? Are they scattered over the world, all awaiting their common heritage of horror? I must recall the place where I once so particularly noticed the name of Sleght.

I wish I could be sure that these pictures stay always in their frames. For several hours now I have been seeing momentary presences like the earlier paws and shadow-faces and forms, but closely duplicating some of the ancient portraits. Somehow I can never glimpse a presence and the portrait it resembles at the same time – the light is always wrong for one or the other, or else the presence and the portrait are in different rooms.

Perhaps, as I have hoped, the presences are mere figments of imagination, but I cannot be sure now. Some are female, and of the same hellish beauty as the picture in the little locked room. Some are like no portrait I have seen, yet make me feel that their painted features lurk unrecognized beneath the mold and soot of canvases I cannot decipher. A few, I desperately fear, have approached materialization in solid or semi-solid form – and some have a dreaded and unexplained familiarity.

There is one woman who in full loveliness excels all the rest. Her poisonous charms are like a honeyed flower growing on the brink of hell. When I look at her closely she vanishes, only to reappear later. Her face has a greenish cast, and now and then I fancy I can spy a suspicion of the squamous in its smooth texture. Who is she? Is she that being who must have dwelt in the little locked room a century and more ago?

My supplies were again left in the front hall – that, clearly, is to be the custom. I had sprinkled dust about to catch footprints, but this morning the whole hall was swept clean by some unknown agency.

April 22

This has been a day of horrible discovery. I explored the cobwebbed attic again, and found a carved, crumbling chest – plainly from Holland – full of blasphemous books and papers far older than any hitherto encountered here. There was a Greek *Necronomicon*, a Norman-French *Livre d'Eibon*, and a first edition of old Ludvig Prinn's *De Vermis Mysteriis.* But the old bound manuscript was the worst. It was in Low Latin, and full of the strange, crabbed handwriting of Claes van der Heyl, being evidently the diary or notebook kept by him between 1560 and 1580. When I unfastened the blackened silver clasp and opened the yellowed leaves a colored drawing fluttered out – the likeness of a monstrous creature resembling nothing so much as a squid, beaked and tentacled, with great yellow eyes, and with certain abominable approximations to the human form in its contours.

I had never before seen so utterly loathsome and nightmarish a form. On the paws, feet, and head-tentacles were curious claws – reminding me of the colossal shadow-shapes which had groped so horribly in my path – while the entity as a whole sat upon a great throne-like pedestal inscribed with unknown hieroglyphs of vaguely Chinese cast. About both writing and image there hung an air of sinister evil so profound and pervasive that I could not think it the product of any one world or age. Rather must that monstrous shape be a focus for all the evil in unbounded space, throughout the eons past and to come – and those eldritch symbols be vile sentient ikons endowed with a morbid life of their own and ready to wrest themselves from the parchment for the reader's destruction. To the meaning of that monster and of those hieroglyphs I had no clue, but I knew that both had been traced with a hellish precision and for no nameable purpose. As I studied the leering characters, their kinship to the symbols on that ominous lock in the cellar became more and more manifest. I left the picture in the attic, for never could sleep come to me with such a thing near by.

All the afternoon and evening I read in the manuscript book of old Claes van der Heyl; and what I read will cloud and make horrible whatever period of life lies ahead of me. The genesis of the world, and of previous worlds, unfolded itself before my eyes. I learned of the city of Shambaliah, built by the Lemurians fifty million years ago, yet inviolate still behind its wall of psychic force in the eastern desert. I learned of the *Book of Dzyan*, whose first six chapters antedate the Earth, and which was old when the lords of Venus came through space in their ships to civilize our planet. And I saw recorded in writing for the first time that name which others had spoken to me in whispers, and which I had known in a closer and more horrible way – the shunned and dreaded name of *Yian-Ho*.

In several places I was held up by passages requiring a key. Eventually, from various allusions, I gathered that old Claes had not dared to embody all his knowledge in one book, but had left certain points for another. Neither volume can be wholly intelligible without its fellow; hence I have resolved to find the second one if it lies anywhere within this accursed house. Though plainly a prisoner, I have not lost my life-long zeal for the unknown; and am determined to probe the cosmos as deeply as possible before doom comes.

April 23

Searched all the morning for the second diary, and found it about noon in a desk in the little locked room. Like the first, it is in Claes van der Heyl's barbarous Latin, and it seems to consist of disjointed notes referring to various sections of the other. Glancing through the leaves, I spied at once the abhorred name of Yian-Ho – of Yian-Ho, that lost and hidden city wherein brood eon-old secrets, and of which dim memories older than the body lurk behind the minds of all men. It was repeated many times, and the text around it was strewn with crudely-drawn hieroglyphs plainly akin to those on the pedestal in that hellish drawing I had seen. Here, clearly, lay the key to that monstrous tentacled shape and its forbidden message. With this knowledge I ascended the creaking stairs to the attic of cobwebs and horror.

When I tried to open the attic door it stuck as never before. Several times it resisted every effort to open it, and when at last it gave way I had a distinct feeling that some colossal, unseen shape had suddenly released it – a shape that soared away on non-material but audibly beating wings. When I found the horrible drawing I felt that it was not precisely where I had left it. Applying the key in the other book, I soon saw that the latter was no instant guide to the secret. It was only a clue – a clue to a secret too black to be left lightly guarded. It would take hours – perhaps days – to extract the awful message.

Shall I live long enough to learn the secret? The shadowy black arms and paws haunt my vision more and more now, and seem even more titanic than at first. Nor am I ever long free from those vague, unhuman presences whose nebulous bulk seems too vast for the chambers to contain. And now and then the grotesque, evanescent faces and forms, and the mocking portrait-shapes, troop before me in bewildering confusion.

Truly, there are terrible primal arcana of Earth which had better be left unknown and unevoked; dread secrets which have nothing to do with man, and which man may learn only in exchange for peace and sanity; cryptic truths which make the knower evermore an alien among his kind, and cause him to walk alone on Earth. Likewise are there dread survivals of things older and more potent than man; things that have blasphemously straggled down through the eons to ages never meant for them; monstrous entities that have lain sleeping endlessly in incredible crypts and remote caverns, outside the laws of reason and causation, and ready to be waked by such blasphemers as shall know their dark forbidden signs and furtive passwords.

April 24

Studied the picture and the key all day in the attic. At sunset I heard strange sounds, of a sort not encountered before and seeming to come from far away. Listening, I realized that they must flow from that queer abrupt hill with the circle of standing stones, which lies behind the village and some distance north of the house. I had heard that there was a path from the house leading up that hill to the primal cromlech, and had suspected that at certain seasons the van der Heyls had much occasion to use it; but the whole matter had hitherto lain latent in my consciousness. The present sounds consisted of a shrill piping intermingled with a peculiar and hideous sort of hissing or whistling, a bizarre, alien kind of music, like nothing which the annals of Earth describe. It was very faint, and soon faded, but the matter has set me thinking. It is toward the hill that the long, northerly 'ell' with the secret chute, and the locked brick vault under it, extend. Can there be any connection which has so far eluded me?

April 25

I have made a peculiar and disturbing discovery about the nature of my imprisonment. Drawn toward the hill by a sinister fascination, I found the briars giving way before me, *but in that direction only.* There is a ruined gate, and beneath the bushes the traces of an old path no doubt exist. The briars extend part-way up and all around the hill, though the summit with the standing stones bears only a curious growth of moss and stunted grass. I climbed the hill and spent several hours there, noticing a strange wind which seems always to sweep around the forbidding monoliths and which sometimes seems to whisper in an oddly articulate though darkly cryptic fashion.

These stones, both in color and texture, resemble nothing I have seen elsewhere. They are neither brown nor gray, but rather of a dirty-yellow merging into an evil green and having a suggestion of chameleon-like variability. Their texture is queerly that of a scaled serpent, and is inexplicably nauseous to the touch – being as cold and clammy as the skin of a toad or other reptile. Near the central menhir is a singular stone-rimmed hollow which I cannot explain, but which may possibly form the entrance to a long-choked well or tunnel. When I sought to descend the hill at points away from the house I found the briars intercepting me as before, though the path toward the house was easily retraceable.

April 26

Up on the hill again this evening, and found that windy whispering much more distinct. The almost angry humming came close to actual speech, of a vague, sibilant sort, and reminded me of the strange piping chant I had heard from afar. After sunset there came a curious flash of premature summer lightning on the northern horizon, followed almost at once by a queer detonation high in the fading sky. Something about this phenomenon disturbed me greatly, and I could not escape the impression that the noise ended in a kind of unhuman hissing speech which trailed off into guttural cosmic laughter. Is my mind tottering at last, or has my unwarranted curiosity evoked unheard-of horrors from the twilight spaces? The Sabbat is close at hand now. What will be the end?

April 27

At last my dreams are to be realized! Whether or not my life or spirit or body will be claimed, I shall enter the gateway! Progress in deciphering those crucial hieroglyphs in the picture has been slow, but this afternoon I hit upon the final clue. By evening I knew their meaning – and that meaning can apply in only one way to the things I have encountered in this house.

There is beneath this house – sepulchered I know not where – an Ancient One who will show me the gateway I would enter, and give me the lost signs and words I shall need. How long It has lain buried here, forgotten save by those who reared the stones on the hill, and by those who later sought out this place and built this house, I cannot conjecture, It was in search of this Thing, beyond question, that Hendrik van der Heyl came to New-Netherland in 1638. Men of this Earth know it not, save in the secret whispers of the fear-shaken few who have found or inherited the key. No human eye has even yet glimpsed It – unless, perhaps, the vanished wizards of this house delved farther than has been guessed.

With knowledge of the symbols came likewise a mastery of the Seven Lost Signs of Terror, and a tacit recognition of the hideous and unutterable Words of Fear. All that remains for me to accomplish is the Chant which will transfigure that Forgotten One Who is Guardian of the Ancient Gateway. I marvel much at the Chant. It is composed of strange and repellent gutturals and disturbing sibilants resembling no language I have ever encountered, even in the blackest chapters of the *Livre d'Eibon.* When I visited the hill at sunset I tried to read it aloud, but evoked in response only a vague, sinister rumbling on the far horizon, and a thin cloud of elemental dust that writhed and whirled like some evil living thing. Perhaps I do not pronounce the alien syllables correctly, or perhaps it is only on the Sabbat – that hellish Sabbat for which the Powers in this house are without question holding me – that the great Transfiguration can occur.

Had an odd spell of fright this morning. I thought for a

moment that I recalled where I had seen that baffling name of Sleght before, and the prospect of realization filled me with unutterable horror.

April 28

Today dark ominous clouds have hovered intermittently over the circle on the hill. I have noticed such clouds several times before, but their contours and arrangements now hold a fresh significance. They are snake-like and fantastic, and curiously like the evil shadow-shapes I have seen in the house. They float in a circle around the primal cromlech, revolving repeatedly as though endowed with a sinister life and purpose. I could swear that they give forth an angry murmuring. After some fifteen minutes they sail slowly away, ever to the eastward, like the units of a straggling battalion. Are they indeed those dread Ones whom Solomon knew of old – those giant black beings whose number is legion and whose tread doth shake the earth?

I have been rehearsing the Chant that will transfigure the Nameless Thing; yet strange fears assail me even when I utter the syllables under my breath. Piecing all evidence together, I have now discovered that the only way to It is through the locked cellar vault. That vault was built with a hellish purpose, and must cover the hidden burrow leading to the Immemorial Lair. What guardians live endlessly within, flourishing from century to century on an unknown nourishment, only the mad may conjecture. The warlocks of this house, who called them out of inner Earth, have known them only too well, as the shocking portraits and memories of the place reveal.

What troubles me most is the limited nature of the Chant. It evokes the Nameless One, yet provides no method for the control of That Which is evoked. There are, of course, the general signs and gestures, but whether they will prove effective toward such a One remains to be seen. Still, the rewards are great enough to justify any danger, and I could not retreat if I would, since an unknown force plainly urges me on.

I have discovered one more obstacle. Since the locked cellar vault must be traversed, the key to that place must be found. The lock is far too strong for forcing. That the key is somewhere hereabouts cannot be doubted, but the time before the Sabbat is very short. I must search diligently and thoroughly.

It will take courage to unlock that iron door, for what prisoned horrors may not lurk within?

Later

I have been shunning the cellar for the past day or two, but late this afternoon I again descended to those forbidding precincts.

At first all was silent, but within five minutes the menacing padding and muttering began once more beyond the iron door. This time it was loud and more terrifying than on any previous occasion, and I likewise recognized the slithering that bespoke some monstrous sea-beast – now swifter and nervously intensified, as if the thing were striving to force its way through the portal to where I stood.

As the pacing grew louder, more restless, and more sinister, there began to pound through it those hellish and unidentifiable reverberations which I had heard on my second visit to the cellar – those muffled reverberations which seemed to echo from far horizons like distant thunder. Now, however, their volume was magnified an hundredfold, and their timbre freighted with new and terrifying implications. I can compare the sound to nothing more aptly than to the roar of some dread monster of the vanished saurian age, when primal horrors roamed the Earth, and Valusia's serpent-men laid the foundation-stones of evil magic. To such a roar – but swelled to deafening heights reached by no known organic throat – was this shocking sound akin. Dare I unlock the door and face the onslaught of what lies beyond?

April 29

The key to the vault is found. I came upon it this noon in the little locked room – buried beneath rubbish in a drawer of the ancient desk, as if some belated effort to conceal it had been made. It was wrapped in a crumbling newspaper dated October 31, 1872; but there was an inner wrapping of dried skin – evidently the hide of some unknown reptile – which bore a Low Latin message in the same crabbed writing as that of the notebooks I found. As I had thought, the lock and key were vastly older than the vault. Old Claes van der Heyl had them ready for something he or his descendants meant to do – and how much older than he they were I could not estimate. Deciphering the Latin message, I trembled in a fresh access of clutching terror and nameless awe.

'The secrets of the monstrous primal Ones,' ran the crabbed text, 'whose cryptic words relate the hidden things that were before man; the things no one of Earth should learn, lest peace be for ever forfeited; shall by me never suffer revelation. To Yian-Ho, that lost and forbidden city of countless eons whose place may not be told, I have been in the veritable flesh of this body, as none other among the living has been. Therein have I found, and thence have I borne away, that knowledge which I would gladly lose, though I may not. I have learnt to bridge a gap that should not be bridged, and must call out of the Earth That Which should not be waked nor called. And what is sent to follow me will not sleep till I or those after me have found and done what is to be found and done.

'That which I have awaked and borne away with me, I may not part with again. So is it written in the *Book of Hidden Things*. That which I have willed to be has twined its dreadful shape around me, and – if I live not to do the bidding – around those children born and unborn who shall come after me, until the bidding be done. Strange may be their joinings, and awful the aid they may summon till the end be reached. Into lands unknown and dim must the seeking go, and a house must be built for the outer guardians.

'This is the key to that lock which was given me in the dreadful, eon-old and forbidden city of Yian-Ho; the lock which I or mine must place upon the vestibule of That Which is to be found. And may the Lords of Yaddith succor me – or him – who must set that lock in place or turn the key thereof.'

Such was the message – a message which, once I had read it, I seemed to have known before. Now, as I write these words, the key is before me. I gaze on it with mixed dread and longing, and cannot find words to describe its aspect. It is of the same unknown, subtly greenish frosted metal as the lock; a metal best compared to brass tarnished with verdigris. Its design is alien and fantastic, and the coffin-shaped end of the ponderous bulk leaves no doubt of the lock it was meant to fit. The handle roughly forms a strange, nonhuman image, whose exact outlines and identity cannot now be traced. Upon holding it for any length of time I seem to feel an alien, anomalous life in the cold metal – a quickening or pulsing too feeble for ordinary recognition.

Below the eidolon is graven a faint, eon-worn legend in those blasphemous, Chinese-like hieroglyphs I have come to know so well. I can make out only the beginning – the words: 'My vengeance lurks . . .' – before the text fades to indistinctness. There is some fatality in this timely finding of the key – for tomorrow night comes the hellish Sabbat. But strangely enough, amidst all this hideous expectancy, that question of the Sleght name bothers me more and more. Why should I dread to find it linked with the van der Heyls?

Walpurgis-Eve – April 30

The time has come. I waked last night to see the key glowing with a lurid greenish radiance – that same morbid green which I have seen in the eyes and skin of certain portraits here, on the shocking lock and key, on the monstrous menhirs of the hill, and in a thousand other recesses of my consciousness. There were strident whispers in the air – sibilant whistlings like those of the wind around that dreadful cromlech. Something spoke to me out of the frore aether of space, and it said, 'The hour falls.' It is an omen, and I laugh at my own fears. Have I not the dread words and the Seven Lost Signs of Terror – the power coercive of any Dweller in the cosmos or in the unknown darkened spaces? I will no longer hesitate.

The heavens are very dark, as if a terrific storm were coming on – a storm even greater than that of the night when I reached here, nearly a fortnight ago. From the village, less than a mile away, I hear a queer and unwonted babbling. It is as I thought – these poor degraded idiots are within the secret, and keep the awful Sabbat on the hill.

Here in the house the shadows gather densely. In the darkness the sky before me almost glows with a greenish light of its own. I have not yet been to the cellar. It is better that I wait, lest the sound of that muttering and padding – those slitherings and muffled reverberations – unnerve me before I can unlock the fateful door.

Of what I shall encounter, and what I must do, I have only the most general idea. Shall I find my task in the vault itself, or must I burrow deeper into the nighted heart of our planet? There are things I do not yet understand – or at least, prefer not to understand – despite a dreadful, increasing, and inexplicable sense of bygone familiarity with this fearsome house. That chute, for instance, leading down from the little locked room. But I think I know why the wing with the vault extends toward the hill.

6 P.M.

Looking out the north windows, I can see a group of villagers on the hill. They seem unaware of the lowering sky, and are digging near the great central menhir. It occurs to me that they are working on that stone-rimmed hollow place which looks like a long-choked tunnel entrance. What is to come? How much of the olden Sabbat rites have these people retained? That key glows horribly – it is not imagination. Dare I use it as it must be used? Another matter has greatly disturbed me. Glancing nervously through a book in the library I came upon an ampler form of the name that has teased my memory so sorely: 'Trintje, wife of Adriaen Sleght.' The *Adriaen* leads me to the very brink of recollection.

Midnight

Horror is unleashed, but I must not weaken. The storm has broken with pandemoniac fury, and lightning has struck the hill three times, yet the hybrid, malformed villagers are gathering within the cromlech. I can see them in the almost constant flashes. The great standing stones loom up shockingly, and have a dull green luminosity that reveals them even when the lightning is not there. The peals of thunder are deafening, and every one seems to be horribly *answered* from some indeterminate direction. As I write, the creatures on the hill have begun to chant and howl and scream in a degraded, half-simian version of the ancient ritual. Rain pours down like a flood, yet they leap and emit sounds in a kind of diabolic ecstasy.

'Iä, Shub-Niggurath! The Goat With a Thousand Young!'

But the worst thing is within the house. Even at this height, I have begun to hear sounds from the cellar. *It is the padding and muttering and slithering and muffled reverberations within the vault. . . .*

Memories come and go. That name *Adriaen Sleght* pounds oddly at my consciousness. Dirck van der Heyl's son-in-law . . . his child old Dirck's granddaughter and Abaddon Corey's great granddaughter. . . .

Later

Merciful God! *At last I know where I saw that name.* I know, and am transfixed with horror. All is lost. . . .

The key has begun to feel warm as my left hand nervously clutches it. At times that vague quickening or pulsing is so distinct that I can almost feel the living metal move. It came from Yian-Ho for a terrible purpose, and to me – who all too late know the thin stream of van der Heyl blood that trickles down through the Sleghts into my own lineage – has descended the hideous task of fulfilling that purpose. . . .

My courage and curiosity wane. I know the horror that lies beyond that iron door. What if Claes van der Heyl was my ancestor – need I expiate his nameless sin? *I will not – I swear I will not!* . . . (the writing here grows indistinct) . . . too late – cannot help self – black paws materialize – am dragged away toward the cellar. . . .

THE ELECTRIC EXECUTIONER

by Adolphe de Castro

For one who has never faced the danger of legal execution, I have a rather queer horror of the electric chair as a subject. Indeed, I think the topic gives me more of a shudder than it gives many a man who has been on trial for his life. The reason is that I associate the thing with an incident of forty years ago – a very strange incident which brought me close to the edge of the unknown's black abyss.

In 1889 I was an auditor and investigator connected with the Tlaxcala Mining Company of San Francisco, which operated several small silver and copper properties in the San Mateo Mountains in Mexico. There had been some trouble at Mine No. 3, which had a surly, furtive assistant superintendent named Arthur Feldon; and on August sixth the firm received a telegram saying that Feldon had decamped, taking with him all the stock records, securities, and private papers, and leaving the whole clerical and financial situation in dire confusion.

This development was a severe blow to the company, and late in the afternoon President McComb called me into his office to give orders for the recovery of the papers at any cost. There were, he knew, grave drawbacks. I had never seen Feldon, and there were only very indifferent photographs to go by. Moreover, my own wedding was set for Thursday of the following week – only nine days ahead – so that I was naturally not eager to be hurried off to Mexico on a man-hunt of indefinite length. The need, however, was so great that McComb felt justified in asking me to go at once; and I for my part decided that the effect on my status with the company would make ready acquiescence eminently worth while.

I was to start that night, using the president's private car as far as Mexico City, after which I would have to take a narrow-gage railway to the mines. Jackson, the superintendent of No. 3, would give me all details and any possible clues upon my arrival; and then the search would begin in earnest – through the mountains, down to the coast, or among the byways of Mexico City, as the case might be. I set out with a grim determination to get the matter done – and successfully done – as swiftly as possible; and tempered my discontent with pictures of an early return with papers and culprit, and of a wedding which would be almost a triumphal ceremony.

Having notified my family, fiancee, and principal friends, and made hasty preparations for the trip, I met President McComb at eight P.M. at the Southern Pacific depot, received from him some written instructions and a check-book, and left in his car attached to the eight-fifteen eastbound transcontinental train. The journey that followed seemed destined for uneventfulness, and after a good night's sleep I revelled in the ease of the private car so thoughtfully assigned me; reading my instructions with care, and formulating plans for the capture of Feldon and the recovery of the documents. I knew the Tlaxcala country quite well – probably much better than the missing man – hence had a certain amount of advantage in my search unless he had already used the railway.

According to the instructions, Feldon had been a subject of worry to Superintendent Jackson for some time; acting secretively, and working unaccountably in the company's laboratory at odd hours. That he was implicated with a Mexican boss and several peons in some thefts of ore was strongly suspected; but though the natives had been discharged, there was not enough evidence to warrant any positive step regarding the subtle official. Indeed, despite his furtiveness, there seemed to be more of defiance than of guilt in the man's bearing. He wore a chip on his shoulder, and talked as if the company were cheating him instead of his cheating the company. The obvious surveillance of his colleagues, Jackson wrote, appeared to irritate him increasingly; and now he had gone with everything of importance in the office. Of his possible whereabouts no guess could be made; though Jackson's final telegram suggested the wild slopes of the Sierra de Malinche, that tall, myth-surrounded peak with the corpse-shaped silhouette, from whose neighborhood the thieving natives were said to have come.

At El Paso, which we reached at two A.M. of the night following our start, my private car was detached from the transcontinental train and joined to an engine specially ordered by telegraph to take it southward to Mexico City. I continued to drowse till dawn, and all the next day grew bored on the flat, desert Chihuahua landscape. The crew had told me we were due in Mexico City at noon Friday, but I soon saw that countless delays were wasting precious hours. There were waits on sidings all along the single-tracked route, and now and then a hot-box or other difficulty would further complicate the schedule.

At Torreon we were six hours late, and it was almost eight o'clock on Friday evening – fully twelve hours behind schedule – when the conductor consented to do some speeding in an effort to make up time. My nerves were on edge, and I could do nothing but pace the car in desperation. In the end I found that the speeding had been purchased at a high cost indeed, for within a half-hour the symptoms of a hot-box had developed in my car itself; so that after a maddening wait the crew decided that all the bearings would have to be overhauled after a quarter-speed limp ahead to the next station with shops – the factory town of Queretaro. This was the last straw, and I almost stamped like a child. Actually I sometimes caught myself pushing at my chair-arm as if trying to urge the train forward at a less snail-like pace.

It was almost ten in the evening when we drew into Queretaro, and I spent a fretful hour on the station platform while my car was side-tracked and tinkered at by a dozen native mechanics. At last they told me the job was too much for them, since the forward truck needed new parts which could not be obtained nearer than Mexico City. Everything indeed seemed against me, and I gritted my teeth when I thought of Feldon getting farther and farther away – perhaps to the easy cover of Vera Cruz with its shipping or Mexico City with its varied rail facilities – while fresh delays kept me tied and helpless. Of course Jackson had notified the police in all the cities around, but I knew with sorrow what their efficiency amounted to.

The best I could do, I soon found out, was to take the regular night express for Mexico City, which ran from Aguas Calientes and made a five-minute stop at Queretaro. It would be along at one A.M. if on time, and was due in Mexico City at five o'clock Saturday morning. When I purchased my ticket I found that the train would be made up of European compartment carriages instead of long American cars with rows of two-seat chairs. These had been much used in the early days of Mexican railroading, owing to the European construction interests back of the first lines; and in 1889 the Mexican

Central was still running a fair number of them on its shorter trips. Ordinarily I prefer the American coaches, since I hate to have people facing me; but for this once I was glad of the foreign carriage. At such a time of night I stood a good chance of having a whole compartment to myself, and in my tired, nervously hypersensitive state I welcomed the solitude – as well as the comfortably upholstered seat with soft arm-rests and head cushion, running the whole width of the vehicle. I bought a first-class ticket, obtained my valise from the side-tracked private car, telegraphed both President McComb and Jackson of what had happened, and settled down in the station to wait for the night express as patiently as my strained nerves would let me.

For a wonder, the train was only half an hour late; though even so, the solitary station vigil had about finished my endurance. The conductor, showing me into a compartment, told me he expected to make up the delay and reach the capital on time; and I stretched myself comfortably on the forward-facing seat in the expectation of a quiet three-and-a-half-hour run. The light from the overhead oil lamp was soothingly dim, and I wondered whether I could snatch some much-needed sleep in spite of my anxiety and nerve-tension. It seemed, as the train jolted into motion, that I was alone; and I was heartily glad of it. My thoughts leaped ahead to my quest, and I nodded with the accelerating rhythm of the speeding string of carriages.

Then suddenly I perceived that I was not alone after all. In the corner diagonally opposite me, slumped down so that his face was invisible, sat a roughly clad man of unusual size, whom the feeble light had failed to reveal before. Beside him on the seat was a huge valise, battered and bulging, and tightly gripped even in his sleep by one of his incongruously slender hands. As the engine whistled sharply at some curve or crossing, the sleeper started nervously into a kind of watchful half-awakening; raising his head and disclosing a handsome face, bearded and clearly Anglo-Saxon, with dark, lustrous eyes. At sight of me his wakefulness became complete, and I wondered at the rather hostile wildness of his glance. No doubt, I thought, he resented my presence when he had hoped to have the compartment alone all the way; just as I was myself disappointed to find strange company in the half-lighted carriage. The best we could do, however, was to accept the situation gracefully; so I began apologizing to the man for my intrusion. He seemed to be a fellow-American, and we could both feel more at ease after a few civilities. Then we could leave each other in peace for the balance of the journey.

To my surprise, the stranger did not respond to my courtesies with so much as a word. Instead, he kept staring at me fiercely and almost appraisingly, and brushed aside my embarrassed proffer of a cigar with a nervous lateral movement of his disengaged hand. His other hand still tensely clutched the great, worn valise, and his whole person seemed to radiate some obscure malignity. After a time he abruptly turned his face toward the window, though there was nothing to see in the dense blackness outside. Oddly, he appeared to be looking at something as intently as if there really were something to look at. I decided to leave him to his own curious devices and meditations without further annoyances; so settled back in my seat, drew the brim of my soft hat over my face, and closed my eyes in an effort to snatch the sleep I had half-counted on.

I could not have dozed very long or very fully when my eyes fell open as if in response to some external force. Closing them again with some determination, I renewed my quest of a nap, yet wholly without avail. An intangible influence seemed bent on keeping me awake; so, raising my head, I looked about the dimly lighted compartment to see if anything were amiss. All appeared normal, but I noticed that the stranger in the opposite corner was looking at me very intently – intently, though without any of the geniality or friendliness which would have implied a change from his former surly attitude. I did not attempt conversation this time, but leaned back in my previous sleepy posture; half closing my eyes as if I had dozed off once more, but continuing to watch him curiously from beneath my down-turned hat brim.

As the train rattled onward through the night I saw a subtle and gradual metamorphosis come over the expression of the staring man. Evidently satisfied that I was asleep, he allowed his face to reflect a curious jumble of emotions, the nature of which seemed anything but reassuring. Hatred, fear, triumph and fanaticism flickered compositely over the lines of his lips and the angles of his eyes while his gaze became a glare of really alarming greed and ferocity. Suddenly it dawned upon me that this man was mad and dangerously so.

I will not pretend that I was anything but deeply and thoroughly frightened when I saw how things stood. Perspiration started out all over me and I had hard work to maintain my attitude of relaxation and slumber. Life had many attractions for me just then and the thought of dealing with a homicidal maniac – possibly armed and certainly powerful to a marvelous degree – was a dismaying and terrifying one. My disadvantage in any sort of struggle was enormous; for the man was a virtual giant; evidently in the best of athletic trim, while I have always been rather frail, and was then almost worn out with anxiety, sleeplessness, and nervous tension. It was undeniably a bad moment for me, and I felt pretty close to a horrible death as I recognized the fury of madness in the stranger's eyes. Events from the past came up into my consciousness as if for a farewell – just as a drowning man's whole life is said to resurrect itself before him at the last moment.

Of course I had my revolver in my coat pocket, but any motion of mine to reach and draw it would be instantly obvious. Moreover, if I did secure it, there was no telling what effect it would have on the maniac. Even if I shot him once or twice he might have enough remaining strength to get the gun from me and deal with me in his own way; or if he were armed himself he might shoot or stab without trying to disarm me. One can cow a sane man by covering him with a pistol, but an insane man's complete indifference to consequences gives him a strength and menace quite superhuman for the time being. Even in those pre-Freudian days I had a common-sense realization of the dangerous power of a person without normal inhibitions. That the stranger in the corner was indeed about to start some murderous action, his burning eyes and twitching facial muscles did not permit me to doubt for a moment.

Suddenly I heard his breath begin to come in excited gasps, and saw his chest heaving with mounting excitement. The time for a showdown was close, and I tried desperately to think of the best thing to do. Without interrupting my pretense of sleep, I began to slide my right hand gradually and inconspicuously toward the pocket containing my pistol; watching the madman closely as I did so, to see if he would detect any move. Unfortunately he did – almost before he had time to register the fact in his expression. With a bound so agile and abrupt as to be almost incredible in a man of his size, he was upon me before I knew what had happened; looming up and swaying forward like a giant ogre of legend, and pinioning me with one powerful hand while with the other he forestalled me in reaching the revolver. Taking it from my pocket and placing it in his own, he released me contemptuously, well knowing how fully his physique placed me at his mercy. Then he stood up at his full height – his head almost touching the roof of the carriage – and stared down at me with eyes whose fury had quickly turned to a look of pitying scorn and ghoulish calculation.

I did not move, and after a moment the man resumed his seat opposite me; smiling a ghastly smile as he opened his great bulging valise and extracted an article of peculiar appearance – a rather large cage of semi-flexible wire, woven somewhat like a baseball catcher's mask, but shaped more like the helmet of a diving-suit. Its top was connected with a cord whose other end remained in the valise. This device he fondled with obvious affection, cradling it in his lap as he looked at me afresh and licked his bearded lips with an almost feline motion of the tongue. Then, for the first time, he spoke – in a deep, mellow voice of a softness and cultivation startlingly at variance with his rough corduroy clothes and unkempt aspect.

'You are fortunate, sir. I shall use you first of all. You shall go into history as the first fruits of a remarkable invention. Vast sociological consequences – I shall let my light shine, as it were. I'm radiating all the time, but nobody knows it. Now you shall know. Intelligent guinea-pig. Cats and burros – it worked even with a burro. . . .'

He paused, while his bearded features underwent a convulsive motion closely synchronized with a vigorous gyratory shaking of the whole head. It was as though he were shaking clear of some nebulous obstructing medium, for the gesture was followed by a clarification or subtilization of expression which hid the more obvious madness in a look of suave composure through which the craftiness gleamed only dimly. I glimpsed the difference at once, and put in a word to see if I could lead his mind into harmless channels. 'You seem to have a marvelously fine instrument, if I'm any judge. Won't you tell me how you came to invent it?'

He nodded.

'Mere logical reflection, dear sir. I consulted the needs of the age and acted upon them. Others might have done the same had their minds been as powerful – that is, as capable of sustained concentration – as mine. I had the sense of conviction – the available will-power – that is all. I realized, as no one else has yet realized, how imperative it is to remove everybody from the earth before Quetzalcoatl comes back, and realized also that it must be done elegantly. I hate butchery of any kind, and hanging is barbarously crude. You know last year the New York legislature voted to adopt electric execution for condemned men – but all the apparatus they have in mind is as primitive as Stephenson's 'Rocket' or Davenport's first electric engine. I knew of a better way, and told them so, but they paid no attention to me. God, the fools! As if I didn't know all there is to know about men and death and electricity – student, man and boy – technologist and engineer – soldier of fortune. . . .'

He leaned back and narrowed his eyes.

'I was in Maximilian's army twenty years and more ago. They were going to make me a nobleman. Then those damned greasers killed him and I had to go home. But I came back – back and forth, back and forth. I live in Rochester, New York. . . .'

His eyes grew deeply crafty, and he leaned forward, touching me on the knee with the fingers of a paradoxically delicate hand.

'I came back, I say, and I went deeper than any of them. I hate greasers, but I like Mexicans! A puzzle? Listen to me, young fellow – you don't think Mexico is really Spanish, do you? God, if you knew the tribes I know! In the mountains – in the mountains – Anahuac – Tenochtitlan – the old ones. . . .'

His voice changed to a chanting and not unmelodious howl.

'Iä! Huitzilopotchli! . . . Nahuatlacatl! Seven, seven, seven . . . Xochimilca, Chalca, Tepaneca, Acolhua, Tlahuica, Tlascalteca, Azteca! . . . Iä! Iä! I have been to the Seven Caves of Chicomoztoc, but no one shall ever know! I tell you *because you will never repeat it. . . .*'

He subsided, and resumed a conversational tone.

'It would surprise you to know what things are told in the mountains. Huitzilopotchli is coming back . . . of that there can be no doubt. Any peon south of Mexico City can tell you that. But I meant to do nothing about it. I went home, as I tell you, again and again, and was going to benefit society with my electric executioner when that cursed Albany legislature adoped the other way. A joke, sir, a joke! Grandfather's chair – sit by the fireside – Hawthorne—'

The man was chuckling with a morbid parody of good nature.

'Why, sir, I'd like to be the first man to sit in their damned chair and feel their little two-bit battery current! It wouldn't make a frog's legs dance! And they expect to kill murderers with it – reward of merit – everything! But then, young man, I saw the uselessness – the pointless illogicality, as it were – of killing just a few. Everybody is a murderer – they murder ideas – steal inventions – stole mine by watching, and watching, and watching—'

The man choked and paused, and I spoke soothingly.

'I'm sure your invention was much the better, and probably they'll come to use it in the end.'

Evidently my tact was not great enough, for his response showed fresh irritation.

'"Sure," are you? Nice, mild, conservative assurance! Cursed lot you care – *but you'll soon know!* Why, damn you, all the good there ever will be in that electric chair will have been stolen from me. The ghost of Nezahualpilli told me that on the sacred mountain. They watched, and watched, and watched—'

He choked again, then gave another of those gestures in which he seemed to shake both his head and his facial expression. That seemed temporarily to steady him.

'What my invention needs is testing. That is it – here. The wire hood or head-net is flexible, and slips on easily. Neck-piece binds but doesn't choke. Electrodes touch forehead and base of cerebellum – all that's necessary. Stop the head, and what else can go? The fools up at Albany, with their carved oak easy-chair, think they've got to make it a head-to-foot affair. Idiots! – don't they know that you don't need to shoot a man through the body after you've plugged him through the brain? I've seen men die in battle – I know better. And then their silly high-power circuit – dynamos – all that. Why didn't they see what I've done with the storage-battery? Not a hearing – nobody knows – I alone have the secret alone – I and they, if I choose to let them. . . . But I must have experimental subjects – subjects – *do you know whom I've chosen for the first?*'

I tried jocoseness, quickly merging into friendly seriousness, as a sedative. Quick thought and apt words might save me yet.

'Well, there are lots of fine subjects among the politicians of San Francisco, where I come from! They need your treatment, and I'd like to help you introduce it! But really, I think I can help you in all truth. I have some influence in Sacramento, and if you'll go back to the States with me after I'm through with my business in Mexico, I'll see that you get a hearing.'

He answered soberly and civilly.

'No – I can't go back. I swore not to when those criminals at Albany turned down my invention and set spies to watch me, and steal from me. But I must have American subjects. Those greasers are under a curse, and would be too easy; and the full-blood Indians – the real children of the feathered serpent – are sacred and inviolate except for proper sacrificial victims . . . and even those must be slain according to ceremony. I must have Americans without going back – and the first man I choose will be signally honored. Do you know who he is?'

I temporized desperately.

'Oh, if that's all the trouble, I'll find you a dozen first-rate Yankee specimens as soon as we get to Mexico City! I know where there are lots of small mining men who wouldn't be missed for days—'

But he cut me short with a new and sudden air of authority which had a touch of real dignity in it.

'That'll do – we've trifled long enough. Get up and stand erect like a man. You're the subject I've chosen, and you'll thank me for the honor in the other world, just as the sacrificial victim thanks the priest for transferring him to eternal glory. A new principle – no other man alive has dreamed of such a battery, and it might never again be hit on if the world experimented a thousand years. Do you know that atoms aren't what they seem? Fools! A century after this some dolt would be guessing if I were to let the world live!'

As I arose at his command, he drew additional feet of cord from the valise and stood erect beside me; the wire helmet outstretched toward me in both hands, and a look of real exaltation on his tanned and bearded face. For an instant he seemed like a radiant Hellenic mystagogue or hierophant.

'Here, O Youth – a libation! Wine of the cosmos – nectar

of the starry spaces – Linos – Iacchus – Ialemus – Zagreus – Dionysos – Atys – Hylas – sprung from Apollo and slain by the hounds of Argos – seed of Psamathe – child of the sun – Evoe! Evoe!'

He was chanting again, and this time his mind seemed far back amongst the classic memories of his college days. In my erect posture I noticed the nearness of the signal cord overhead, and wondered whether I could reach it through some gesture of ostensible response to his ceremonial mood. It was worth trying, so with an antiphonal cry of 'Evoe!' I put my arms forward and upward toward him in a ritualistic fashion, hoping to give the cord a tug before he could notice the act. But it was useless. He saw my purpose, and moved one hand toward the right-hand coat pocket where my revolver lay. No words were needed, and we stood for a moment like carven figures. Then he quietly said, 'Make haste!'

Again my mind rushed frantically about seeking avenues of escape. The doors, I knew, were not locked on Mexican trains; but my companion could easily forestall me if I tried to unlatch one and jump out. Besides, our speed was so great that success in that direction would probably be as fatal as failure. The only thing to do was to play for time. Of the three-and-a-half-hour trip a good slice was already worn away, and once we got to Mexico City the guards and police in the station would provide instant safety.

There would, I thought, be two distinct times for diplomatic stalling. If I could get him to postpone the slipping on of the hood, that much time would be gained. Of course I had no belief that the thing was really deadly; but I knew enough of madmen to understand what would happen when it failed to work. To his disappointment would be added a mad sense of my responsibility for the failure which would hold his attention and lead him into more or less extended searches for corrective influences. I wondered just how far his credulity went, and whether I could prepare in advance a prophecy of failure which would make the failure itself stamp me as a seer or initiate, or perhaps a god. I had enough of a smattering of Mexican mythology to make it worth trying; though I would try other delaying influences first and let the prophecy come as a sudden revelation. Would he spare me in the end if I could make him think me a prophet or divinity? Could I 'get by' as Quetzalcoatl or Huitzilopotchli? Anything to drag matters out till five o'clock, when we were due in Mexico City.

But my opening 'stall' was the veteran will-making ruse. As the maniac repeated his command for haste, I told him of my family and intended marriage, and asked for the privilege of leaving a message and disposing of my money and effects. If, I said, he would lend me some paper and agree to mail what I should write, I could die more peacefully and willingly. After some cogitation he gave a favorable verdict and fished in his valise for a pad, which he handed me solemnly as I resumed my seat. I produced a pencil, artfully breaking the point at the outset and causing some delay while he searched for one of his own. When he gave me this, he took my broken pencil and proceeded to sharpen it with a large, horn-handled knife which had been in his belt under his coat. Evidently a second pencil-breaking would not profit me greatly.

What I wrote, I can hardly recall at this date. It was largely gibberish, and composed of random scraps of memorized literature when I could think of nothing else to set down. I made my handwriting as illegible as I could without destroying its nature as writing; for I knew he would be likely to look at the result before commencing his experiment, and realized how he would react to the sight of obvious nonsense. The ordeal was a terrible one, and I chafed each second at the slowness of the train. In the past I had often whistled a brisk gallop to the sprightly 'tac' of wheels on rails, but now the tempo seemed slowed down to that of a funeral march – my funeral march, I grimly reflected.

My ruse worked till I had covered over four pages, six by nine; when at last the madman drew out his watch and told me I could have but five minutes more. What should I do next? I was hastily going through the form of concluding the will when a new idea struck me. Ending with a flourish and handing him the finished sheets, which he thrust carelessly into his left-hand coat pocket, I reminded him of my influential Sacramento friends who would be so much interested in his invention.

'Oughtn't I give you a letter of introduction to them?' I said. 'Oughtn't I to make a signed sketch and description of your executioner so that they'll grant you a cordial hearing? They can make you famous, you know – and there's no question at all but that they'll adopt your method for the state of

California if they hear of it through someone like me, whom they know and trust.'

I was taking this tack on the chance that his thoughts as a disappointed inventor would let him forget the Aztec-religious side of his mania for a while. When he veered to the latter again, I reflected, I would spring the 'revelation' and 'prophecy.' The scheme worked, for his eyes glowed an eager assent, though he bruskly told me to be quick. He further emptied the valise, lifting out a queer-looking congeries of glass cells and coils to which the wire from the helmet was attached, and delivering a fire of running comment too technical for me to follow yet apparently quite plausible and straightforward. I pretended to note down all he said, wondering as I did so whether the queer apparatus was really a battery after all. Would I get a slight shock when he applied the device? The man surely talked as if he were a genuine electrician. Description of his own invention was clearly a congenial task for him, and I saw he was not as impatient as before. The hopeful gray of dawn glimmered red through the windows before he wound up, and I felt at last that my chance of escape had really become tangible.

But he, too, saw the dawn, and began glaring wildly again. He knew the train was due in Mexico City at five, and would certainly force quick action unless I could override all his judgement with engrossing ideas. As he rose with a determined air, setting the battery on the seat beside the open valise, I reminded him that I had not made the needed sketch, and asked him to hold the headpiece so that I could draw it near the battery. He complied and resumed his seat, with many admonitions to me to hurry. After another moment I paused for some information, asking him how the victim was placed for execution, and how his presumable struggles were overcome.

'Why,' he replied, 'the criminal is securely strapped to a post. It does not matter how much he tosses his head, for the helmet fits tightly and draws even closer when the current comes on. We turn the switch gradually – you see it here, a carefully arranged affair with a rheostat.'

A new idea for delay occurred to me as the tilled fields and increasingly frequent houses in the dawnlight outside told of our approach to the capital at last.

'But,' I said, 'I must draw the helmet in place on a human

head as well as beside the battery. Can't you slip it on yourself a moment so that I can sketch you with it? The papers as well as the officials will want all this, and they are strong on completeness.'

I had, by chance, made a better shot than I had planned; for at my mention of the press the madman's eyes lit up afresh.

'The papers? Yes – damn them, you can make even the papers give me a hearing! They all laughed at me and wouldn't print a word. Here, you hurry up! We've not a second to lose!

'Now, curse 'em, they'll print pictures! I'll revise your sketch if you make any blunders – must be accurate at any cost. Police will find you afterward – they'll tell how it works. Associated Press item – back up your letter – immortal fame. . . . Hurry, I say – hurry, confound you!'

The train was lurching over the poorer roadbed near the city, and we swayed disconcertingly now and then. With this excuse I managed to break the pencil again, but of course the maniac at once handed me my own which he had sharpened. My first batch of ruses was about used up, and I felt that I should have to submit to the headpiece in a moment. We were still a good quarter-hour from the terminal, and it was about time for me to divert my companion to his religious side and spring the divine prophecy.

Mustering up my scraps of Nahuan-Aztec mythology, I suddenly threw down pencil and paper and commenced to chant.

'Iä! Iä! Tloquenahuaque. Thou Who Art All In Thyself! Thou, too, Ipalnemoan, By Whom We Live! I hear, I hear! I see, I see! Serpent-bearing Eagle, hail! A message! A message! Huitzilopotchli, in my soul echoes thy thunder!'

At my intonations the maniac stared incredulously through his odd mask, his handsome face shown in a surprise and perplexity which quickly changed to alarm. His mind seemed to go blank a moment, and then to recrystallize in another pattern. Raising his hands aloft, he chanted as if in a dream.

'Mictlanteuctli, Great Lord, a sign! A sign from within thy black cave! Iä! Tonatiuh-Metztli! Cthulhu! Command, and I serve!'

Now in all this responsive gibberish there was one word which struck an odd chord in my memory. Odd, because it never occurs in any printed account of Mexican mythology, yet had been overheard by me more than once as an awe-struck whisper amongst the peons in my own firm's Tlaxcala mines. It seemed to be part of an exceedingly secret and ancient ritual; for there were characteristic whispered responses which I had caught now and then, and which were as unknown as itself to academic scholarship. This maniac must have spent considerable time with the hill peons and Indians, just as he had said; for surely such unrecorded lore could have come from no mere book-learning. Realizing the importance he must attach to this doubly esoteric jargon, I determined to strike at his most vulnerable spot and give him the gibberish responses the natives used.

'Ya-R'lyeh! Ya-R'lyeh!' I shouted. 'Cthulhu fhtaghn! Nigurat-Yig! Yog-Sototl—'

But I never had a chance to finish. Galvanized into a religious epilepsy by the exact response which his subconscious mind had probably not really expected, the madman scrambled down to a kneeling posture on the floor, bowing his wire-helmeted head again and again, and turning it to the right and left as he did so. With each turn his obeisances became more profound, and I could hear his foaming lips repeating the syllable 'kill, kill, kill,' in a rapidly swelling monotone. It occurred to me that I had overreached myself, and that my response had unloosed a mounting mania which would rouse him to the slaying-point before the train reached the station.

As the arc of the madman's turnings gradually increased, the slack in the cord from his headpiece to the battery had naturally been taken up more and more. Now, in an all-forgetting delirium of ecstasy, he began to magnify his turns to complete circles, so that the cord wound round his neck and began to tug at its moorings to the battery on the seat. I wondered what he would do when the inevitable would happen, and the battery would be dragged to presumable destruction on the floor.

Then came the sudden cataclysm. The battery, yanked over the seat's edge by the maniac's last gesture of orgiastic frenzy, did indeed fall; but it did not seem to have wholly broken. Instead, as my eye caught the spectacle in one too-fleeting instant, the actual impact was borne by the rheostat, so that the switch was jerked over instantly to full current. And the marvelous thing is that there *was* a current. The invention was no mere dream of insanity.

I saw a blinding blue auroral coruscation, heard an ululating shriek more hideous than any of the previous cries of that mad, horrible journey, and smelled the nauseous odor of burning flesh. That was all my overwrought consciousness could bear, and I sank instantly into oblivion.

When the train guard at Mexico City revived me, I found a crowd on the station platform around my compartment door. At my involuntary cry the pressing faces became curious and dubious, and I was glad when the guard shut out all but the trim doctor who had pushed his way through to me. My cry was a very natural thing, but it had been prompted by something more than the shocking sight on the carriage floor which I had expected to see. Or should say, by something *less*, because in truth there was not anything on the floor at all.

Nor, said the guard, had there been when he opened the door and found me unconscious within. My ticket was the only one sold for that compartment and I was the only person found within it. Just myself and my valise, nothing more. I had been alone all the way from Queretaro. Guard, doctor, and spectator alike tapped their foreheads significantly at my frantic and insistent questions.

Had it all been a dream, or was I indeed mad? I recalled my anxiety and overwrought nerves, and shuddered. Thanking the guard and doctor, and shaking free of the curious crowd, I staggered into a cab and was taken to the Fonda Nacional, where, after telegraphing Jackson at the mine, I slept till afternoon in an effort to get a fresh grip on myself. I had myself called at one o'clock, in time to catch the narrow-gage for the mining country, but when I got up I found a telegram under the door. It was from Jackson, and said that Feldon had been found dead in the mountains that morning, the news reaching the mine about ten o'clock. The papers were all safe, and the San Francisco office had been duly notified. So the whole trip, with its nervous haste and harrowing mental ordeal, had been for nothing!

Knowing that McComb would expect a personal report despite the course of events, I sent another wire ahead and took the narrow-gage after all. Four hours later I was rattled and jolted into the station of Mine No. 3, where Jackson was waiting to give a cordial greeting. He was so full of the affair at the mine that he did not notice my still shaken and seedy appearance.

The superintendent's story was brief, and he told me it as he led me toward the shack up the hillside above the *arrastra,* where Feldon's body lay. Feldon, he said, had always been a queer, sullen character, even since he was hired the year before; working at some secret mechanical device and complaining of constant espionage, and being disgustingly familiar with the native workmen. But he certainly knew the work, the country, and the people. He used to make long trips into the hills where the peons lived, and even to take part in some of their ancient, heathenish ceremonies. He hinted at odd secrets and strange powers as often as he boasted of his mechanical skill. Of late he had disintegrated rapidly; growing morbidly suspicious of his colleagues, and undoubtedly joining his native friends in ore-thieving after his cash got low. He needed unholy amounts of money for something or other – was always having boxes come from laboratories and machine shops in Mexico City or the States.

As for the final absconding with all the papers – it was only a crazy gesture of revenge for what he called 'spying.' He was certainly stark mad, for he had gone across country to a hidden cave on the wild slope of the haunted Sierra de Malinche, where no white men live, and had done some amazingly queer things. The cave, which would never have been found but for the final tragedy, was full of hideous old Aztec idols and altars; the latter covered with the charred bones of recent burnt-offerings of doubtful nature. The natives would tell nothing – indeed, they swore they knew nothing – but it was easy to see that the cave was an old rendezvous of theirs, and that Feldon had shared their practises to the fullest extent.

The searchers had found the place only because of the chanting and the final cry. It had been close to five that morning, and after an all-night encampment the party had begun to pack up for its empty-handed return to the mines. Then somebody had heard faint rhythms in the distance, and knew that one of the noxious old native rituals was being howled from some lonely spot up the slope of the corpse-shaped mountain. They heard the same old names – Mictlanteuctli, Tonatiuh-Metzli, Cthulhu, Ya-R'lyeh, and all the rest – but the queer thing was that some English words were mixed with them. Real white man's English, and no greaser patter. Guided by the sound, they had hastened up the weed-entangled mountainside toward it, when after a spell of quiet the shriek had burst upon them. It was a terrible thing – a worse thing than any of them had ever heard before. There seemed to be some smoke, too, and a morbid acrid smell.

Then they stumbled on the cave, its entrance screened by scrub mesquites, but now emitting clouds of fetid smoke. It was lighted within, the horrible altar and grotesque images revealed flickeringly by candles which must have been changed less than a half-hour before; and on the gravelly floor lay the horror that made all the crowd reel backward. It was Feldon, head burned to a crisp by some odd device he had slipped over it – a kind of wire cage connected with a rather shaken-up battery which had evidently fallen to the floor from a nearby altar-pot. When the men saw it they exchanged glances, thinking of the 'electric executioner' Feldon had always boasted of inventing – the thing which everyone had rejected, but had tried to steal and copy. The papers were safe in Feldon's open portmanteau which stood close by, and an hour later the column of searchers started back for No. 3 with a grisly burden on an improvised stretcher.

That was all, but it was enough to make me turn pale and falter as Jackson led me up past the *arrastra* to the shed where he said the body lay. For I was not without imagination, and knew only too well into what hellish nightmare this tragedy somehow supernaturally dovetailed. I knew what I should see inside that gaping door around which the curious miners clustered, and did not flinch when my eyes took in the giant form, the rough corduroy clothes, the oddly delicate hands, the wisps of burnt beard, and the hellish machine itself – battery slightly broken, and headpiece blackened by the charring of what was inside. The great, bulging portmanteau did not surprise me, and I quailed only at two things – the folded sheets of paper sticking out of the left-hand pocket. In a moment when no one was looking I reached out and seized the too-familiar sheets, crushing them in my hand without daring to look at their penmanship. I ought to be sorry now that a kind of panic fear made me burn them that night with averted eyes. They would have been a positive proof or disproof of something – but for that matter I could still have proof by asking about the revolver the coroner afterward took from that sagging right-hand coat pocket. I never had the courage to ask about that – because my own revolver was missing after the night on the train. My pocket pencil, too, showed signs of a crude and hasty sharpening unlike the precise pointing I had given it Friday afternoon on the machine in President McComb's private car.

So in the end I went home still puzzled – mercifully puzzled, perhaps. The private car was repaired when I got back to Queretaro, but my greatest relief was crossing the Rio Grande into El Paso and the States. By the next Friday I was in San Francisco again, and the postponed wedding came off the following week.

As to what really happened that night – as I've said, I simply don't dare to speculate. That chap Feldon was insane to start with, and on top of his insanity he had piled a lot of prehistoric Aztec witchlore that nobody has any right to know. He was really an inventive genius, and that battery must have been the genuine stuff. I heard later how he had been brushed aside in former years by press, public, and potentates alike. Too much disappointment isn't good for men of a certain kind. Anyhow, some unholy combination of influences was at work. He had really, by the way, been a soldier of Maximilian's.

When I tell my story most people call me a plain liar. Others lay it to abnormal psychology – and Heaven knows I *was* overwrought – while still others talk of 'astral projection' of some sort. My zeal to catch Feldon certainly sent my thoughts ahead toward him, and with all his Indian magic he'd be about the first one to recognize and meet them. Was he in the railway carriage or was I in the cave on the corpse-shaped haunted mountain? What would have happened to me, had I not delayed him as I did? I'll confess I don't know, and I'm not sure that I want to know. I've never been in Mexico since – and as I said at the start, I don't enjoy hearing about electric executions.

THE MOUND

by Zealia Bishop

It is only within the last few years that most people have stopped thinking of the West as a new land. I suppose the idea gained ground because our own special civilization happens to be new there; but nowadays explorers are digging beneath the surface and bringing up whole chapters of life that rose and fell among these plains and mountains before recorded history began. We think nothing of a Pueblo village 2,500 years old, and it hardly jolts us when archaeologists put the subpedregal culture of Mexico back to 17,000 or 18,000 B.C. We hear rumors of still older things, too; of primitive men contemporaneous with extinct animals and known today only through a few fragmentary bones and artifacts, so that the idea of newness is fading out pretty rapidly. Europeans usually catch the sense of immemorial ancientness and deep deposits from successive life streams better than we do. Only a couple of years ago a British author spoke of Arizona as a 'moon-dim region, very lovely in its way, and stark and old – an ancient, lonely land.'

Yet I believe I have a deeper sense of the stupefying, almost horrible, ancientness of the West than any European. It rises from an incident that happened in 1928; an incident which I'd like to dismiss as three-quarters hallucination, but which has left such a frightfully firm impression on my memory that I can't put it off very easily. It was in Oklahoma, where my work as an American-Indian ethnologist constantly takes me and where I had come upon some devilishly strange and disconcerting matters before. Make no mistake: Oklahoma is a lot more than a mere pioneer's and promoter's frontier. There are old, old tribes with old, old memories there; and when the tom-toms beat ceaselessly over brooding plains in the autumn the spirits of men are brought dangerously close to the primal, whispered things. I am white and Eastern enough myself, but anybody is welcome to know that the rites of Yig, Father of Snakes, can get a real shudder out of me any day. I have heard and seen too much to be 'sophisticated' in such matters.

I had gone into Oklahoma to track down and correlate one of the many ghost tales which were current among the white settlers, but which had strong Indian corroboration, and, I felt sure, an ultimate Indian source. They were curious, these open-air ghost tales; and though they sounded flat and prosaic in the mouths of the white people, they had earmarks of linkage with some of the richest and obscurest phases of native mythology. All were woven around the vast, lonely, artificial-looking mounds in the western part of the state, and all involved apparitions of exceedingly strange aspect and equipment.

The commonest and among the oldest became quite famous in 1892, when a government marshal named John Willis went into the mound region after horse thieves and came out with a wild yarn of nocturnal cavalry battles in the air between great armies of invisible spectres – battles that involved the rush of hooves and feet, the thud of blows, the clank of metal on metal, the muffled cries of warriors, and the fall of human and equine bodies. These things happened by moonlight, and frightened his horse as well as himself. The sounds persisted for an hour at a time; vivid, but subdued as if brought from a distance by a wind, and unaccompanied by any glimpse of the armies themselves. Later on, Willis learned that the seat of the sounds was a notoriously haunted spot, shunned by settlers and Indians alike. Many had seen, or half seen, the warring horsemen in the sky; and had furnished dim, ambiguous descriptions. The settlers described the ghostly fighters as Indians; though of no familiar tribe, and having the most singular costumes and weapons. They even went so far as to say that they could not be sure the horses were really horses.

The Indians, on the other hand, did not seem to claim the spectres as kinfolk. They referred to them as 'those people', 'the old people', or 'they who dwell below'; and appeared to hold them in too great a frightened veneration to talk much about them. No ethnologist had been able to pin any tale-teller down to a specific description of the beings, and apparently nobody had ever had a very clear look at them. The Indians had one or two old proverbs about these phenomena, saying that 'men very old, make very big spirit; not so old, not so big; older than all time, then spirit he so big he near flesh; those old people and spirits they mix up – get all the same.'

Now all of this, of course, is 'old stuff' to an ethnologist: of a piece with the persistent legends of rich hidden cities and buried races which abound among the Pueblo and plains Indians, and which lured Coronado centuries ago on his vain search for the fabled Quivira. What took me into western Oklahoma was something far more definite and tangible: a local and distinctive tale which, though really old, was wholly new to the outside world of research; and which involved the first clear descriptions of the ghosts of which it treated. There was an added thrill in the fact that it came from the remote town of Binger, in Caddo County, a place I had long known as the scene of a very terrible and partly inexplicable occurrence connected with the old snake-god myth.

The tale, outwardly, was an extremely naive and simple one, and centered in a huge, lone mound or small hill that rose above the plain about a third of a mile west of the village, a mound which some thought a product of nature, but which others believed to be a burial-place or ceremonial dais constructed by prehistoric tribes. The mound, the villagers said, was constantly haunted by two Indian figures which appeared in alternation; an old man who paced back and forth along the top from dawn till dusk, regardless of the weather and with only brief intervals of disappearance, and a squaw who took his place at night with a blue-flamed torch that glimmered continuously till morning. When the moon was bright, the squaw's peculiar figure could be seen fairly plainly, and over half the villagers agreed that the apparition was headless.

Local opinion was divided as to the motives and relative ghostliness of the two visions. Some held that the man was not a ghost at all, but a living Indian who had killed and beheaded a squaw for gold and buried her somewhere on the mound. According to these theorists he was pacing the eminence through sheer remorse, bound by the spirit of his victim which took visible shape after dark. But other theorists, more uniform in their spectral beliefs, held that both man and woman were ghosts; the man having killed the squaw and himself as well at some very distant period. These and minor variant versions seemed to have been current ever since the settlement of the Wichita country in 1889; and were, I was told, sustained to an astonishing degree by still-existing phenomena which anyone might observe for himself. Not many ghost tales offer such free and open proof, and I was very eager to see what bizarre wonders might be lurking in this small, obscure village so far from the beaten path of crowds and from the ruthless searchlight of scientific knowledge. So, in the late summer of 1928 I entrained for Binger and brooded on strange mysteries as the train rattled timidly along the single track through a lonelier and lonelier landscape.

My train drew into Binger at twilight, and I felt rather lost and uneasy, cut off from wholesome and everyday things, as it puffed southward without me. The station platform was filled with curious loafers, all of whom seemed eager to direct me when I asked for the man to whom I had letters of introduction. I was ushered along a commonplace main street whose rutted surface was red with the sandstone soil of the country, and finally delivered at the door of my prospective host. Those who had arranged things for me had done well; for Mr Compton was a man of high intelligence and local responsibility, while his mother, who lived with him and was familiarly known as 'Grandma Compton,' was one of the first pioneer generation, and a veritable mine of anecdote and folklore.

That evening the Comptons summed up for me all the legends current among the villagers, proving that the phenomenon I had come to study was indeed a baffling and important one. The ghosts, it seems, were accepted almost as a matter of course by everyone in Binger. Two generations had been born and grown up within sight of that queer, lone tumulus and its restless figures. The neighborhood of the mound was naturally feared and shunned, so that the village and the farms had not spread toward it in all four decades of settlement; yet venturesome individuals had several times visited it. Some had come back to report that they saw no ghosts at all when they neared the dreaded hill; that somehow the lone sentinel had stepped out of sight before they reached the spot, leaving them free to climb the steep slope and explore the flat summit. There was nothing up there, they said – merely a rough expanse of underbrush. Where the Indian watcher could have vanished to, they had no idea. He must, they reflected, have descended the slope and somehow managed to escape unseen along the plain; although there was no convenient cover within sight. At any rate, there did not appear to be any opening into the mound; a conclusion which was reached after considerable exploration of the shrubbery and tall grass on all sides. In a few cases some of the more sensitive searchers declared that they felt a sort of invisible restraining presence; but they could describe nothing more definite than that. It was simply as if the air thickened against them in the direction they wished to move. It is needless to mention that all these daring surveys were conducted by day. Nothing in the universe could have induced any human being, white or red, to approach that sinister elevation after dark; and indeed, no Indian would have thought of going near it even in the brightest sunlight.

But it was not from the tales of these sane, observant seekers that the chief terror of the ghost-mound sprang; indeed, had their experience been typical, the phenomenon would have bulked far less prominently in the local legendry. The most evil thing was the fact that many other seekers had come back strangely impaired in mind and body, or had not come back at all.

The first of these cases had occurred in 1891, when a young man named Heaton had gone with a shovel to see what hidden secrets he could unearth. He had heard curious tales from the Indians, and had laughed at the barren report of another youth who had been out to the mound and had found nothing. Heaton had watched the mound with a spy-glass from the village while the other youth made his trip; and as the explorer neared the spot, he saw the sentinel Indian walk deliberately down into the tumulus as if a trap-door and staircase existed on the top. The other youth had not noticed how the Indian disappeared, but had merely found him gone upon arriving at the mound.

When Heaton made his own trip he resolved to get to the bottom of the mystery, and watchers from the village saw him hacking diligently at the shrubbery atop the mound. Then they saw his figure melt slowly into invisibility; not to reappear for long hours, till after the dusk drew on, and the torch of the headless squaw glimmered ghoulishly on the distant elevation. About two hours after nightfall he staggered into the village minus his spade and other belongings, and burst into a shrieking monologue of disconnected ravings. He howled of shocking abysses and monsters, of terrible carvings and statues, of inhuman captors and grotesque tortures, and of other fantastic abnormalities too complex and chimerical even to remember. 'Old! Old! Old!' he would moan over and over again, 'Great God, they are older than the earth, and came here from somewhere else – they know what you think, and make you know what they think – they're half man, half ghost – crossed the line – melt and take shape again – getting more and more so, yet we're all descended from them in the beginning – children of Tulu – everything made of gold – monstrous animals, half human – dead slaves – madness – Iä! Shub-Niggurath! – that white man – oh, my God, what they did to him! . . .'

Heaton was the village idiot for about eight years when he died. Since his ordeal, there had been two more cases of mound-madness, and eight of total disappearance. Immediately after Heaton's mad return, three desperate and determined men had gone out to the lone hill together; heavily armed, and with spades and pickaxes. Watching villagers saw the Indian ghost melt away as the explorers drew near, and afterward saw the men climb the mound and begin scouting around through the underbrush. All at once they faded into nothingness, and were never seen again. One watcher, with an especially powerful telescope, thought he saw other forms dimly materialize beside the hapless men and drag them down into the mound; but this account remained uncorroborated. It is needless to say that no searching party went out after the lost ones, and that for many years the mound was wholly unvisited.

Only when the incidents of 1891 were largely forgotten did anybody dare to think of further explorations. Then, about 1910, a fellow too young to recall the old horrors made a trip to the shunned spot and found nothing at all.

By 1915 the acute dread and wild legendry of '91 had largely faded into the commonplace and unimaginative ghost-tales at present surviving – that is, had so faded among the white people. On the nearby reservation were old Indians who thought much and kept their own counsel. About this time a second wave of active curiosity and adventuring developed, and several bold searchers made the trip to the mound and returned. Then came a trip of two Eastern visitors with spades and other apparatus; a pair of amateur archaeologists connected with a small college, who had been making studies among the Indians. No one watched this trip from the village, but they never came back. The searching party that went out after them, among whom was my host Clyde Compton, found nothing whatsoever amiss at the mound.

The next trip was the solitary venture of old Captain Lawton, a grizzled pioneer who had helped to open up the region in 1889, but who had never been there since. He had recalled the mound and its fascination all through the years; and being now in comfortable retirement, resolved to have a try at solving the ancient riddle. Long familiarity with Indian myth had given him ideas rather stranger than those of the simple villagers, and he had made preparations for some extensive delving. He ascended the mound on the morning of Thursday, May 11, 1916, watched through spy-glasses by more than twenty people in the village and on the adjacent plain. His disappearance was very sudden, and occurred as he was hacking at the shrubbery with a brushcutter. No one could say more than that he was there one moment and absent the next. For over a week no tidings of him reached Binger, and then, in the middle of the night, there dragged itself into the village the object about which dispute still rages.

It said it was – or had been – Captain Lawton, but it was definitely younger by as much as forty years than the old man who had climbed the mound. Its hair was jet black, and its face, now distorted with nameless fright, free from wrinkles. But it did remind Grandma Compton most uncannily of the captain as he had looked back in '89. Its feet were cut off neatly at the ankles, and the stumps were smoothly healed to an extent almost incredible if the being really were the man who had walked upright a week before. It babbled of incomprehensible things, and kept repeating the name 'George Lawton, George B. Lawton' as if trying to reassure itself of its own identity. The things it babbled of, Grandma Compton thought, were curiously like the hallucinations of poor young Heaton in '91; though there were minor differences. 'The blue light! – the blue light! . . .' muttered the object, 'always down there, before there were any living things – older than the dinosaurs – always the same, only weaker – never death – brooding and brooding and brooding – the same people, half man and half gas – the dead that walk and walk – oh, those beasts, those half-human unicorns – houses and cities of gold – old, old, old, older than time – came down from the stars – Great Tulu – Azathoth – Nyarlathotep – waiting, waiting. . . .' The object died before dawn.

Of course there was an investigation, and the Indians at the reservation were grilled unmercifully. But they knew nothing, and had nothing to say. At least, none of them had anything to say except old Grey Eagle, a Wichita chieftain whose more than a century of age put him above common fears. He alone deigned to grunt some advice.

'You let um 'lone, white man. No good – those people. All under here, all under there, them old ones. Yig, big father of snakes, he there. Yig is Yig, Tirawa, big father of men, he there. Tirawa is Tirawa. No die. No get old. Just same like air. Just live and wait. One time they come out here, live and fight. Build um dirt tepee. Bring up gold – they got plenty. Go off and make new lodges. Me them. You them. Then big waters come. All change. Nobody come out, let nobody in. Get in, no get out. You let um 'lone, you have no bad medicine. Red man know, he no get catch. White man meddle, he no come back. Keep 'way little hills. No good. Grey Eagle say this.'

If Joe Norton and Rance Wheelock had taken the old chief's advice, they would probably be here today; but they didn't. They were great readers and materialists, and feared nothing in heaven or earth; and they thought that some Indian fiends had a secret headquarters inside the mound. They had been to the mound before, and now they went again to avenge old Captain Lawton – boasting that they'd do it if they had to tear the mound down altogether. Clyde Compton watched them with a pair of prism binoculars and saw them round the base of the sinister hill. Evidently they meant to survey their territory very gradually and minutely. Minutes passed, and they did not reappear. Nor were they ever seen again.

Once more the mound was a thing of panic fright, and only the excitement of the Great War served to restore it to the farther background of Binger folklore. It was unvisited from 1916 to 1919, and would have remained so but for the dare-devilry of some of the youths back from service in France. From 1919 to 1920, however, there was a veritable epidemic of mound-visiting among the prematurely hardened young veterans: an epidemic that waxed as one youth after another returned unhurt and contemptuous. By 1920, so short is human memory, the mound was almost a joke; and the tame story of the murdered squaw began to displace the darker whispers on everybody's tongues. Then two reckless young brothers – the especially unimaginative and hard-boiled Clay boys – decided to go and dig up the buried squaw and the gold for which the old Indian had murdered her.

They went out on a September afternoon – about the time the Indian tom-toms begin their incessant annual beating over the flat, red-dusty plains. Nobody watched them, and their parents did not become worried at their non-return for several hours. Then came an alarm and a searching-party, and another resignation to the mystery of silence and doubt.

But one of them came back after all. It was Ed, the elder, and his straw-coloured hair and beard had turned an albino white for two inches from the roots. On his forehead was a queer scar like a branded hieroglyphic. Three months after he and his brother Walker had vanished he skulked into his house at night, wearing nothing but a queerly patterned blanket which he thrust into the fire as soon as he had got into a suit of his own clothes. He told his parents that he and Walker had been captured by some strange Indians: not Wichitas or Caddos: and held prisoners somewhere towards the west. Walker had died under torture, but he himself had managed to escape at a high cost. The experience had been particularly terrible, and he could not talk about it just then. He must rest, and anyway, it would do no good to give an alarm and try to find and punish the Indians. They were not of a sort that could be caught or punished, and it was especially important for the good of Binger, for the good of the world, that they be not pursued into their secret lair. As a matter of fact, they were not altogether what one could call real Indians; he would explain about that later. Meanwhile he must rest. Better not to rouse the village with the news of his return; he would go upstairs and sleep. Before he climbed the rickety flight to his room he took a pad and pencil from the living-room table, and an automatic pistol from his father's desk drawer.

Three hours later the shot rang out. Ed Clay had put a bullet through his temple with a pistol clutched in his left hand, leaving a sparsely written sheet of paper on the rickety table near his bed. He had, it later appeared from the whittled pencil-stub and stove full of charred paper, originally written much more; but had finally decided not to tell what he knew beyond vague hints. The surviving fragment was only a mad warning scrawled in a curiously backhanded script – the ravings of a mind obviously deranged by hardships – and it read thus: rather surprisingly for the utterance of one who had always been stolid and matter-of-fact:

> For gods sake never go near that mound it is part of some kind of a world so devilish and old it cannot be spoke about me and Walker went and was took into the thing just melted at times and made up agen and the whole world outside is helpless alongside of what they can do – they what live forever young as they like and you cant tell if they are really men or just gostes – and what they do cant be spoke about and this is only I entrance – you cant tell how big the whole thing is – after what we seen I dont want to live any more France was nothing besides this – and see that people always keep away an god they wood if they see poor walker like he was in the end.
>
> Yrs truely
>
> Ed Clay

At the autopsy it was found that all of young Clay's organs were transposed from right to left within his body, as if he had been turned inside out. Whether they had always been so, no one could say at the time, but it was later learned from army records that Ed had been perfectly normal when mustered out of the services in May, 1919. Whether there was a mistake somewhere, or whether some unprecedented metamorphosis had indeed occurred, is still an unsettled question, as is also the origin of the hieroglyphic-like scar on the forehead.

That was the end of the explorations of the mound. In the eight intervening years no one had been near the place, and few indeed had even cared to level a spyglass at it. From time to time people continued to glance nervously at the lone hill as it rose starkly from the plain against the western sky, and to shudder at the small dark speck that paraded by day and the glimmering will-o-the-wisp that danced by night. The thing was accepted at face value as a mystery not to be probed, and by common consent the village shunned the subject. It was, after all, quite easy to avoid the hill; for space was unlimited in every direction, and community life always follows beaten trails. The mound side of the village was simply kept trail-less, as if it had been water or swampland or desert. And it is a curious commentary on the stolidity and imaginative sterility of the human animal that the whispers with which children and strangers were warned away from the mound quickly sank once more into the flat tale of a murderous Indian ghost and his squaw victim. Only the tribesmen on the reservation, and thoughtful old-timers like Grandma Compton, remembered the overtones of unholy vistas and deep cosmic menace which clustered around the ravings of those who had come back changed and shattered.

It was very late, and Grandma Compton had long gone upstairs to bed, when Clyde finished telling me this. I hardly knew what to think of the frightful puzzle, yet rebelled at any notion to conflict with sane materialism. What influence had brought madness, or the impulse of flight and wandering, to so many who had visited the mound? Though vastly impressed, I was spurred on rather than deterred. Surely I must get to the bottom of this matter, as well I might if I kept a cool head and an unbroken determination. Compton saw my mood and shook his head worriedly. Then he motioned me to follow him outdoors.

We stepped from the frame house to the quiet side street or lane, and walked a few paces in the light of a waning August moon to where the houses were thinner. The half-moon was still low, and had not blotted many stars from the sky; so that I could see not only the westering gleams of Altair and Vega, but the mystic shimmering of the Milky Way, as I looked out over the vast expanse of earth and sky in the direction that Compton pointed. Then all at once I saw a spark that was not a star – a bluish spark that moved and glimmered against the Milky Way near the horizon, and that seemed in a vague way more evil and malevolent than anything in the vault above. In another moment it was clear that this spark came from the top of a long distant rise in the outspread and faintly-litten plain; and I turned to Compton with a question.

'Yes,' he answered, 'it's the blue ghost-light – and that is the mound. There's not a night in history that we haven't seen it – and not a living soul in Binger that would walk out over that plain toward it. It's a bad business, young man, and if you're wise you'll let it rest where it is. Better call your search off, Son, and tackle some of the other Injun legends around here. We've plenty to keep you busy, Heaven knows!'

II

But I was in no mood for advice; and though Compton gave me a pleasant room, I could not sleep a wink through eagerness for the next morning with its chances to see the daytime ghost and to question the Indians at the reservation. I meant to go about the whole thing slowly and thoroughly, equipping myself with all the available data both white and red before I commenced any actual archaeological investigations. I rose and dressed at dawn, and when I heard others stirring I went downstairs. Compton was building the kitchen fire while his mother was busy in the pantry. When he saw me he nodded, and after a moment invited me out into the glamorous young sunlight. I knew where we were going, and as we walked along the lane I strained my eyes westward over the plains.

There was the mound, far away and very curious in its aspect of artificial regularity. It must have been from thirty to forty feet high, and all of a hundred yards from north to south as I looked at it. It was not as wide as that from east to west, Compton said, but had the contour of a rather thinnish ellipse. He, I knew, had been safely out to it and back several times. As I looked at the rim silhouetted against the deep blue of the west I tried to follow its minor irregularities, and became impressed with a sense of something moving upon it. My pulse mounted a bit feverishly, and I seized quickly on the high-powered binoculars which Compton quietly offered me. Focussing them hastily, I saw at first only a tangle of underbrush on the distant mound's rim – and then something stalked into the field.

It was unmistakably a human shape, and I knew at once that I was seeing the daytime 'Indian ghost'. I did not wonder at the description, for surely the tall, lean, darkly robed being with the filleted black hair and seamed, coppery, expressionless, aquiline face looked more like an Indian than anything else in my previous experience. And yet my trained ethnologist's eye told me at once that this was no redskin of any sort hitherto known to history, but a creature of vast racial variation and of a wholly different culture-stream. Modern Indians are brachycephalic; round-headed; and you can't find any dolichocephalic or long-headed skulls except in ancient Pueblo deposits dating back 2,500 years or more, yet this man's long-headedness was so pronounced that I recognized it at once, even at this vast distance and in the uncertain field of the binoculars. I saw, too, that the pattern of his robe represented a decorative tradition utterly remote from anything we recognize in south-western native art. There were shining metal trappings, likewise, and a short sword or kindred weapon at his side, all wrought in a fashion wholly alien to anything of which I had ever heard.

As he paced back and forth along the top of the mound I followed him for several minutes with the glass, noting the kinaesthetic quality of his stride and the poised way he carried his head; and there was borne in upon me the strong, persistent conviction that this man, whoever or whatever he might be, was certainly not a savage. He was the product of a civilization, I felt instinctively, though of what civilization I could not guess. At length he disappeared beyond the farther edge of the mound, as if descending the opposite and unseen slope; and I lowered the glass with a curious mixture of puzzled feelings.

Compton was looking quizzically at me, and I nodded non-committally. 'What do you make of that? he ventured. 'This is what we've seen here in Binger every day of our lives.'

That noon found me at the Indian reservation talking with old Grey Eagle, who, through some miracle, was still alive, though he must have been close to a hundred and fifty years old. He was a strange, impressive figure, this stern, fearless leader of his kind who had talked with outlaws and traders in fringed buckskin and French officials in knee-breeches and three-cornered hats, and I was glad to see that, because of my air of deference toward him, he appeared to like me. His liking, however, took an unfortunately obstructive form as soon as he learned what I wanted; for all he would do was to warn me against the search I was about to make.

'You good boy, you no bother that hill. Bad medicine. Plenty devil under there, catchum when you dig. No dig, no hurt. Go and dig, no come back. Just same when my boy, just same when my father and he father boy. All time buck he walk in day, squaw with no head she walk in night. All time since white men with tin coats they come from sunset and below big river – long way back – three, four times more back than Grey Eagle – two times more back than Frenchmen – all same after then. More back than that, nobody go near little hills nor deep valleys with stone caves. Still more back, those old ones no hide, come out and make villages. Bring plenty gold. Me them. You them. Then big waters come. All change. Nobody come out, let nobody in. Get in, no get out. They no die – no get old like Grey Eagle with valleys in face and snow on head. Just same like air – some man, some spirit. Bad medicine. Sometimes at night spirit come out on half-man-horse with horn and fight where men once fight. Keep 'way them place. No good. You good boy, go 'way and let them old ones 'lone.'

That was all I could get out of the ancient chief, and the rest of the Indians would say nothing at all. But if I was troubled, Grey Eagle was clearly more so; for he obviously felt a real regret at the thought of my invading the region he feared so abjectly. As I turned to leave the reservation he stopped me for a final ceremonial farewell, and once more tried earnestly to get my promise to abandon my search. When he saw that he could not, he produced something half-timidly from a buckskin pouch he wore, and extended it toward me very solemnly. It was a worn but finely minted metal disc about two inches in diameter, oddly figured and perforated, and suspended from a leather cord.

'You no promise, then Grey Eagle no can tell what get you. But if anything help um, this good medicine. Come from my father – he get from he father – he get from he father – all way back, close to Tirawa, all men's father. My father he say, "You keep 'way from those old ones, keep 'way from little hills and valleys with stone caves. But if old ones they come out to get you, then you show um this medicine. They know. They make him long way back. They look, then they no do such bad medicine maybe. But no can tell. You keep 'way, just same. Them no good. No tell what they do." '

As he spoke, Grey Eagle was hanging the thing around my neck, and I saw it was a very curious object indeed. The more I looked at it, the more I marvelled, for not only was its heavy, darkish, lustrous and richly mottled substance an absolutely strange and utterly unknown workmanship. One side, so far as I could see, had borne an exquisitely modelled serpent design; whilst the other side had depicted a kind of octopus or other tentacled monster. There were some half-effaced hieroglyphs, too, of a kind which no archaeologist could identify or even place conjecturally. With Grey Eagle's permission I later had expert historians, anthropologists, geologists and chemists pass carefully upon the disc, but from them I obtained only a chorus of bafflement. It defied either classification or analysis. The chemists called it an amalgam of unknown metallic elements of heavy atomic weight, and one geologist suggested that the substance must be of meteoric origin, shot from unknown gulfs of interstellar space. Whether it really saved my life or sanity or existence as a human being I cannot attempt to say, but Grey Eagle is sure of it. He has it again, now, and I wonder if it has any connection with his inordinate age.

When I returned to the village, I tried to secure more moundlore, but found only excited gossip and opposition. It was really flattering to see how solicitous the people were about my safety, but I had to set their almost frantic remonstrances aside. I showed them Grey Eagle's charm, but none of them had ever heard of it before, or seen anything even remotely like it. They agreed that it could not be an Indian relic, and imagined that the old chief's ancestors must have obtained it from some trader.

When they saw they could not deter me from my trip, the Binger citizens sadly did what they could to aid my outfitting. Having known before my arrival the sort of work to be done, I had most of my supplies already with me; machete and trench-knife for shrub-clearing and excavating, electric torches for any underground phase which might develop, rope, field-glasses; tape measure, microscope, and incidentals for emergencies; as much, in fact, as might be comfortably stowed in a convenient handbag. To this equipment I added only the heavy revolver which the sheriff forced upon me, and the pick and shovel which I thought might expedite my work.

I decided to carry these latter things slung over my shoulder with a stout cord, for I soon saw that I could not hope for any helpers or fellow-explorers. The village would watch me, no doubt, with all its available telescopes and field-glasses; but it would not send any citizen so much as a yard over the flat plain toward the lone hillock. My start was timed for early the next morning, and all the rest of that day I was treated with the awed and uneasy respect which people give to a man about to set out for certain doom.

When morning came, a cloudy though not a threatening morning, the whole village turned out to see me start across the dust-blown plain. Binoculars showed the lone man at his usual pacing on the mound, and I resolved to keep him in sight as steadily as possible during my approach. At the last moment a vague sense of dread oppressed me, and I was just weak and whimsical enough to let Grey Eagle's talisman swing on my chest in full view of any beings or ghosts who might be inclined to heed it. Bidding au revoir to Compton and his mother I started off at a brisk stride despite the bag in my left hand and the clanking pick and shovel strapped to my back; holding my field-glasses in my right hand and taking a glance at the silent pacer from time to time. As I neared the mound I saw the man very clearly, and fancied I could trace an expression of infinite evil and decadence on his seamed, hairless features. I was startled, too, to see that his goldenly gleaming weapon-case bore hieroglyphics very similar to those on the unknown talisman I wore. All the creature's costume and trappings bespoke exquisite workmanship and civilization. Then, all too abruptly, I saw him start down the farther side of the mound and out of sight. When I reached the place, about ten minutes after I set out, there was no one there.

There is no need of relating how I spent the early part of my search in surveying and circumnavigating the mound, taking measurements and stepping back to view the thing from different angles. It had impressed me tremendously as I approached it, and there seemed to be a kind of latent menace in its too regular outlines. It was the only elevation of any sort on the wide, level plain; and I could not doubt for a moment that it was an artificial tumulus. The steep sides seemed wholly unbroken, and without marks of human tenancy or passage. There were no signs of a path toward the top; and, burdened as I was, I managed to scramble up only with considerable difficulty. When I reached the summit I found a roughly level elliptical plateau about 300 by 50 feet in dimensions; uniformly covered with rank grass and dense underbrush, and utterly incompatible with the constant presence of a pacing sentinel. This condition gave me a real shock, for it showed beyond question that the 'Old Indian', vivid though he had seemed, could not be other than a collective hallucination.

I looked about with considerable perplexity and alarm, glancing wistfully back at the village and the mass of black dots which I knew was the watching crowd. Training my glasses upon them, I saw that they were studying me avidly with their glasses; so to reassure them I waved my cap in the air with a show of jauntiness which I was far from feeling. Then, settling to my work I flung down pick, shovel, and bag; taking my machete from the latter and commencing to clear away underbrush. It was a weary task, and now and then I felt a curious shiver as some perverse gust of wind arose to hamper my motion with a skill approaching deliberateness. At times it seemed as if a half-tangible force were pushing me back as I worked, almost as if the air thickened in front of me, or as if formless hands tugged at my wrists. My energy seemed used up without producing adequate results, yet for all that I made some progress.

By afternoon I had clearly perceived that, toward the northern end of the mound, there was a slight bowl-like depression in the root-tangled earth. While this might mean nothing, it would be a good place to begin when I reached the digging stage, and I made a mental note of it. At the same time I noticed another and very peculiar thing – namely, that the Indian talisman swinging from my neck seemed to behave oddly at a point about seventeen feet southeast of the suggested bowl. Its gyrations were altered whenever I happened to stoop around that point, and it tugged downward as if attracted by some magnetism in the soil. The more I noticed this, the more it struck me, till at length I decided to do a little preliminary digging there without further delay.

As I turned up the soil with my trench-knife I could not help wondering at the relative thinness of the reddish regional layer. The country as a whole was all red sandstone earth, but here I found a strange black loam less than a foot down. It was such soil as one finds in the strange, deep valleys farther west and south, and must surely have been brought from a considerable distance in the prehistoric age when the mound was reared. Kneeling and digging, I felt the leathern cord around my neck tugged harder and harder, more vigorously as something in the soil seemed to draw the heavy metal talisman more and more toward it. Then I felt my implements strike a hard surface, and wondered if a rock layer rested beneath. Prying about with the trench-knife, I found that such was not the case. Instead, to my intense surprise and feverish interest, I brought up a mould-clogged, heavy object of cylindrical shape, about a foot long and four inches in diameter, to which my hanging talisman clove with gluelike tenacity. As I cleared off the black loam my wonder and tension increased at the bas-reliefs revealed by the process. The whole cylinder, ends and all, was covered with figures and hieroglyphics; and I saw with growing excitement that these things were in the same unknown tradition as those on Grey Eagle's charm and on the yellow metal trappings of the ghost I had seen through my binoculars.

Sitting down, I further cleaned the magnetic cylinder against the rough corduroy of my knickerbockers, and observed that it was made of the same heavy, lustrous unknown metal as the charm – hence, no doubt, the singular attraction. The carvings and chasings were very strange and very horrible; nameless monsters and designs fraught with insidious evil: and all were of the highest finish and craftsmanship. I could not at first make head or tail of the thing, and handled it aimlessly until I spied a cleavage near one end. Then I sought eagerly for some mode of opening, discovering at last that the end simply unscrewed.

The cap yielded with difficulty, but at last it came off, liberating a curious aromatic odour. The sole contents was a bulky roll of a yellowish, paper-like substance inscribed in greenish characters, and for a second I had the supreme thrill of fancying that I held a written key to unknown elder worlds and abysses beyond time. Almost immediately, however, the unrolling of one end showed that the manuscript was in Spanish – albeit the formal, pompous Spanish of a long-departed day. In the golden sunset light I looked at the heading and the opening paragraph, trying to decipher the wretched and ill-punctuated script of the vanished writer. What manner of relic was this? Upon what sort of a discovery had I stumbled? The first words set me in a new fury of excitement and curiosity, for instead of diverting me from my original quest they startlingly confirmed me in that very effort.

The yellow scroll with the green script began with a bold, identifying caption and a ceremoniously desperate appeal for belief in incredible revelations to follow:

RELIGION DE PANFILO DE ZAMACONA Y NUNEZ HIDALGO DE LUARCA EN ASTURIAS, TOGANTE AL MUNDO SOTERRANEO DE XINAIAN. A. D. MDXLV

En el nombre de la santisima Trinidad, Padre, Hijo, y Espiritu-Santo, tres personas distin-

tas y un solo. Dios verdadero, y de la santi-
sima Virgen nuestra Senora, YO PANFILO DE
ZAMACONA, HIJO DE PEDRO GUZMAN Y ZAMACONA

HIDALGO, Y DE LA DONA YNES ALVARADO Y NUNEZ
DE LUARCA EN ASTURIAS, juro para que todo que
deco esta verdadero como sacramento. . . .

I paused to reflect on the portentous significance of what I was reading. 'The Narrative of Panfilo de Zamacona y Nunez, gentleman, of Luarca in Astorias, Concerning the Subterranean World of Xinaian, A.D. 1545'. . . . Here surely, was too much for any mind to absorb all at once. A subterranean world – again that persistent idea which filtered through all the Indian tales and through all the utterances of those who had come back from the mound. And the date: 1545: what could this mean? In 1540 Coronado and his men had gone north from Mexico into the wilderness but had they not turned back in 1542? My eye ran questioningly down the opened part of the scroll and almost at once seized on the name Francisco Varquez de Coronado. The writer of this thing clearly was one of Coronado's men, but what had he been doing in this remote realm three years after his party had gone back? I must read further, for another glance told me that what was now unrolled was merely a summary of Coronado's northward march, differing in no essential way from the account known to history.

It was only the waning light which checked me before I could unroll and read more, and in my impatient bafflement I almost forgot to be frightened at the onrush of night in this sinister place. Others, however, had not forgotten the lurking terror, for I heard a loud distant hallooing from a knot of men who had gathered at the edge of the town. Answering the anxious hail, I restored the manuscript to its strange cylinder, to which the disc around my neck still clung until I pried it off and packed it and my smaller implements for departure. Leaving the pick and shovel for the next day's work, I took up my handbag, scrambled down the steep side of the mound, and in another quarter-hour was back in the village explaining and exhibiting my curious find. As darkness drew on, I glanced back at the mound I had so lately left, and saw with a shudder that the faint bluish torch of the nocturnal squaw-ghost had begun to glimmer.

It was hard work waiting to get at the bygone Spaniard's narrative; but I knew I must have quiet and leisure for a good translation, so reluctantly saved the task for the later hours of night. Promising the townsfolk a clear account of my findings in the morning, and giving them an ample opportunity to examine the bizarre and provocative cylinder, I accompanied Clyde Compton home and ascended to my room for the translating process as soon as I possibly could. My host and his mother were intensely eager to hear the tale, but I thought they had better wait till I could thoroughly absorb the text myself and give them the gist concisely and unerringly.

Opening my handbag in the light of a single electric bulb, I again took out the cylinder and noted the instant magnetism which pulled the Indian talisman to its carven surface. The designs glimmered evilly on the richly lustrous and unknown metal, and I could not help shivering as I studied the abnormal and blasphemous forms that leered at me with such exquisite workmanship. I wish now that I had carefully photographed all these designs – though perhaps it is just as well that I did not. Of one thing I am really glad, and that is that I could not then identify the squatting octopus-headed thing which dominated most of the ornate cartouches, and which the manuscript called 'Tulu'. Recently I have associated it, and the legends in the manuscript connected with it, with some new-found folklore of monstrous and unmentioned Cthulhu, a horror which seeped down from the stars while the young earth was still half formed; and had I known of the connection then, I could not have stayed in the same room with the thing. The secondary motif, a semi-anthropomorphic serpent, I did quite readily place as a prototype of the Yig, Quetzalcoatl, and Kukulkan conceptions. Before opening the cylinder I tested its magnetic powers on metals other than that of Grey Eagle's disc, but found that no attraction existed. It was no common magnetism which pervaded this morbid fragment of unknown worlds and linked it to its kind.

At last I took out the manuscript and began translating – jotting down a synoptic outline in English as I went, and now and then regretting the absence of a Spanish dictionary when I came upon some especially obscure or archaic word or construction. There was a sense of ineffable strangeness in thus being thrown back nearly four centuries in the midst of my continuous quest, thrown back to a year when my own forebears were settled, home-keeping gentlemen of Somerset and Devon under Henry the Eighth, with never a thought of the adventure that was to take their blood to Virginia and the New World, yet when that new world possessed, even as now, the same brooding mystery of the mound which formed my present sphere and horizon. The sense of throwback was all the stronger because I felt instinctively that the common problem of the Spaniard and myself was one of such abysmal timelessness, of such unholy and unearthly eternity, that the scant four hundred years between us bulked as nothing in comparison. It took no more than a single look at that monstrous and insidious cylinder to make me realize the dizzying gulfs that yawned between all men of the known earth and the primal mysteries it represented. Before that gulf Panfilo de Zamacona and I stood side by side; just as Aristotle and I, or Cheops and I might have stood.

III

Of his youth, in Luarca, a small, placid port on the Bay of Biscay, Zamacona told little. He had been wild, and a younger son, and had come to New Spain in 1532, when only twenty years old. Sensitively imaginative, he had listened spellbound to the floating rumors of rich cities and unknown worlds to the north – and especially to the tale of the Franciscan friar Marcos de Niza, who came back from a trip in 1539 with glowing accounts of fabulous Cibola and its great walled towns with terraced stone houses. Hearing of Coronado's contemplated expedition in search of these wonders, and of the greater wonders whispered to lie beyond them in the land of buffaloes, young Zamacona managed to join the picked party of three hundred, and started north with the rest in 1540.

History knows the story of that expedition: how Cibola was found to be merely the squalid Pueblo village of Zuni, and how de Niza was sent back to Mexico in disgrace for his florid exaggerations; how Coronado first saw the Grand Canyon, and how at Cicuye, on the Pecos, he heard from the Indian called El Turco of the rich and mysterious land of Quivira, far to the northeast, where gold, silver, and buffaloes abounded, and where there flowed rivers two leagues wide. Zamacona told briefly of the winter camp at Tiguex on the

Pecos, and of the northward start in April, when the native guide proved false and led the party astray amidst a land of prairie-dogs, salt pools, and roving, bison-hunting tribes.

When Coronado dismissed his larger force and made his final forty-two-day march with a very small and select detachment, Zamacona managed to be included in the advancing party. He spoke of the fertile country and of the great ravines with trees visible only from the edge of their steep banks; and of how all the men lived solely on buffalo-meat. And then came mention of the expedition's farthest limit – of the presumable but disappointing land of Quivira with its villages of great houses, its brooks and rivers, its good black soil, its plums, nuts, grapes, and mulberries, and its maize-growing and copper-using Indians. The execution of El Turco, the false native guide, was casually touched upon, and there was a mention of the cross which Coronado raised on the bank of a great river in the autumn of 1541 – a cross bearing the inscription, 'Thus far came the great general, Francisco Vasquez de Coronado'.

This supposed Quivira lay at about the fortieth parallel of north latitude, and I see that quite lately the New York archaeologist, Dr Hodge, had identified it with the course of the Arkansas River through Barton and Rice Counties, Kansas. It is the old home of the Wichitas, before the Sioux drove them into what is now Oklahoma, and some of the grass-house village sites have been found and excavated for artifacts. Coronado did considerable exploring hereabouts, led hither and thither by the persistent rumors of rich cities and hidden worlds which floated fearfully around on the Indians' tongues. These northerly natives seemed more afraid and reluctant to talk about the rumored cities and worlds than the Mexican Indians had been; yet at the same time seemed as if they could reveal a good deal more than the Mexicans had they been willing or dared to do so. Their vagueness exasperated the Spanish leader and after many disappointing searches he began to be very severe toward those who brought him stories. Zamacona, more patient than Coronado, found the tales especially interesting; and learned enough of the local speech to hold long conversations with a young buck named Charging Buffalo, whose curiosity had led him into much stranger places than any of his fellow-tribesmen had dared to penetrate.

It was Charging Buffalo who told Zamacona of the queer

stone doorways, gates, or cave-mouths at the bottom of some of those deep, steep, wooded ravines which the party had noticed on the northward march. These openings, he said, were mostly concealed by shrubbery; and few had entered them for untold aeons. Those who went to where they led, never returned – or in a few cases returned mad or curiously maimed. But all this was legend, for nobody was known to have gone more than a limited distance inside any of them within the memory of the grandfathers of the oldest living men. Charging Buffalo himself had probably been farther than anyone else, and he had seen enough to curb both his curiosity and his greed for the rumored gold below.

Beyond the aperture he had entered there was a long passage running crazily up and down and round about, and covered with frightful carvings of monsters and horrors that no man had ever seen. At last, after untold miles of windings and descents, there was a glow of terrible blue light; and the passage opened upon a shocking nether world. About this the Indian would say no more, for he had seen something that had sent him back in haste. But the golden cities must be somewhere down there, he added, and perhaps a white man with the magic of the thunderstick might succeed in getting to them. He would not tell the big chief Coronado what he knew, for Coronado would not listen to Indian talk any more. Yes – he could show Zamacona the way if the white man would leave the party and accept his guidance. But he would not go inside the opening with the white man. It was bad in there.

The place was about a five days' march to the south, near the region of great mounds. These mounds had something to do with the evil world down there; they were probably ancient closed-up passages to it, for once the Old Ones below had had colonies on the surface and had traded with men everywhere, even in the lands that had sunk under the big waters. It was when those lands had sunk that the Old Ones closed themselves up below and refused to deal with surface people. The refugees from the sinking places had told them that the gods of outer earth were against men, and that no men could survive on the outer earth unless they were demons in league with the evil gods. That is why they shut out all surface folk, and did fearful things to any who ventured down where they dwelt. There had been sentries once at the various openings, but after ages they were no longer needed. Not many people cared to talk about the hidden Old Ones, and the legends about them would probably have died out but for certain ghostly reminders of their presence now and then. It seemed that the infinite ancientness of these creatures had brought them strangely near to the borderline of spirit, so that their ghostly emanations were more commonly frequent and vivid. Accordingly, the region of the great mounds was often convulsed with spectral nocturnal battles reflecting those which had been fought in the days before the openings were closed.

The Old Ones themselves were half ghost – indeed, it was said that they no longer grew old or reproduced their kind, but flickered eternally in a state between flesh and spirit. The change was not complete, though, for they had to breathe. It was because the underground world needed air that the openings in the deep valleys were not blocked up as the mound openings on the plains had been. These openings, Charging Buffalo added, were probably based on natural fissures in the earth. It was whispered that the Old Ones had come down from the stars to the world when it was very young, and had gone inside to build cities of solid gold because the surface was not then fit to live on. They were the ancestors of all men, yet none could guess from what star – or what place beyond the stars – they came. Their hidden cities were still full of gold and silver, but men had better let them alone unless protected by very strong magic.

They had frightful beasts with a faint strain of human blood, on which they rode, and which they employed for other purposes. The things, so people hinted, were carnivorous, and like their masters, preferred human flesh; so that although the Old Ones themselves did not breed, they had a sort of half-human slave class which also served to nourish the human and animal population. This had been very oddly recruited, and was supplemented by a second slave class of reanimated corpses. The Old Ones knew how to make a corpse into an automaton which would last almost indefinitely and perform any sort of work when directed by streams of thought. Charging Buffalo said that the people had all come to talk by means of thought only; speech having been found crude and needless, except for religious devotions and emotional expression, as aeons of discovery and study rolled by. They worshipped Yig, the great father of serpents, and Tulu, the octopus-headed entity that had brought them down from the stars; appeasing both of these hideous monstrosities by means of human sacrifices offered up in a very curious manner which Charging Buffalo did not care to describe.

Zamacona was held spellbound by the Indian's tale, and at once resolved to accept his guidance to the cryptic doorway in the ravine. He did not believe the accounts of strange ways attributed by legend to the hidden people, for the experiences of the party had been such as to disillusion one regarding native myths of unknown lands; but he did feel that some sufficiently marvellous field of riches and adventure must indeed lie beyond the weirdly carved passages in the earth. At first he thought of persuading Charging Buffalo to tell his story to Coronado – offering to shield him against any effects of the leader's testy scepticism – but later he decided that a lone adventure would be better. If he had no aid, he would not have to share anything he found, but might perhaps become a great discoverer and the owner of fabulous riches. Success would make him a greater figure than Coronado himself, perhaps a greater figure than anyone else in New Spain, including even the mighty viceroy Don Antonio de Mendoza.

On October 7, 1541, at an hour close to midnight, Zamacona stole out of the Spanish camp near the grass-house village and met Charging Buffalo for the long southward journey. He travelled as lightly as possible, and did not wear his heavy helmet and breastplate. Of the details of the trip the manuscript told very little, but Zamacona records his arrival at the great ravine on October 13th. The descent of the thickly wooded slope took no great time; and though the Indian had trouble in locating the shrubbery-hidden stone door again amidst the twilight of the deep gorge, the place was finally found. It was a very small aperture as doorways go, formed of monolithic sandstone jambs and lintel, and bearing signs of nearly effaced and now undecipherable carvings. Its height was perhaps seven feet, and its width not more than four. There were drilled places in the jambs which argued the bygone presence of a hinged door or gate, but all other traces of such a thing had long since vanished.

At sight of this black gulf, Charging Buffalo displayed considerable fear, and threw down his pack of supplies with signs of haste. He had provided Zamacona with a good stock of resinous torches and provisions, and had guided him honestly and well; but refused to share in the venture that lay ahead.

Zamacona gave him the trinkets he had kept for such an occasion, and obtained his promise to return to the region in a month; afterward showing the way southward to the Pecos villages. A prominent rock on the plain above them was chosen as a meeting place; the one arriving first to pitch camp until the other should arrive.

In the manuscript Zamacona expressed a wistful wonder as to the Indian's length of waiting at the rendezvous – for he himself could never keep that tryst. At the last moment Charging Buffalo tried to dissuade him from his plunge into the darkness, but soon saw it was futile, and gestured a stoical farewell. Before lighting his first torch and entering the opening with his ponderous pack, the Spaniard watched the lean fôrm of the Indian scrambling hastily and rather relievedly upward among the trees. It was the cutting of his last link with the world – though he did not know that he was never to see a human being, in the accepted sense of that term, again.

Zamacona felt no immediate premonition of evil upon entering that ominous doorway, though from the first he was surrounded by a bizarre and unwholesome atmosphere. The passage, slightly taller and wider than the aperture, was for many yards a level tunnel of cyclopean masonry, with heavily worn flagstones under foot, and grotesquely carved granite and sandstone blocks in sides and ceiling. The carvings must have been loathsome and terrible indeed, to judge from Zamacona's description; according to which most of them involved the monstrous beings Yig and Tulu. They were unlike anything the adventurer had ever seen before, though he added that the native architecture of Mexico came closest to them of all things in the outer world. After some distance the tunnel began to dip abruptly, and irregular natural rock appeared on all sides. The passage seemed only partly artificial, and decorations were limited to occasional cartouches with shocking bas-reliefs.

Following an enormous descent, whose steepness at times produced an acute danger of slipping and tobogganing, the passage became exceedingly uncertain in its direction and variable in contour. At times it narrowed almost to a slit or grew so low that stooping and even crawling were necessary, while at other times it broadened out into sizeable caves or chains of caves. Very little human construction, it was plain, had gone into this part of the tunnel; though occasionally a sinister cartouche or hieroglyphic on the wall, or a blocked-up lateral passageway, would remind Zamacona that this was in truth the aeon-forgotten highroad to a primal and unbelievable world of living things.

For three days, as best as he could reckon, Panfilo de Zamacona scrambled down, up, along, and around, but always predominantly downward through the dark region of palaeogean night. Once in a while he heard some secret being of darkness patter or flap out of his way, and on just one more occasion he half-glimpsed a great bleached thing that set him trembling. The quality of the air was mostly very tolerable; though foetid zones were now and then met with, while one great cavern of stalactites and stalagmites afforded a depressing dampness. This latter, when Charging Buffalo had come upon it, had quite seriously barred the way; since the limestone deposits of ages had built fresh pillars in the path of the primordial abyss-denizens. The Indian, however, had broken through these; so that Zamacona did not find his course impeded. It was an unconscious comfort to him to reflect that someone else from the outside world had been there before – and the Indian's careful descriptions had removed the element of surprise and unexpectedness. More – Charging Buffalo's knowledge of the tunnel had led him to provide so good a torch supply for the journey in and out, that there would be no danger of becoming stranded in darkness. Zamacona camped twice, building a fire whose smoke seemed well taken care of by the natural ventilation.

At what he considered the end of the third day (though his cocksure guesswork chronology is not at any time to be given the easy faith that he gave it) Zamacona encountered the prodigious descent and subsequent prodigious climb which Charging Buffalo had described as the tunnel's last phase. As at certain earlier points, marks of artificial improvement were here discernible; and several times the steep gradient was eased by a flight of rough-hewn steps. The torch showed more and more of the monstrous carvings on the walls, and finally the resinous flare seemed mixed with a fainter and more diffusive light as Zamacona climbed up and up after the last downward stairway. At length the ascent ceased, and a level passage of artificial masonry with dark, basaltic blocks led straight ahead. There was no need for a torch now, for all the air was glowing with a bluish quasi-electric radiance that flickered like an aurora. It was the strange light of the inner world that the Indian had described – and in another moment Zamacona emerged from the tunnel upon a bleak, rocky hillside which climbed above him to a seething, impenetrable sky of bluish coruscations, and descended dizzily below him to an apparently illimitable plain shrouded in bluish mist.

He had come to the unknown world at last, and from his manuscript it is clear that he viewed the formless landscape as proudly and exaltedly as ever his fellow-countryman Balboa viewed the new-found Pacific from that unforgettable peak in Darien. Charging Buffalo had turned back at this point, driven by fear of something which he would only describe vaguely and evasively as a herd of bad cattle, neither horse nor buffalo, but like the things the mound-spirits rode at night – but Zamacona could not be deterred by such a trifle. Instead of fear, a strange sense of glory filled him; for he had imagination enough to know what it meant to stand alone in an inexplicable nether world whose existence no other white man suspected.

The soil of the great hill that surged upward behind him and spread steeply downward below him was dark-grey, rock-strewn, without vegetation, and probably basaltic in origin; with an unearthly cast which made him feel like an intruder on an alien planet. The vast distant plain, thousands of feet below, had no features he could distinguish; especially since it appeared to be largely veiled in a curling bluish vapor. But more than hill or plain or cloud, the bluely luminous coruscating sky impressed the adventurer with a sense of supreme wonder and mystery. What created this sky within a world he could not tell; though he knew of the northern lights, and had even seen them once or twice. He concluded that this subterraneous light was something vaguely akin to the aurora; a view which moderns may well endorse, though it seems likely that certain phenomena of radio-activity may also enter it.

At Zamacona's back the mouth of the tunnel he had traversed yawned darkly; defined by a stone doorway very like the one he had entered in the world above, save that it was of greyish-black basalt instead of red sandstone. There were hideous sculptures, still in good preservation and perhaps corresponding to those on the outer portal which time had largely weathered away. The absence of weathering here argued a dry, temperate climate; indeed the Spaniard already began to note the delightfully springlike stability of temperature which marks the air of the earth's interior. On the stone jambs were works proclaiming the bygone presence of hinges, but of any actual door or gate no trace remained. Seating himself for rest and thought, Zamacona lightened his pack by removing an amount of food and torches sufficient to take him back through the tunnel. These he proceeded to cache at the opening, under a cairn hastily formed of the rock fragments which everywhere lay around. Then, readjusting his lightened pack, he commenced his descent toward the distant plain; preparing to invade a region which no living thing of outer earth had penetrated in a century or more, which no white man had ever penetrated, and from which, if legend were to be believed, no organic creature had ever returned sane.

Zamacona strode briskly along down the steep, interminable slope; his progress checked at times by the bad walking that came from loose rock fragments, or by the excessive precipitousness of the grade. The distance to the mist-shrouded plain must have been enormous, for many hours' walking brought him apparently no closer to it than he had been before. Behind him was always the great hill stretching upward into a bright aerial sea of bluish coruscations. Silence was universal; so that his own footsteps, and the fall of stones that he dislodged, struck on his ears with startling distinctness. It was at what he regarded as about noon that he first saw the abnormal footprints which set him to thinking of Charging Buffalo's terrible hints, precipitate flight, and strangely abiding horror.

The rock-strewn nature of the soil gave few opportunities for tracks of any kind, but at one point a rather level interval had caused the loose detritus to accumulate in a ridge, leaving a considerable area of dark-grey loam absolutely bare. Here, in a rambling confusion indicating a large herd aimlessly wandering, Zamacona found the abnormal prints. It is to be regarded that he could not describe them more exactly, but the manuscript displayed far more vague fear than accurate observation. Just what it was that so frightened the Spaniard can only be inferred from his later hints regarding the beasts. He referred to the prints as 'not hooves, nor hands, nor feet, nor precisely paws, nor so large to cause alarm on that account'. Just why or how long ago the things had been there, was not easy to guess. There was no vegetation visible, hence grazing was out of the question; but of course if the beasts were carnivorous they might well have been hunting smaller animals, whose tracks their own would tend to obliterate.

Glancing backward from this plateau to the heights above, Zamacona thought he detected traces of a great winding road which had once led from the tunnel downward to the plain. One could get the impression of this former highway only from a broad panoramic view, since a trickle of loose rock fragments had long ago obscured it; but the adventurer felt nonetheless certain that it had existed. It had not, probably, been an elaborately paved trunk route; for the smaller tunnel it reached seemed scarcely like a main avenue to the outer world. In choosing a straight path of descent Zamacona had not followed its curving course, though he must have crossed it once or twice. With his attention now called to it, he looked ahead to see if he could trace it downward toward the plain; and this he finally thought he could do. He resolved to investigate its surface when next he crossed it, and perhaps to pursue its line for the rest of the way if he could distinguish it.

Having resumed his journey Zamacona came some time later upon what he thought was a bend of the ancient road. There were signs of grading and of some primal attempt at rock-surfacing, but not enough was left to make the route worth following. While rummaging about in the soil with his sword the Spaniard turned up something that glittered in the eternal blue daylight, and was thrilled at beholding a kind of coin or medal of a dark, unknown, lustrous metal, with hideous designs on each side. It was utterly and bafflingly alien to him, and from his description I have no doubt but that it was a duplicate of the talisman given me by Grey Eagle almost four centuries afterward. Pocketing it after a long and curious examination, he strode onward, finally pitching camp at an hour which he guessed to be the evening of the outer world.

The next day Zamacona rose early and resumed his descent through this blue-litten world of mist and desolation and preternatural silence. As he advanced, he at last became able to distinguish a few objects on the distant plain below; trees, bushes, rocks and a small river that came into view from the right and curved forward at a point to the left of his contemplated course. This river seemed to be spanned by a bridge connected with the descending roadway, and with care the explorer could trace the route of the road beyond it in a straight line over the plain. Finally he even thought he could detect towns scattered along the rectilinear ribbon; towns whose left-hand edges reached the river and sometimes crossed it. Where such crossings occurred, he saw as he descended, there were always signs of bridges either ruined or surviving. He was now in the midst of a sparse grassy vegetation, and saw that below him the growth became thicker and thicker. The road was easier to define now, since its surface discouraged the grass which the looser soil supported. Rock fragments were less frequent, and the barren upward vista behind him looked bleak and forbidding in contrast to his present milieu.

It was on this day that he saw the blurred mass moving over the distant plain. Since his first sight of the sinister footprints he had met with no more of these, but something about that slowly and deliberately moving mass peculiarly sickened him. Nothing but a herd of grazing animals could move just like that, and after seeing the footprints he did not wish to meet the things which had made them. Still, the moving mass was not near the road - and his curiosity and greed for fabled gold were great. Besides, who could really judge things from vague, jumbled footprints or from the panic-twisted hints of an ignorant Indian?

In straining his eyes to view the moving mass Zamacona became aware of several other interesting things. One was that certain parts of the now unmistakable towns glittered oddly in the misty blue light. Another was that, besides the towns, several similarly glittering structures of a more isolated sort were scattered here and there along the road and over the plain. They seemed to be embowered in clumps of vegetation, and those off the road had small avenues leading to the highway. No smoke or other signs of life could be discerned about any of the towns or buildings. Finally Zamacona saw that the plain was not infinite in extent, though the half-concealing blue mists had hitherto made it seem so. It was bounded in the remote distance by a range of low hills, toward a gap in which the river and roadway seemed to lead. All this - especially the glittering of certain pinnacles in the towns - had become very vivid when Zamacona pitched his second camp amidst the endless blue day. He likewise noticed the flocks of high-soaring birds, whose nature he could not clearly make out.

The next afternoon, to use the language of the outer world as the manuscript did at all times, Zamacona reached the silent plain and crossed the soundless, slow-running river on a curiously carved and fairly well-preserved bridge of black basalt. The water was clear, and contained large fishes of a wholly strange aspect. The roadway was now paved and somewhat overgrown with weeds and creeping vines, and its course was occasionally outlined by small pillars bearing obscure symbols. On every side the grassy level extended, with here and there a clump of trees or shrubbery, and with unidentifiable bluish flowers growing irregularly over the whole area. Now and then some spasmodic motion of the grass indicated the presence of serpents. In the course of several hours the traveller reached a grove of old and alien-looking evergreen trees which he knew, from distant viewing, protected one of the glittering-roofed isolated structures. Amidst the encroaching vegetation he saw the hideously sculptured pylons of a stone gateway leading off the road, and was presently forcing his way through briars above a moss-crusted tessellated walk lined with huge trees and low monolithic pillars.

At last, in this hushed green twilight, he saw the crumbling and ineffably ancient facade of the building; a temple, he had no doubt. It was a mass of nauseous bas-reliefs; depicting scenes and beings, objects and ceremonies, which could certainly have no place on this or any sane planet. In hinting of these things Zamacona displays for the first time that shocked and pious hesitancy which impairs the informative value of the rest of his manuscript. We cannot help regretting that the Catholic ardour of Renaissance Spain had so thoroughly permeated his thought and feeling. The door of the place stood wide open, and absolute darkness filled the windowless interior. Conquering the repulsion which the mural sculptures had excited, Zamacona took out flint and steel, lighted a resinous torch, pushed aside curtaining vines, and sallied boldly across the ominous threshold.

For a moment he was quite stupefied by what he saw. It was not the all-covering dust and cobwebs of immemorial aeons, the fluttering winged things, the shriekingly loathsome sculptures on the walls, the bizarre form of the many basins and braziers, the sinister pyramidal altar with the hollow top, or the monstrous, octopus-headed abnormality in some strange, dark metal leering and squatting broodingly on its hieroglyphed pedestal which robbed him of even the power to give a startled cry. It was nothing so unearthly as all this: but merely the fact that, with the exception of the dust, the cobwebs, the winged things, and the gigantic emerald-eyed idol, every particle of substance in sight was composed of pure and evidently solid gold.

Even the manuscript, written in retrospect after Zamacona knew that gold is the most common structural metal of a nether world containing limitless lodes and veins of it, reflects the frenzied excitement which the traveller felt upon suddenly finding the real source of all the Indian legends of golden cities. For a time the power of detailed observation left him, but in the end his faculties were recalled by a peculiar tugging sensation in the pocket of his doublet. Tracing the feeling, he realized that the disc of strange metal he had found in the abandoned road was being attracted strongly by the vast octopus-headed, emerald-eyed idol on the pedestal, which he now saw to be composed of the same unknown exotic metal. He was later to learn that this strange magnetic substance - as alien to the inner world as to the outer world of men - is the one precious metal of the blue-lighted abyss. None knows what it is or where it occurs in nature, and the amount of it on this planet came down from the stars with the people when great Tulu, the octopus-headed god, brought them for the first time to this earth. Certainly, its only known source was a stock of pre-existing artifacts, including multitudes of cyclopean idols. It could never be placed or analyzed, and even its magnetism was exerted only on its own kind. It was the supreme ceremonial metal of the hidden people, its use being regulated by custom in such a way that its magnetic properties might cause no inconvenience. A very weakly magnetic alloy of it with such base metals as iron, gold, silver, copper, or zinc, had formed the sole monetary standard of the hidden people at one period of their history.

Zamacona's reflection on the strange idol and its magnetism were disrupted by a tremendous wave of fear as, for the first time in this silent world, he heard a rumble of very definite and obviously approaching sound. There was no mistaking its nature. It was a thunderously charging herd of large animals; and, remembering the Indian's panic, the footprints, and the moving mass distantly seen, the Spaniard shuddered in terrified anticipation. He did not analyze his position, or the significance of this onrush of great lumbering beings, but merely responded to an elemental urge toward self-protection.

Charging herds do not stop to find victims in obscure places, and on the outer earth Zamacona would have felt little or no alarm in such a massive, grove-girt edifice. Some instinct, however, now bred a deep and peculiar terror in his soul; and he looked about frantically for any means of safety.

There being no available refuge in the great, gold-patinaed interior, he felt that he must close the long-disused door; which still hung on its ancient hinges, doubled back against the inner wall. Soil, vines, and moss had entered the opening from outside, so that he had to dig a path for the great gold portal with his sword; but he managed to perform this work very swiftly under the frightful stimulus of the approaching noise. The hoofbeats had grown still louder and more menacing by the time he began tugging at the heavy door itself; and for a while his fears reached a frantic height, as hope of moving the age-clogged metal grew faint. Then, with a creak, the thing responded to his youthful strength, and a frenzied siege of pulling and pushing ensued. Amidst the roar of unseen stampeding feet success came at last, and the ponderous golden door clanged shut, leaving Zamacona in darkness but for the single lighted torch he had wedged between the pillars of a basin-tripod. There was a latch, and the frightened man blessed his patron saint that it was still effective.

Sound alone told the fugitive the sequel. When the roar grew very near it resolved itself into separate footfalls, as if the evergreen grove had made it necessary for the herd to slacken speed and disperse. But feet continued to approach, and it became evident that the beasts were advancing among the trees and circling the hideously carven temple walls. In the curious deliberation of their tread Zamacona found something very alarming and repulsive, nor did he like the scuffling sounds which were audible even through the thick stone walls and heavy golden door. Once the door rattled ominously on its archaic hinges, as if under a heavy impact, but fortunately it still held. Then, after a seemingly endless interval, he heard retreating steps and realized that his unknown visitors were leaving. Since the herds did not seem to be very numerous, it would have perhaps been safe to venture out within a half-hour or less; but Zamacona took no chances. Opening his pack, he prepared his camp on the golden tiles of the temple's floor, with the great door still securely latched against all comers; drifting eventually into a sounder sleep than he could have known in the blue-litten spaces outside. He did not even mind the hellish, octopus-headed bulk of great Tulu, fashioned of unknown metal and leering with fishy, sea-green eyes, which squatted in the blackness above him on its monstrously hieroglyphed pedestal.

Surrounded by darkness for the first time since leaving the tunnel, Zamacona slept profoundly and long. He must have more than made up the sleep he had lost at his two previous camps, and when the ceaseless glare of the sky had kept him awake despite his fatigue, for much distance was covered by other living feet while he lay in his healthily dreamless rest. It is well that he rested deeply, for there were many strange things to be encountered in his next period of consciousness.

IV

What finally roused Zamacona was a thunderous rapping at the door. It beat through his dreams and dissolved all the lingering mists of drowsiness as soon as he knew what it was. There could be no mistake about it - it was a definite, human, and peremptory rapping; performed apparently with some metallic object, and with all the measured quality of conscious thought or will behind it. As the awakening man rose clumsily to his feet, a sharp vocal note was added to the summons - someone calling out in a not unmusical voice, a formula which the manuscript tries to represent as 'oxi, oxi, ginathcan yca relex.' Feeling sure that his visitors were men and not daemons, and arguing that they could have no reason for considering him an enemy, Zamacona decided to face them openly and at once; and accordingly fumbled with the ancient latch till the golden door creaked open from the pressure of those outside.

As the great portal swung back, Zamacona stood facing a group of about twenty individuals of an aspect not calculated to give him alarm. They seemed to be Indians; though their tasteful robes and trappings and swords were not such as he had seen among any of the tribes of the outer world, while their faces had many subtle differences from the Indian type. That they did not mean to be irresponsibly hostile, was very clear; for instead of menacing him in any way they merely probed him attentively and significantly with their eyes, as if they expected their gaze to open up some sort of communication. The longer they gazed, the more he seemed to know about them and their mission; for although not one had spoken since the vocal summons before the opening of the door, he found himself slowly realizing that they had come from the great city beyond the low hills, mounted on animals, and that they had been summoned by animals who had reported his presence; that they were not sure what kind of a person he was or just where he had come from, but that they knew he must be associated with that dimly remembered outer world which they sometimes visited in curious dreams. How he read all this in the gaze of the two or three leaders he could not possibly explain; though he learned why a moment later.

As it was, he attempted to address his visitors in the Wichita dialect he had picked up from Charging Buffalo: and after this failed to draw a vocal reply he successively tried the Aztec, Spanish, French, and Latin tongues – adding so many scraps of lame Greek, Galician and Portuguese, and of the Bable peasant patois of his native Asturias, as his memory could recall. But not even this polyglot array – his entire linguistic stock – could bring a reply in kind. When, however, he paused in perplexity, one of the visitors began speaking in an utterly strange and rather fascinating language whose sounds the Spaniard later had much difficulty in representing on paper. Upon his failure to understand this, the speaker pointed first to his own eyes, then to his forehead, and then to his eyes again, as if commanding the other to gaze at him in order to absorb what he wanted to transmit.

Zamacona, obeying, found himself rapidly in possession of certain information. The people, he learned, conversed nowadays by means of unvocal radiations of thought; although they had formerly used a spoken language which still survived as the written tongue, and into which they still dropped orally for tradition's sake, or when strong feeling demanded a spontaneous outlet. He could understand them merely by concentrating his attention upon their eyes; and could reply by summoning up a mental image of what he wished to say, and throwing the substance of this into his glance. When the thought-speaker paused, apparently inviting a response, Zamacona tried his best to follow the prescribed pattern, but did not appear to succeed very well. So he nodded, and tried to describe himself and his journey by signs. He pointed upward, as if to the outer world, then closed his eyes and made signs as of a mole burrowing. Then he opened his eyes again and pointed downward, in order to indicate his descent of the great slope. Experimentally he blended a spoken word or two with his gestures – for example, pointing successively to himself and to all of his visitors and saying 'un hombre,' and then pointing to himself alone and very carefully pronouncing his individual name, Panfilo de Zamacona.

Before the strange conversation was over, a good deal of data had passed in both directions. Zamacona had begun to learn how to throw his thoughts, and had likewise picked up several words of the region's archaic spoken language. His visitors, moreover, had absorbed many beginnings of an elementary Spanish vocabulary. Their own old language was utterly unlike anything the Spaniard had ever heard, though there were .imes later on when he was to fancy an indefinitely remote linkage with the Aztec, as if the latter represented some far stage of corruption, or some very thin infiltration of loan-words. The underground world, Zamacona learned, bore an ancient name which the manuscript records as 'Xinaian,' but which, from the writer's supplementary explanations and diacritical marks, could probably be best represented to Anglo-Saxon ears by the phonetic arrangement 'K'n-yan.'

It is not surprising that this preliminary discourse did not go beyond the merest essentials, but those essentials were highly important. Zamacona learned that the people of K'n-yan were almost infinitely ancient and that they had come from a distant part of space where physical conditions are much like those of the earth. All this, of course, was legend now; and one could not say how much truth was in it, or how much worship was really due to the octopus-headed being Tulu who had traditionally brought them hither and whom they still reverenced for aesthetic reasons. But they knew of the outer world, and were indeed the original stock which had peopled it as soon as its crust was fit to live on. Between glacial ages they had had some remarkable surface civilizations, especially one at the South Pole near the mountain Kadath.

At some time infinitely in the past most of the outer world had sunk beneath the ocean, so that only a few refugees remained to bear the news of K'n-yan. This was undoubtedly due to the wrath of space-devils hostile alike to men and to men's gods – for it bore out rumors of a primordially earlier sinking which had submerged the gods themselves, including great Tulu, who still lay prisoned and dreaming in the watery vaults of the half-cosmic city Relex. No man not a slave of the space-devils, it was argued, could live long on the outer earth; and it was decided that all beings who remained there must be evilly connected. Accordingly traffic with the lands of sun and starlight abruptly ceased. The subterraneous approaches to K'n-yan, or such as could be remembered, were either blocked up or carefully guarded; and all encroachers were treated as dangerous spies and enemies.

But this was long ago. With the passing of ages fewer and fewer visitors came to K'n-yan, and eventually sentries ceased to be maintained at the unblocked approaches. The mass of the people forgot, except through distorted memories and myths and some very singular dreams, that an outer world existed; though educated folk never ceased to recall the essential facts. The last visitors ever recorded, centuries in the past, had not even been treated as devil-spies; faith in the old legendry having long before died out. They had been questioned eagerly about the fabulous outer regions; for scientific curiosity in K'n-yan was keen, and the myths, memories, dreams and historical fragments relating to the earth's surface had often tempted scholars to the brink of an external expedition which they had not quite dared to attempt. The only thing demanded of such visitors was that they refrain from going back and informing the outer world of K'n-yan's positive existence; for after all, one could not be sure about these outer lands. They coveted gold and silver, and might prove highly troublesome intruders. Those who had obeyed the injunction had lived happily, though regrettably briefly, and had told all they could about their world – little enough, however, since their accounts were all so fragmentary and conflicting that one could hardly tell what to believe and what to doubt. One wished that more of them would come. As for those who disobeyed and tried to escape; it was unfortunate about them. Zamacona himself was very welcome, for he appeared to be a higher-grade man, and to know much more about the outer world, than anyone else who had come down within memory. He could tell them much – and they hoped he would be reconciled to his lifelong stay.

Many things which Zamacona learned about K'n-yan in

that first colloquy left him quite breathless. He learned, for instance, that during the past few thousand years the phenomena of old age and death had been conquered; so that men no longer grew feeble or died except through violence or will. By regulating the system, one might be as physiologically young and immortal as he wished; and the only reason why any allowed themselves to age, was that they enjoyed the sensation in a world where stagnation and commonplaceness reigned. They could easily become young again when they felt like it. Births had ceased, except for experimental purposes, since a large population had been found needless by a master-race which controlled nature and organic rivals alike. Many, however, chose to die after a while; since despite the cleverest efforts to invent new pleasures, the ordeal of consciousness became too dull for sensitive souls - especially those in whom time and satiation had blinded the primal instincts and emotions of self-preservation. All the members of the group before Zamacona were from five hundred to fifteen hundred years old; and several had seen surface visitors before, though time had blurred the recollection. These visitors, by the way, had often tried to duplicate the longevity of the underground race; but had been able to do so only fractionally, owing to evolutionary differences developing during the million or two years of cleavage.

Those evolutionary differences were even more strikingly shown in another particular: one far stranger than the wonder of immortality itself. This was the ability of the people of K'n-yan to regulate the balance between matter and abstract energy, even where the bodies of living organic beings were concerned, by the sheer force of the technically trained will. In other words, with suitable effort a learned man of K'n-yan could dematerialize and rematerialize himself, or, with somewhat greater effort and subtler technique, any other object he chose; reducing solid matter to free external particles and recombining the particles again without damage. Had not Zamacona answered his visitor's knock when he did, he would have discovered this accomplishment in a highly puzzling way, for only the strain and bother of the process prevented the twenty men from passing bodily through the golden door without pausing for a summons.

This art was much older than the art of perpetual life, and it could be taught to some extent, though never perfectly, to any intelligent person. Rumors of it had reached the outer world in past aeons; surviving in secret traditions and ghostly legendry. The men of K'n-yan had been amused by the primitive and imperfect spirit tales brought down by outer-world stragglers. In practical life this principle had certain industrial applications, but was generally suffered to remain neglected through lack of any particular incentive to its use. Its chief surviving form was in connection with sleep, when for excitement's sake many dream-connoisseurs resorted to it to enhance the vividness of their visionary wanderings. By the aid of this method certain dreamers even paid half-material visits to a strange, nebulous realm of mounds and valleys and varying light which some believed to be the forgotten outer world. They would go thither on their beasts, and in an age of peace live over the old, glorious battles of their forefathers. Some philosophers thought that in such cases they actually coalesced with immaterial forces left behind by these warlike ancestors themselves.

The people of K'n-yan all dwelt in the great, tall city of Tsath beyond the mountains. Formerly several races of them had inhabited the entire underground world, which stretched down to unfathomable abysses and which included besides the blue-litten region a red-litten region called Yoth, where relics of a still older and non-human race were found by archaeologists. In the course of time, however, the men of Tsath had conquered and enslaved all the rest: interbreeding them with certain horned and four-footed animals of the red-litten region, whose semi-human learnings were very peculiar, and which, though containing a certain artificially created element, may have been in part the degenerate descendants of those peculiar entities who had left the relics. As aeons passed, and mechanical discoveries made the business of life extremely easy, a concentration of the people in the city of Tsath took place; so that all the rest of K'n-yan became relatively deserted.

It was easier to live in one place, and there was no object in maintaining a population of overflowing proportions. Many of the old mechanical devices were still in use, though others had been abandoned when it was seen that they failed to give pleasure, or that they were not necessary for a race of reduced numbers whose mental force could govern an extensive array of inferior and semi-human industrial organisms. This extensive slave class was highly composite, being bred from ancient conquered enemies, from outer-world stragglers, from dead bodies curiously galvanized into effectiveness, and from the naturally inferior members of the ruling race of Tsath. The ruling type itself had become highly superior through selective breeding and social evolution – the nation having passed through a period of idealistic industrial democracy which gave equal opportunities to all, and thus, by raising the naturally intelligent to power, drained the masses of all their stamina. Industry, being found fundamentally futile except for the supplying of basic needs and the gratification of inescapable yearnings, had become very simple. Physical comfort was ensured by an urban mechanization of standardized and easily maintained pattern; and other elemental needs were supplied by scientific agriculture and stock-raising. Long travel was abandoned, and people went back to using the horned, half-human beasts instead of maintaining the profusion of gold, silver, and steel transportation machines which had once threaded land, water, and air. Zamacona could scarcely believe that such things had ever existed outside dreams, but was told he could see specimens of them in museums. He could also see the ruins of other vast magical devices by travelling a day's journey to the valley of Do-Hna, to which the race had spread during its period of greatest numbers. The cities and temples of this present plain were of a far more archaic period, and had never been other than religious and antiquarian shrines during the supremacy of the men of Tsath.

In government, Tsath was a kind of communistic or semi-anarchical state; habit rather than law determining the daily order of things. This was made possible by the age-old experience and paralyzing ennui of the race, whose wants and needs were limited to physical fundamentals and to new sensations. An aeon-long tolerance not yet undermined by growing reaction had abolished all illusions of values and principles, and nothing but an approximation to custom was ever sought or expected. To see that the mutual encroachments of pleasure-seeking never crippled the massed life of the community – this was all that was desired. Family organization had long ago perished, and the civil and social distinction of the sexes had disappeared. Daily life was organized in ceremonial patterns; with intoxication, torture of slaves, day-dreaming, gastronomic and emotional orgies, religious exercises, exotic experiments, artistic and philosophical discussions, and the like, as the principal occupations. Property: chiefly land, slaves, animals, shares in the common city enterprise of Tsath, and ingots of magnetic Tulu-metal, the former universal money standard was allocated on a very complex basis which included a certain amount equally divided among all the freemen. Poverty was unknown, and labour consisted only of certain administrative duties imposed by an intricate system of testing and selection. Zamacona found difficulty in describing conditions so unlike anything he had previously known; and the text of his manuscript proved unusually puzzling at this point.

Art and intellect, it appeared, had reached very high levels in Tsath; but had become listless and decadent. The dominance of machinery had at one time broken up the growth of normal aesthetics, introducing a lifelessly geometrical tradition fatal to sound expression. This had soon been outgrown, but had left its mark upon all pictorial and decorative attempts; so that except for conventionalized religious designs, there was little depth or feeling in any later work. Archaistic reproductions of earlier work had been found much preferable for general enjoyment. Literature was all highly individual and analytical, so much so as to be wholly incomprehensible to Zamacona. Science had been profound and accurate, and all-embracing save in the one direction of astronomy. Of late, however, it was falling into decay, as people found it increasingly useless to tax their minds by recalling its maddening infinitude of details and ramifications. It was thought more sensible to abandon the deepest speculations and to confine philosophy to conventional forms. Technology, of course, could be carried on by rule of thumb. History was more and more neglected, but exact and copious chronicles of the past existed in the libraries. It was still an interesting subject, and there would be a vast number to rejoice at the fresh outer-world knowledge brought in by Zamacona. In general, though, the modern tendency was to feel rather than to think; so that men were now more highly esteemed for inventing new diversions than for preserving old facts or pushing back the frontier of cosmic mystery.

Religion was a leading interest in Tsath, though very few actually believed in the supernatural. What was desired was the aesthetic and emotional exaltation bred by the mystical moods and sensuous rites which attended the colourful ancestral faith. Temples to Great Tulu, a spirit of universal harmony anciently symbolized as the octopus-headed god who had brought all men down from the stars, were the most richly constructed objects in all K'n-yan; while the cryptic shrines of Yig, the principle of life symbolized as the Father of all Serpents, were almost as lavish and remarkable. In time Zamacona learned much of the orgies and sacrifices connected with this religion, but seemed piously reluctant to describe them in his manuscript. He himself never participated in any of the rites save those which he mistook for perversions of his own faith; nor did he ever lose an opportunity to try to convert the people to the faith of the Cross which the Spaniards hoped to make universal.

Prominent in the contemporary religion of Tsath was a revived and almost genuine veneration for the rare, sacred metal of Tulu – that dark, lustrous, magnetic stuff which was nowhere found in nature, but which had always been with men in the form of idols and hieratic implements. From the earliest times any sight of it in its unalloyed form had impelled respect, while all the sacred archives and litanies were kept in cylinders wrought of its purest substance. Now, as the neglect of science and intellect was dulling the critically analytical spirit, people were beginning to weave around the metal once more that same fabric of awe-struck superstition which had existed in primitive times.

Another function of religion was the regulation of the calendar, born of a period when time and speed were regarded as prime fetishes in man's emotional life. Periods of alternate waking and sleeping, prolonged, abridged and inverted as mood and convenience dictated, and timed by the tail-beats of Great Yig, the Serpent, corresponded very roughly to terrestrial days and nights; though Zamacona's sensations told him they must actually be almost twice as long. The year-unit, measured by Yig's annual shedding of his skin, was equal to about a year and a half of the outer world. Zamacona thought he had mastered this calendar very well when he wrote his manuscript, whence the confidently given date of 1545; but the document failed to suggest that his assurance in this matter was fully justified.

As the spokesman of the Tsath party proceeded with his information, Zamacona felt a growing repulsion and alarm.

It was not only what was told, but the strange, telepathic manner of telling, and the plain inference that return to the outer world would be impossible, that made the Spaniard wish he had never descended to this region of magic, abnormality, and decadence. But he knew that nothing but friendly acquiescence would do as a policy, hence decided to cooperate in all his visitors' plans and furnish all the information they might desire. They, on their part, were fascinated by the outer-world data which he managed haltingly to convey.

It was really the first draught of reliable surface information they had had since the refugees straggled back from Atlantis and Lemuria aeons before, for all their subsequent emissaries from outside had been members of narrow and local groups without any knowledge of the world at large: Mayas, Toltecs, and Aztecs at best, and mostly ignorant tribes of the plains. Zamacona was the first European they had ever seen, and the fact that he was a youth of education and brilliancy made him of still more emphatic value as a source of knowledge. The visiting party showed their breathless interest in all he contrived to convey, and it was plain that his coming would do much to revive the flagging interest of weary Tsath in matters of geography and history.

The only thing which seemed to displease the men of Tsath was the fact that curious and adventurous strangers were beginning to pour into those parts of the upper world where the passages to K'n-yan lay. Zamacona told them of the founding of Florida and New Spain, and made it clear that a great part of the world was stirring with the zest of adventure and discovery – Spanish, Portuguese, French, and English. Sooner or later Mexico and Florida must meet in one great colonial Empire, and then it would be hard to keep outsiders from the rumored gold and silver of the abyss. Charging Buffalo knew of Zamacona's journey into the earth. Would he tell Coronado, or somehow let a report get to the great viceroy, when he failed to find the traveller at the promised meeting place? Alarm for the continued secrecy and safety of K'n-yan showed in the faces of the visitors, and Zamacona absorbed from their minds the fact that from now on sentries would undoubtedly be posted once more at all the unblocked passages to the outside world which the men of Tsath could remember.

V

The long conversation of Zamacona and his visitors took place in the green-blue twilight of the grove just outside the temple door. Some of the men reclined on the weeds and moss beside the half-vanished walk, while others, including the Spaniard and the chief spokesman of the Tsath party, sat on the occasional low, monolithic pillars that lined the temple approach. Almost a whole terrestrial day must have been consumed in the colloquy, for Zamacona felt the need of food several times, and ate from his well-stocked pack while some of the Tsath party went back for provisions to the roadway, where they had left the animals on which they had ridden. At length the prime leader of the party brought the discourse to a close, and indicated that the time had come to proceed to the city.

There were, he affirmed, several extra beasts in the cavalcade, upon one of which Zamacona could ride. The prospect of mounting one of those ominous hybrid entities whose fabled nourishment was so alarming, and a single sight of which had set Charging Buffalo into such a frenzy of flight, was by no means reassuring to the traveller. There was, moreover, another point about the things which disturbed him greatly; the apparently preternatural intelligence with which some members of the previous day's roving pack had reported his presence to the men of Tsath and brought out the present expedition. But Zamacona was not a coward, and followed the men boldly down the weed-grown walk toward the road where the things were stationed.

And yet he could not refrain from crying out in terror at what he saw when he passed through the great vine-draped pylons and emerged upon the ancient road. He did not wonder that the curious Wichita had fled in panic, and had to close his eyes a moment to retain his sanity. It is unfortunate that some sense of pious reticence prevented him from describing fully in his manuscript the nameless sight he saw. As it is, he merely hinted at the shocking morbidity of these great floundering white things with black fur on their backs, a rudimentary horn in the centre of their foreheads, and an unmistakable trace of human or anthropoid blood in their flat-nosed, bulging-lipped faces. They were, he declared later in his manuscript, the most terrible, objective entities he ever saw in his life, either in K'n-yan or in the outer world. And the specific quality of their supreme terror was something apart from any easily recognizable or describable feature. The main trouble was that they were not wholly products of nature. The party observed Zamacona's fright, and hastened to reassure him as much as possible. The beasts or *gyaa-yothn*, they explained, surely were curious things; but were really very harmless. The flesh they ate was not that of intelligent people of the master race, but merely that of a special slave class which had for the most part ceased to be thoroughly human, and which indeed was the principal meat stock of K'n-yan. They – or their principal ancestral element – had first been found in a wild state amidst the cyclopean ruins of the deserted red-litten world of Yoth which lay below the blue-litten world of K'n-yan. That part of them was human, seemed quite clear; but men of science could never decide whether they were actually the descendants of the bygone entities who had lived and reigned in the strange ruins. The chief ground for such a supposition was the well-known fact that the vanished inhabitants of Yoth had been quadrupedal. This much was known from the very few manuscripts and carvings found in the vaults of Zin, beneath the largest ruined city of Yoth. But it was also known from these manuscripts that the beings of Yoth had possessed the art of synthetically creating life, and had made and destroyed several efficiently designed races of industrial and transportational animals in the course of their history – to say nothing of concocting all manner of fantastic living shapes for the sake of amusement and new sensations during the long period of decadence. The beings of Yoth had undoubtedly been reptilian in affiliations, and most physiologists of Tsath agreed that the present beasts had been very much inclined toward reptilianism before they had been crossed with the mammal slave class of K'n-yan.

It argues well for the intrepid fibre of those Renaissance Spaniards who conquered half the unknown world, that Panfilo de Zamacona y Nunez actually mounted one of the morbid beasts of Tsath and fell into place beside the leader of the cavalcade: the man named Gll'-Hthaa-Ynn, who had been most active in the previous exchange of information. It was a repulsive business; but after all, the seat was very easy, and the gait of the clumsy *gyaa-yoth* surprisingly even and regular. No saddle was necessary, and the animal appeared to require no guidance whatever. The procession moved forward at a brisk gait, stopping only at certain abandoned cities and temples about which Zamacona was curious, and which Gll'-Hthaa-Ynn was obligingly ready to display and explain. The largest of these towns, B'graa, was a marvel of finely wrought gold, and Zamacona studied the curiously ornate architecture with avid interest. Buildings tended toward height and slenderness, with roofs bursting into a multitude of pinnacles. The streets were narrow, curving, and occasionally picturesquely hilly, but Gll'-Hthaa-Ynn said that the later cities of K'n-yan were far more spacious and regular in design. All these old cities of the plain showed traces of levelled walls – reminders of the archaic days when they had been successively conquered by the now dispersed armies of Tsath.

There was one object along the route which Gll'-Hthaa-Ynn exhibited on his own initiative, even though it involved a detour of about a mile along a vine-tangled side path. This was a squat, plain temple of black basalt blocks without a single carving, and containing only a vacant onyx pedestal. The remarkable thing about it was its story, for it was a link with a fabled elder world compared to which even cryptic Yoth was a thing of yesterday. It had been built in imitation of certain temples depicted in the vaults of Zin, to honor a very terrible black toad-idol found in the red-litten world and called Tsathoggua in the Yothic manuscripts. It had been a potent and widely worshipped god, and after its adoption by the people of K'n-yan had lent its name to the city which was later to become dominant in that region. Yothic legend said that it had come from a mysterious inner realm beneath the red-litten world – a black realm of peculiar-sensed beings which had no light at all, but which had had great civilizations and mighty gods before ever the reptilian quadrupeds of Yoth had come into being. Many images of Tsathoggua existed in Yoth, all of which were alleged to have come from the black inner realm, and which were supposed by Yothic archaeologists to represent the aeon-extinct race of that realm. The black realm called N'kai in the Yothic manuscripts, had been explored as thoroughly as possible by these archaeologists, and its singular stone troughs or burrows had excited infinite speculations.

When the men of K'n-yan discovered the red-litten world and deciphered its strange manuscripts, they took over the Tsathoggua cult and brought all the frightful toad images up to the land of blue light – housing them in shrines of Yoth-quarried basalt like the one Zamacona now saw. The cult flourished until it almost rivalled the ancient cults of Yig and Tulu, and one branch of the race even took it to the outer world, where the smallest of the images eventually found a shrine at Olathoe, in the land of Lomar near the earth's north pole. It was rumored that this outer-world cult survived even after the great ice-sheet and the hairy Gnophkehs destroyed Lomar, but of such matters not much was definitely known in K'n-yan. In that world of blue light the cult came to an abrupt end, even though the name of Tsath was suffered to remain.

What ended the cult was the partial exploration of the black realm of N'kai beneath the red-litten world of Yoth. According to the Yothic manuscripts, there was no surviving life in N'kai, but something must have happened in the aeons between the days of Yoth and the coming of men to the earth; something perhaps not unconnected with the end of Yoth. Probably it had been an earthquake, opening up lower chambers of the lightless world which has been closed against the Yothic archaeologists; or perhaps some more frightful juxtaposition of energy and electrons, wholly inconceivable to any sort of vertebrate minds, had taken place. At any rate, when the men of K'n-yan went down into N'kai's black abyss with their great atom-power searchlights they found living things – living things that oozed along stone channels and worshipped onyx and basalt images of Tsathoggua. But they were not toads like Tsathoggua himself. Far worse – they were amorphous lumps of viscous black slime that took temporary shapes for various purposes. The explorers of K'n-yan did not pause for detailed observations, and those who escaped alive sealed the passage leading from red-litten Yoth down into the gulfs of nether horror. Then all the images of Tsathoggua in the land of K'n-yan were dissolved into the ether by disintegrating rays, and the cult was abolished forever.

Aeons later, when naive fears were outgrown and supplanted by scientific curiosity, the old legends of Tsathoggua and N'kai were recalled, and a suitably armed and equipped exploring party went down to Yoth to find the closed gate of the black abyss and see what might still lie beneath. But they could not find the gate, nor could any man ever do so in all the ages that followed. Nowadays there were those who doubted that any abyss had ever existed, but the few scholars who could still decipher the Yothic manuscripts believed that the evidence for such a thing was adequate, even though the middle records of K'n-yan, with accounts of the one frightful expedition into N'kai, were more open to question. Some of the later religious cults tried to suppress remembrance of N'kai's existence, and attached severe penalties to its mention; but these had not begun to be taken seriously at the time of Zamacona's advent to K'n-yan.

As the cavalcade returned to the old highway and approached the low range of mountains, Zamacona saw that the river was very close on the left. Somewhat later, as the terrain rose, the stream entered a gorge and passed through the hills, while the road traversed the gap at a rather higher level close to the brink. It was about this time that light rainfall came. Zamacona noticed the occasional drops and drizzle, and looked up at the coruscating blue air, but there was no diminution of the strange radiance. Gll'-Hthaa-Ynn then told him that such condensations and precipitations of water-vapour were not uncommon, and that they never dimmed the glare of the vault above. A kind of mist, indeed, always hung about the lowlands of K'n-yan, and compensated for the complete absence of true clouds.

The slight rise of the mountain pass enabled Zamacona, by looking behind, to see the ancient and deserted plain in panorama as he had seen it from the other side. He seems to have appreciated its strange beauty, and to have vaguely regretted leaving it; for he speaks of being urged by Gll'-Hthaa-Ynn to drive his beast more rapidly. When he faced frontward again he saw that the crest of the road was very near; the weed-grown way leading starkly up and ending against a blank void of blue light. The scene was undoubtedly highly impressive – a steep green mountain wall on the right, a deep river-chasm on the left with another green mountain wall beyond it, and ahead, the churning sea of bluish coruscations into which the upward path dissolved. Then came the crest itself, and with it the world of Tsath outspread in a stupendous forward vista.

Zamacona caught his breath at the great sweep of peopled

landscape, for it was a hive of settlement and activity beyond anything he had ever seen or dreamed of. The downward slope of the hill itself was relatively thinly strewn with small farms and occasional temples; but beyond it lay an enormous plain covered like a chessboard with planted areas, irrigated by narrow canals cut from the river, and threaded by wide, geometrically precise roads of gold or basalt blocks. Great silver cables borne aloft on golden pillars linked the low, spreading buildings and clusters of buildings which rose here and there, and in some places one could see lines of partly ruinous pillars without cables. Moving objects showed the fields to be under tillage, and in some cases Zamacona saw that men were ploughing with the aid of the repulsive, half-human quadrupeds.

But most impressive of all was the bewildering vision of clustered spires and pinnacles which rose afar off across the plain and shimmered flower-like and spectral in the coruscating blue light. At first Zamacona thought it was a mountain covered with houses and temples, like some of the picturesque hill cities of his own Spain, but a second glance showed him that it was not indeed such. It was a city of the plain, but fashioned of such heaven-reaching towers that its outline was truly that of a mountain. Above it hung a curious greyish haze, through which the blue light glistened and took added overtones of radiance from the million golden minarets. Glancing at Gll'-Hthaa-Ynn, Zamacona knew that this was the monstrous, gigantic and omnipotent city of Tsath.

As the road turned downward toward the plain, Zamacona felt a kind of uneasiness and sense of evil. He did not like the beast he rode, or the world that could provide such a beast, and he did not like the atmosphere that brooded over the distant city of Tsath. When the cavalcade began to pass occasional small farms, the Spaniard noticed the forms that worked in the fields: and did not like their motions and proportions, or the mutilations he saw on most of them. Moreover, he did not like the way that some of these forms were herded in corrals, or the way they grazed on the heavy verdure. Gll'-Hthaa-Ynn indicated that these beings were members of the slave class, and that their acts were controlled by the master of the farm, who gave them hypnotic impressions in the morning of all they were to do during the day. As semi-conscious machines, their industrial efficiency was nearly perfect. Those in the corrals were inferior specimens, classified merely as livestock.

Upon reaching the plain, Zamacona saw the larger farms and noted the almost human work performed by the repulsive horned *gyaa-yothn*. He likewise observed the more manlike shapes that toiled along the furrows, and felt a curious fright and disgust toward certain of them whose motions were more mechanical than those of the rest. These, Gll'-Hthaa-Ynn explained, were what men called the *y'm-bhi* – organisms which had died, but which had been mechanically reanimated for industrial purposes by means of atomic energy and thought-power. The slave class did not share the immortality of the free-men of Tsath, so that with time the number of *y'm-bhi* had become very large. They were doglike and faithful, but not so readily amenable to thought-commands as were living slaves. Those which most repelled Zamacona were those whose mutilations were greatest – for some were wholly headless, while others had suffered singular and seemingly capricious subtractions, distortions, transpositions, and graftings in various places. The Spaniard could not account for this condition, but Gll'-Hthaa-Ynn made it clear that these were slaves who had been used for the amusement of the people in some of the vast arenas; for the men of Tsath were connoisseurs of delicate sensation, and required a constant supply of fresh and novel stimuli for their jaded impulses. Zamacona, though by no means squeamish, was not favourably impressed by what he saw and heard.

Approached more closely, the vast metropolis became dimly horrible in its monstrous extent and inhuman height. Gll'-Hthaa-Ynn explained that the upper parts of the great towers were no longer used, and that many had been taken down to avoid the bother of maintenance. The plain around the original urban area was covered with newer and smaller dwellings, which in many cases were preferred to the ancient towers. From the whole mass of gold and stone a monotonous roar of activity droned outward over the plain, while cavalcades and streams of wagons were constantly entering and leaving over the great gold- or stone-paved roads.

Several times Gll'-Hthaa-Ynn paused to show Zamacona some particular object of interest, especially the temples of Yig, Tulu, Nug, Yeb, and the Not-to-be-Named One which lined the road at infrequent intervals, each in its embowering grove according to the custom of K'n-yan. These temples, unlike those of the deserted plain beyond the mountains, were still in active use; large parties of mounted worshippers coming and going in constant streams. Gll'-Hthaa-Ynn took Zamacona into each of them, and the Spaniard watched the subtle orgiastic rites with fascination and repulsion. The ceremonies of Nug and Yeb sickened him especially – so much, indeed, that he refrained from describing them in his manuscript. One squat, black temple of Tsathoggua was encountered, but it had been turned into a shrine of Shub-Niggurath, the All-Mother and wife of the Not-to-be-Named One. This deity was a kind of sophisticated Astarte, and her worship struck the pious Catholic as supremely obnoxious. What he liked least of all were the emotional sounds emitted by the celebrants – jarring sounds in a race that had ceased to use vocal speech for ordinary purposes.

Close to the compact outskirts of Tsath, and well within the shadow of its terrifying towers, Gll'-Hthaa-Ynn pointed out a monstrous circular building before which enormous crowds were lined up. This, he indicated, was one of the many amphitheatres where curious sports and sensations were provided for the weary people of K'n-yan. He was about to pause and usher Zamacona inside the vast curved facade, when the Spaniard, recalling the mutilated forms he had seen in the fields, violently demurred. This was the first of those friendly clashes of taste which were to convince the people of Tsath that their guest followed strange and narrow standards.

Tsath itself was a network of strange and ancient streets; and despite a growing sense of horror and alienage, Zamacona was enthralled by its intimations of mystery and cosmic wonder. The dizzy giganticism of its overawing towers, the monstrous surge of teeming life through its ornate avenues, the curious carvings on its doorways and windows, the odd vistas glimpsed from balustraded plazas and tiers of titan terraces, and the enveloping grey haze which seemed to press down on the gorge-like streets in low-ceiling fashion, all combined to produce such a sense of adventurous expectancy as he had never known before. He was taken at once to a council of executives which held forth in a gold and copper palace behind a gardened and fountained park and was for some time subjected to close, friendly questioning in a vaulted hall frescoed with vertiginous arabesques. Much was expected of him, he could see, in the way of historical information about the outside earth; but in return all the mysteries of K'n-yan would be unveiled to him. The one great drawback was the inexorable ruling that he might never return to the world of sun and stars and Spain which was his.

A daily programme was laid down for the visitor, with time apportioned judiciously among several kinds of activities. There were to be conversations with persons of learning in various places, and lessons in many branches of Tsathic lore. Liberal periods of research were allowed for, and all the libraries of K'n-yan both secular and sacred were to be thrown open to him as soon as he might master the written language. Rites and spectacles were to be attended – except when he might especially object – and much time would be left for the enlightened pleasure – seeking an emotional titillation which formed the goal and nucleus of daily life. A house in the suburbs or an apartment in the city would be assigned him, and he would be initiated into one of the large affection-groups, including many noblewomen of the most extreme and art-enhanced beauty, which in latter-day K'n-yan took the place of family units. Several horned *gyaa-yothn* would be provided for his transportation and errand-running, and ten living slaves of intact body would serve to conduct his establishment and protect him from thieves and sadists and religious orgiasts on the public highways. There were many mechanical devices which he must learn to use, but Gll'-Hthaa-Ynn would instruct him immediately regarding the principal ones.

Upon his choosing an apartment in preference to a suburban villa, Zamacona was dismissed by the executives with great courtesy and ceremony, and was led through several gorgeous streets to a cliff-like carven structure of some seventy or eighty floors. Preparations for his arrival had already been instituted, and in a spacious ground-floor suite of vaulted rooms slaves were busy adjusting hangings and furniture. There were lacquered and inlaid tabourets, velvet and silk reclining-corners and squatting-cushions, and infinite rows of teakwood and ebony pigeonholes with metal cylinders containing some of the manuscripts he was soon to read – standard classics which all urban apartments possessed. Desks with great stacks of membrane – paper and pots of prevailing green pigment were in every room – each with graded sets of pigment brushes and other odd bits of stationery. Mechanical writing devices stood on ornate golden tripods, while over all was shed a brilliant blue light from energy-globes set in the ceiling. There were windows, but at this shadowy ground-level they were of scant illuminating value. In some of the rooms were elaborate baths, while the kitchen was a maze of technical contrivances. Supplies were brought, Zamacona was told, through the network of underground passages which lay beneath Tsath, and which had once accommodated curious mechanical transports. There was a stable on that underground level for the beasts, and Zamacona would presently be shown how to find the nearest runway to the street. Before his inspection was finished, the permanent staff of slaves arrived and were introduced; and shortly afterward there came some half-dozen freemen and noblewomen of his future affection-group, who were to be his companions for several days, contributing what they could to his instruction and amusement. Upon their departure, another party would take their place, and so onward in rotation through a group of about fifty members.

VI

Thus was Panfilo de Zamacona y Nunez absorbed for four years into the life of the sinister city of Tsath in the blue-litten nether world of K'n-yan. All that he learned and saw and did is clearly not told in his manuscript; for a pious reticence overcame him when he began to write in his native Spanish tongue, and he dared not set down everything. Much he consistently viewed with repulsion, and many things he steadily refrained from seeing or doing or eating. For other things he atoned by frequent countings of the beads of his rosary. He explored the entire world of K'n-yan, including the deserted machine-cities of the middle period on the gorse-grown plain of Nith, and made one descent into the red-litten world of Yoth to see the cyclopean ruins. He witnessed prodigies of craft and machinery which left him breathless, and beheld human metamorphoses, dematerializations, rematerializations, and reanimations which made him cross himself again and again. His very capacity for astonishment was blunted by the plethora of new marvels which every day brought him.

But the longer he stayed, the more he wished to leave, for the inner life of K'n-yan was based on impulses very plainly outside his radius. As he progressed in historical knowledge, he understood more; but understanding only heightened his distaste. He felt that the people of Tsath were a lost and dangerous race – more dangerous to themselves than they knew – and that their growing frenzy of monotony-warfare and novelty-quest was leading them rapidly toward a precipice of disintegration and utter horror. His own visit, he could see, had accelerated their unrest; not only by introducing fears of outside invasion, but by exciting in many a wish to sally forth and taste the diverse external world he described. As time progressed, he noticed an increasing tendency of the people to resort to dematerialization as an amusement; so that the apartments and amphitheatres of Tsath became a veritable witches' sabbath of transmutations, age-adjustments, death-experiments, and projections. With the growth of boredom and restlessness, he saw cruelty and subtlety and revolt were growing apace. There was more and more cosmic abnormality, more and more curious sadism, more and more ignorance and superstition, and more and more desire to escape out of physical life into a half-spectral state of electronic dispersion.

All his efforts to leave, however, came to nothing. Persuasion was useless, as repeated trials proved; though the mature disillusion of the upper classes at first prevented them from resenting their guest's open wish for departure. In a year which he reckoned as 1543 Zamacona made an actual attempt to escape through the tunnel by which he had entered K'n-yan, but after a weary journey across the deserted plain he encountered forces in the dark passage which discouraged him from future attempts in that direction. As a means of sustaining hope and keeping the image of home in mind, he began about this time to make rough drafts of the manuscript relating his adventures; delighting in the loved, old, Spanish words and the familiar letters of the Roman alphabet. Somehow he fancied he might get the manuscript to the outer world; and to make it convincing to his fellows he resolved to enclose it in one of the Tulu-metal cylinders used for sacred archives. That alien, magnetic substance could not but support the incredible story he had to tell.

But even as he planned, he had little real hope of ever reestablishing contact with the earth's surface. Every known gate, he knew, was guarded by persons and forces that it were better not to oppose. His attempt to escape had not helped matters, for he could now see a growing hostility to the outer world he represented. He hoped that no other European would find his way in, for it was possible that later comers might not fare as well as he. He himself had been a cherished fountain of data, and as such had enjoyed a privileged status. Others, deemed less necessary, might receive rather different treatment. He even wondered what would happen to him when the sages of Tsath considered him drained dry of fresh facts; and in self-defense began to be more gradual in his talks on earth-lore, conveying whenever he could the impression of vast knowledge held in reserve.

One other thing which endangered Zamacona's status in Tsath was his persistent curiosity regarding the ultimate abyss of N'kai, beneath red-litten Yoth, whose existence the dominant religious cults of K'n-yan were more and more inclined to deny. When exploring Yoth he had vainly tried to find the blocked-up entrance; and later on he experimented in the arts of dematerialization and projection, hoping that he might thereby be able to throw his consciousness downward into the gulfs which his physical eyes could not discover. Though never becoming truly proficient in these processes, he did manage to achieve a series of monstrous and portentous dreams which he believed included some elements of actual projection into N'kai; dreams which greatly shocked and perturbed the leaders of Yig and Tulu-worship when he related them, and which he was advised by friends to conceal rather than exploit. In time those dreams became very frequent and maddening; containing things which he dared not record in his main manuscript, but of which he prepared a special record for the benefit of certain learned men in Tsath.

It may have been unfortunate, or it may have been mercifully fortunate, that Zamacona practised so many reticences and reserved so many themes and descriptions for subsidiary manuscripts. The main document leaves one to guess much about the detailed manners, customs, thoughts, language, and history of K'n-yan, as well as to form any adequate picture of the visual aspect and daily life of Tsath. One is left puzzled, too, about the real motivations of the people; their strange passivity and craven unwarlikeness and their almost cringing fear of the outer world despite their possession of atomic and dematerializing powers which would have made them unconquerable had they taken the trouble to organize armies as in the old days. It is evident that K'n-yan was far along in its decadence – reacting with mixed apathy and hysteria against the standardized and time-tabled life of stultifying regularity which machinery had brought it during its middle period. Even the grotesque and repulsive customs and modes of thought and feeling can be traced to this source; for in his historical research Zamacona found evidence of bygone eras in which K'n-yan had held ideas much like those of the classic and renaissance outer world, and had possessed a national character and art full of what Europeans regard as dignity, kindness, and nobility.

The more Zamacona studied these things, the more apprehensive about the future he became; because he saw that the omnipresent moral and intellectual disintegration was a tremendously deep-seated and ominously accelerating movement. Even during his stay the signs of decay multiplied. Rationalism degenerated more and more into fanatical and orgiastic superstition, centering in a lavish adoration of the magnetic Tulu-metal, and tolerance steadily dissolved into a series of frenzied hatreds, especially toward the outer world of which the scholars were learning so much from him. At times he almost feared that the people might some day lose their age-long apathy and brokenness and turn like desperate rats against the unknown lands above them, sweeping all before them by virtue of their singular and still-remembered scientific powers. But for the present they fought their boredom and sense of emptiness in other ways; multiplying their hideous emotional outlets and increasing the mad grotesqueness and abnormality of their diversions. The arenas of Tsath must have been accursed and unthinkable places – Zamacona never went near them. And what they would be in another century, or even in another decade, he did not dare to think. The pious Spaniard crossed himself and counted his beads more often than usual in those days.

In the year 1545, as he reckoned it, Zamacona began what may well be accepted as his final series of attempts to leave K'n-yan. His fresh opportunity came from an unexpected source: a female of his affection-group who conceived for him a curious individual infatuation based on some hereditary memory of the days of monogamous wedlock in Tsath. Over this female – a noblewoman of moderate beauty and of at least average intelligence, named T'la-yub – Zamacona acquired the most extraordinary influence; finally inducing her to help him in an escape, under the promise that he would let her accompany him. Chance proved a great factor in the course of events. T'la-yub came of a primordial family of gate-lords who had retained oral traditions of at least one passage to the outer world which the mass of people had forgotten even at the time of the great closing; a passage to a mound on the level plains of earth which had, in consequence, never been sealed up or guarded. She explained that the primordial gate-lords were not guards or sentries, but merely ceremonial and economic proprietors, half-feudal and baronial in status, of an era preceding the severance of surface-relations. Her own family had been so reduced at the time of the closing that their gate had been wholly overlooked; and they had ever afterward preserved the secret of its existence as a sort of hereditary secret – a source of pride, and of a sense of reserve power, to offset the feeling of vanished wealth and influence which so constantly irritated them.

Zamacona, now working feverishly to get his manuscript into final form in case anything untoward should happen to him, decided to take with him on his onward journey only five beast loads of unalloyed gold in the form of the small ingots used for minor decorations – enough, he calculated, to make him a personage of unlimited power in his own world. He had become somewhat hardened to the sight of the monstrous *gyaa-yothn* during his four years of residence in Tsath, hence did not shrink from using the creatures; yet he resolved to kill and bury them, and cache the gold, as soon as he reached the outer world; since he knew that even a glimpse of one of the things would drive any ordinary Indian mad. Later he could arrange for a suitable expedition to transport the treasure to Mexico. T'la-yub he would perhaps allow to share his fortunes, for she was by no means unattractive; though possibly he would arrange for her sojourn amongst the plains Indians, since he was not over-anxious to preserve links with the manner of life of Tsath. For a wife, of course, he would choose a lady of Spain: or at worst, an Indian princess of normal outer-world descent and a regular and approved past. But for the present T'la-yub must be used as a guide. The manuscript he would carry on his own person, encased in a book-cylinder of the sacred and magnetic Tulu-metal.

The expedition itself is described in the addendum to Zamacona's manuscript, written later, and in a hand showing signs of nervous strain. It set out amid the most careful precautions, choosing a rest-period and proceeding as far as possible along the faintly lighted passages beneath the city. Zamacona and T'la-yub, disguised in slaves' garments, bearing provision-knapsacks, and leading the five laden beasts on foot, were readily taken for commonplace workers; and they clung as long as possible to the subterranean way – using a long and little-frequented branch which had formerly conducted the mechanical transports to the now ruined suburb of L'thaa. Amidst the ruins of L'thaa they came to the surface, thereafter passing as rapidly as possible over the deserted, blue-litten plain of Nith toward the Grh-yan range of low hills. There, amidst the tangled underbrush, T'la-yub found the long-disused and half-fabulous entrance to the forgotten tunnel; a thing she had seen but once before – aeons in the past, when her father had taken her thither to show her this monument to their family pride. It was hard work getting the laden *gyaa-yothn* to scrape through the obstructing vines and briars, and one of them displayed a rebelliousness destined to bear dire consequences – bolting away from the party and loping back toward Tsath on its detestable pads, golden burden and all.

It was nightmare work burrowing by the light of blue-ray torches upward, downward, forward and upward again through a dank, choked tunnel that no foot had trodden since ages before the sinking of Atlantis; and at one point T'la-yub had to practice the fearsome art of dematerialization on herself, Zamacona, and the laden beasts in order to pass a point wholly clogged by shifting earth-strata. It was a terrible experience for Zamacona; for although he had often witnessed dematerialization in others, and even practiced it himself to the extent of dream-projection, he had never been fully subjected to it before. But T'la-yub was skilled in the arts of K'n-yan, and accomplished the double metamorphosis in perfect safety.

Thereafter they resumed the hideous burrowing through stalactited crypts of horror where monstrous carvings leered at every turn; alternately camping and advancing for a period which Zamacona reckoned as about three days, but which was probably less. At last they came to a very narrow place where the natural or only slightly hewn cave-walls gave place to walls of wholly artificial masonry, carved into terrible bas-reliefs. These walls, after about a mile of steep ascent, ended with a pair of vast niches, one on each side, in which monstrous, nitre-encrusted images of Yig and Tulu squatted, glaring at each other across the passage as they had glared since the earliest youth of the human world. At this point the passage opened into a prodigious vaulted and circular chamber of human construction; wholly covered with horrible carvings, and revealing at the farther end an arched passage-way with the foot of a flight of steps. T'la-yub knew from family tales that this must be very near the earth's surface, but she could not tell just how near. Here the party camped for what they meant to be their last rest-period in the subterraneous world.

It must have been hours later that the clank of metal and the padding of beasts' feet awakened Zamacona and T'la-yub. A bluish glare was spreading from the narrow passage between the images of Yig and Tulu, and in an instant the truth was obvious. An alarm had been given at Tsath – as was later revealed, by the returning *gyaa-yoth* which had rebelled at the briar-choked tunnel-entrance – and a swift party of pursuers had come to arrest the fugitives. Resistance was clearly useless, and none was offered. The party of twelve beast-riders proved studiously polite, and the return was commenced almost without a word or thought-message on either side.

It was an ominous and depressing journey, and the ordeal of dematerialization and rematerialization at the choked place was all the more terrible because of the lack of that hope and expectancy which had palliated the process on the outward trip. Zamacona heard his captors discussing the imminent clearing of this choked place by intensive radiations, since henceforward sentries must be maintained at the hitherto unknown outer portal. It would not do to let outsiders get within the passage, for then any who might escape without due treatment would have a hint of the vastness of the inner world and would perhaps be curious enough to return in greater strength. As with the other passages since Zamacona's coming, sentries must be stationed all along, as far as the very outermost gate; sentries drawn from amongst the slaves, the dead-alive *y'm-bhi*, or the class of discredited freemen. With the over-running of the American plains by thousands of Europeans, as the Spaniard had predicted, every passage was a potential source of danger; and must be rigorously guarded until the technologists of Tsath could spare the energy to prepare an ultimate entrance-hiding obliteration as they had done for many passages in earlier and more vigorous times.

Zamacona and T'la-yub were tried before three *gn'agn* of the supreme tribunal in the gold and copper palace behind the gardened and fountained park, and the Spaniard was given his liberty because of the vital outer-world information he still had to impart. He was told to return to his apartment and to his affection-group; taking up his life as before, and continuing to meet deputations of scholars according to the latest schedule he had been following. No restriction would be imposed upon him so long as he remained peacefully in K'n-yan – but it was intimated that such leniency would not be repeated after another attempt at escape. Zamacona felt that there was an element of irony in the parting words of the chief *gn'ag* – an assurance that all of his *gyaa-yothn*, including the one which had rebelled, would be returned to him.

The fate of T'la-yub was less happy. There being no object in retaining her, and her ancient Tsathic lineage giving her act a greater aspect of treason than Zamacona's had possessed, she was ordered to be delivered to the curious diversions of the amphitheatre; and afterward, in a somewhat mutilated and half-dematerialized form, to be given the functions of a *y'm-bhi* or animated corpse-slave and stationed among the sentries guarding the passage whose existence she had betrayed. Zamacona soon heard, not without many pangs of regret he could scarcely have anticipated, that poor T'la-yub had emerged from the arena in a headless and otherwise incomplete state, and had been set as an outermost guard upon the mound in which the passage had been found to terminate. She was, he was told, a night-sentinel, whose automatic duty was to warn off all comers with a torch; sending down reports to a small garrison of twelve dead slave *y'm-bhi* and six living but partly dematerialized freemen in the vaulted, circular chamber if the approachers did not heed her warning. She worked, he was told, in conjunction with a day-sentinel – a living freeman who chose this post in preference to other forms of discipline for certain offenses against the state. Zamacona, of course, had long known that most of the chief gate-sentries were such discredited freemen.

It was now made plain to him, though indirectly, that his own penalty for another escape-attempt would be service as a gate-sentry: but in the form of a dead-alive *y'm-bhi* slave, and after amphitheatre-treatment even more picturesque than that which T'la-yub was reported to have undergone. It was intimated that he, or parts of him, would be reanimated to guard some inner section of the passage; within sight of others, where his abridged person might serve as a permanent symbol of the rewards of treason. But, his informants always added, it was of course inconceivable that he would ever court such a fate. So long as he remained peaceably in K'n-yan, he would continue to be a free, privileged, and respected personage.

Yet in the end Panfilo de Zamacona did court the fate so direfully hinted to him. True, he did not really expect to encounter it; but the nervous latter part of his manuscript makes it clear that he was prepared to face its possibility. What gave him a final hope of scatheless escape from K'n-yan was his growing mastery of the art of dematerialization. Having studied it for years, and having learned still more from the two instances in which he had been subjected to it, he now felt increasingly able to use it independently and effectively. The manuscript records several notable experiments in this art – minor successes accomplished in his apartment – and reflects Zamacona's hope that he might soon be able to assume the spectral form in full, attaining complete invisibility and preserving that condition as long as he wished.

Once he reached this stage, he argued, the outward way lay open to him. Of course he could not bear away any gold, but mere escape was enough. He would, though, dematerialize and carry with him his manuscript in the Tulu-metal cylinder, even though it cost additional effort, for this record and proof must reach the outer world at all hazards. He now knew the passage to follow; and if he could thread it in an atom-scattered state, he did not see how any person of force could detect or stop him. The only trouble would be if he failed to maintain his spectral condition at all times. That was the one ever-present peril, as he had learned from his experiments. But must one not always risk death and worse in a life of adventure? Zamacona was a gentleman of Old Spain; of the blood that faced the unknown and carved out half the civilization of the New World.

For many nights after his ultimate resolution Zamacona prayed to St Pamphilus and other guardian saints, and counted the beads of his rosary. The last entry in the manuscript – which toward the end took the form of a diary more and more, was merely a single sentence – *'Es mas tarde de lo que pensaba – tengo que marcharme.'* . . . 'It is later than I thought: I must go.' After that, only silence and conjecture – and such evidence as the presence of the manuscript itself, and what that manuscript could lead to, might provide.

VII

When I looked up from my half-stupefied reading and note-making the morning sun was high in the heavens. The electric bulb was still burning, but such things of the real world – the modern outer world – were far from my whirling brain. I knew I was in my room at Clyde Compton's at Binger, but upon what monstrous vista had I stumbled? Was this thing a hoax or a chronicle of madness? If a hoax, was it a jest of the sixteenth century or of today? The manuscript's age looked appallingly genuine to my not wholly unpracticed eyes, and the problem presented by the strange metal cylinder I dared not even think about.

Moreover, what a monstrously exact explanation it gave of all the baffling phenomena of the mound, of the seemingly meaningless and paradoxical actions of diurnal and nocturnal ghosts, and of the queer cases of madness and disappearance! It was even an accursedly *plausible* explanation, evilly *consistent*, if one could adopt the incredible. It must be a shocking hoax devised by someone who knew all the lore of the mound. There was even a hint of social satire in the account of that unbelievable nether world of horror and decay. Surely this was the clever forgery of some learned cynic, something like the leaden crosses in New Mexico, which a jester once planted and pretended to discover as a relique of some forgotten Dark-Age colony from Europe.

Upon going down to breakfast I hardly knew what to tell Compton and his mother, as well as the curious callers who had already begun to arrive. Still in a daze, I cut the Gordian Knot by giving a few points from the notes I had made, and mumbling my belief that the thing was a subtle and ingenious fraud left there by some previous explorer of the mound, a belief in which everybody seemed to concur when told of the substance of the manuscript. It is curious how all that breakfast group, and all the others in Binger to whom the discussion was repeated, seemed to find a great clearing of the atmosphere in the notion that somebody was playing a joke on somebody. For the time we all forgot that the known, recent history of the mound presented mysteries as strange as any in the manuscript, and as far from acceptable solution as ever.

The fears and doubts began to return when I asked for volunteers to visit the mound with me. I wanted a larger excavating party, but the idea of going to that uncomfortable place seemed no more attractive to the people of Binger than it had seemed on the previous day. I myself felt a mounting horror upon looking toward the mound and glimpsing the moving speck which I knew was the daylight sentinel; for in spite of all my scepticism the morbidities of that manuscript stuck by me and gave everything connected with the place a new and monstrous significance. I absolutely lacked the resolution to look at the moving speck with my binoculars. Instead, I set out with the kind of bravado we display in nightmares – when, knowing we are dreaming, we plunge desperately into still thicker horrors, for the sake of having the whole thing over the sooner. My pick and shovel were already out there, so I had only my handbag of smaller paraphernalia to take. Into this I put the strange cylinder and its contents, feeling vaguely that I might possibly find something worth checking up with some part of the green-lettered Spanish text. Even a clever hoax might be founded on some actual attribute of the mound which a former explorer had discovered – and that magnetic metal was damnably odd! Grey Eagle's cryptic talisman still hung from its leathern cord around my neck.

I did not look very sharply at the mound as I walked toward it, but when I reached it there was nobody in sight. Repeating my upward scramble of the previous day, I was troubled by thoughts of what *might* lie close at hand if, by any miracle, any part of the manuscript *were* actually half-true. In such a case, I could not help reflecting, the hypothetical Spaniard Zamacona must have barely reached the outer world when overtaken by some disaster; perhaps an involuntary rematerialization. He would naturally, in that event, have been seized by whichever sentry happened to be on duty at the time – either the discredited freeman, or, as a matter of supreme irony, the very T'la-yub who had planned and aided his first attempt at escape, and in the ensuing struggle the cylinder with the manuscript might well have been dropped on the mound's summit to be neglected and gradually buried for nearly four centuries. But, I added, as I climbed over the crest, one must not think of extravagant things like that. Still, if there *were* anything in the tale, it must have been a monstrous fate to which Zamacona had been dragged back . . . the amphitheatre . . . mutilation . . . duty somewhere in the dank, nitrous tunnel as a dead-alive . . . a maimed corpse-fragment as an automatic interior sentry. . . .

It was a very real shock which chased this morbid speculation from my head; for upon glancing around the elliptical summit I saw at once that my pick and shovel had been stolen. This was a highly provoking and disconcerting development; baffling, too, in view of the seemed reluctance of all the Binger folk to visit the mound. Was this reluctance a pretended thing, and had the jokers of the village been chuckling over my coming discomfiture as they solemnly saw me off ten minutes before? I took out my binoculars and scanned the gaping crowd at the edge of the village. No – they did not seem to be looking for any comic climax: yet was not the whole affair at bottom a colossal joke in which all the villagers and reservation people were concerned – legends, manuscript, cylinder, and all? I thought of how I had seen the sentry from a distance, and then found him unaccountably vanished; thought also of the conduct of old Grey Eagle, of the speech and expression of Compton and his mother, and of the unmistakable fright of most of the Binger people. On the whole, it could not very well be a village-wide joke. The fear and the problem were surely real, though obviously there were one or two jesting dare-devils in Binger who had stolen out to the mound and made off with the tools I had left.

Everything else on the mound was as I had left it; brush cut by my machete, slight, bow-like depression toward the north end, and the hole I had made with my trench-knife in digging up the magnetism-revealed cylinder. Deeming it too great a concession to the unknown jokers to return to Binger for another pick and shovel, I resolved to carry out my programme as best I could with the machete and trench-knife in my handbag; so extracting these, I set to work excavating the bowl-like depression which my eye had picked as the possible site of a former entrance to the mound. As I proceeded, I felt again the suggestion of a sudden wind blowing against me which I had noticed the day before – a suggestion which seemed stronger, and still more reminiscent of unseen, formless, opposing hands laid on my wrists, as I cut deeper and deeper through the root-tangled red soil and reached the exotic black loam beneath. The talisman around my neck appeared to twitch oddly in the breeze – not in any one direction, as when attracted by the buried cylinder, but vaguely and diffusely, in a manner wholly unaccountable.

Then, quite without warning, the black, root-woven earth beneath my feet began to sink crackingly, while I heard a faint sound of sifting, falling matter far below me. The obstructing wind, or forces, or hands now seemed to be operating from the very seat of the sinking, and I felt that they aided me by pushing as I leaned back out of the hole to avoid being involved in any cave-in. Bending down over the brink and hacking at the mould-caked root-tangle with my machete, I felt that they were against me again, but at no time were they strong enough to stop my work. The more roots I severed, the more falling matter I heard below. Finally the hole began to deepen of itself toward the centre, and I saw that the earth was sifting down into some large cavity beneath, so as to leave a good-sized aperture when the roots that had bound it were gone. A few more hacks of the machete did the trick, and with a parting cave-in and an uprush of curiously chill and alien air the last barrier gave way. Under the morning sun yawned a huge opening at least three feet square, and showing the top of a flight of stone steps down which the loose earth of the collapse was still sliding. My quest had come to something at last! With an elation of accomplishment almost overbalancing fear for the nonce, I replaced the trench-knife and machete in my handbag, took out my powerful electric torch, and prepared for a triumphant, lone, and utterly rash invasion of the fabulous nether world I had uncovered.

It was rather hard getting down the first few steps, both because of the fallen earth which had choked them and because of a singular uprushing of a cold wind from below. The talisman around my neck swayed curiously, and I began to regret the disappearing square of daylight above me. The electric torch showed dank, water-stained and self-encrusted walls fashioned of huge basalt blocks, and now and then I thought I descried some trace of carving beneath the nitrous deposits. I gripped my handbag more tightly, and was glad of the comforting weight of the sheriff's heavy revolver in my right-hand coat pocket. After a time the passage began to wind this way and that, and the staircase became free from obstructions. Carvings on the walls were now definitely traceable, and I shuddered when I saw how clearly the grotesque figures resembled the monstrous bas-reliefs on the cylinder I had found. Winds and forces continued to blow malevolently against me, and at one or two bends I half-fancied the torch gave glimpses of thin, transparent shapes not unlike the sentinel on the mound as my binoculars had showed him. When I reached this stage of visual chaos I stopped for a moment to get a grip of myself. It would not do to let my nerves get the better of me at the very outset of what would surely be a trying experience, and the most important archaeological feat of my career.

But I wished I had not stopped at just that place, for the act fixed my attention on something profoundly disturbing. It was only a small object lying close to the wall on one of the steps below me, but that object was such as to put my reason to a severe test, and bring up a line of the most alarming speculations. That the opening above me had been closed against all material forms for generations was utterly obvious from the growth of shrub-roots and accumulation of drifting soil; yet the object before me was most distinctly *not* many generations old. For it was an electric torch much like the one I now carried – warped and encrusted in the tomb-like dampness, but none the less perfectly unmistakable. I descended a few steps and picked it up, wiping off the evil deposits on my rough coat. One of the nickel bands bore an engraved name and address, and I recognized it with a start the moment I made it out. It read 'Jas C. Williams, 17 Trowbridge St., Cambridge, Mass.' – and I knew that it had belonged to one of the two daring college instructors who had disappeared on June 28, 1915. Only thirteen years ago, and yet I had just broken through the sod of centuries! How had the thing got there? Another entrance – or was there something after all in this mad idea of dematerialization and rematerialization?

Doubt and horror grew upon me as I wound still farther down the seemingly endless staircase. Would the thing never stop? The carvings grew more and more distinct, and assumed a narrative pictorial quality which brought me close to panic as I recognized many unmistakable correspondences with the history of K'n-yan as sketched in the manuscript now resting in my handbag. For the first time, I began seriously to question the wisdom of my descent, and to wonder whether I had not better return to the upper air before I came upon something which would never let me return as a sane man. But I did not hesitate long, for as a Virginian I felt the blood of ancestral fighters and gentleman-adventurers pounding a protest against retreat from any peril known or unknown.

My descent became swifter rather than slower, and I avoided studying the terrible bas-reliefs and intaglios that had unnerved me. All at once I saw an arched opening ahead, and realized that the prodigious staircase had ended at last. But with that realization came horror in mounting magnitude, for before me there yawned a vast vaulted crypt of all-too-familiar outline – a great circular space answering in every least particular to the carving-lined chamber described in the Zamacona manuscript.

It was indeed the place. There could be no mistake. And if any room for doubt yet remained, that doubt was abolished by what I saw directly across the great vault. It was a second arched opening, commencing a long, narrow passage and having at its mouth two huge opposite niches bearing loathsome and titanic images of shockingly familiar pattern. There in the dark, unclean Yig and hideous Tulu squatted eternally, glaring at each other across the passage as they had glared since the earliest youth of the human world.

From this point onward I ask no credence for what I tell – for what I *think* I saw. It is too utterly unnatural, too utterly monstrous and incredible, to be any part of sane human experience or objective reality. My torch, though casting a powerful beam ahead, naturally could not furnish any general illumination of the cyclopean crypt; so I now began moving it about to explore the giant walls little by little. As I did so, I saw to my horror that the space was by no means vacant, but was instead littered with odd furniture and utensils and heaps of packages which bespoke a populous recent occupancy – no nitrous reliques of the past, but queerly-shaped objects and supplies in modern, every-day use. As my torch rested on each article or group of articles, however, the distinctness of the outlines soon began to grow blurred; until in the end I could scarcely tell whether the things belonged to the realm of matter or to the realm of spirit.

All this while the adverse winds blew against me with increasing fury, and the unseen hands plucked malevolently at me and snatched at the strange magnetic talisman I wore. Wild conceits surged through my mind. I thought of the manuscript and what it said about the garrison stationed in this place – twelve dead slave *y'm-bhi* and six living but partly dematerialized freemen – that was in 1545 – three hundred and eighty-three years ago. . . . What since then? Zamacona had predicted change – subtle distintegration . . . more dematerialization . . . weaker and weaker . . . was it Grey Eagle's talisman that held them at bay – their sacred Tulu-metal – and were they feebly trying to pluck it off so that they might do to me what they had done to those who had come before? . . . It occurred to me with shuddering force that I was building my speculations out of a full belief in the Zamacona manuscript – this must not be – I must get a grip on myself—

But, curse it, every time I tried to get a grip I saw some fresh sight to shatter my poise still further. This time, just as my will power was driving the half-seen paraphernalia into obscurity, my glance and torch beam had to light on two things of very different nature; two things of the eminently real and sane world which grew more instead of less distinct the longer I looked at them. I saw they were of the eminently real and sane world; yet they did more to unseat my shaky reason than anything I had seen before – because I knew what they were, and knew how profoundly, in the course of nature, they ought not to be there. *They were my own missing pick and shovel, side by side, and leaning neatly against the blasphemously carved wall of that hellish crypt.* God in Heaven – and I had babbled to myself about daring young jokers from Binger!

That was the last straw. After that the cursed hypnotism of the manuscript got at me, and I actually *saw* the half-transparent shapes of the things that were pushing and plucking; pushing and plucking – those leprous palaeogean things with something of humanity still clinging to them – the *complete* forms, and the forms that were morbidly and perversely *incomplete* . . . all these, and hideous *other entities* – the four-footed blasphemies with ape-like face and projecting horn – and not a sound so far in all that nitrous hell of inner earth. . . .

Then there *was* a sound – a flopping; a padding; a dull,

advancing sound which heralded beyond question a being as structurally material as the pickaxe and the shovel – something wholly unlike the shadow-shapes that ringed me in, yet equally remote from any sort of life as life is understood on the earth's wholesome surface. My shattered brain tried to prepare me for what was coming, but could not frame any adequate image. I could only say over and over again to myself, 'It is of the abyss, but it is *not* dematerialized.' The padding grew more distinct, and from the mechanical cast of the tread I knew it was a dead thing that stalked in the darkness. Then – Oh, God, *I saw it in the full beam of my torch; saw it framed like a sentinel in the narrow passage between the nightmare idols of the serpent Yig and the octopus Tulu. . . .*

Let me collect myself enough to hint at what I saw; to explain why I dropped torch and handbag alike and fled empty-handed in the utter blackness, wrapped in a merciful unconsciousness which did not wear off until the sun and the distant yelling and the shouting from the village roused me as I lay gasping on the top of the accursed mound. I do not yet know what guided me again to the earth's surface. I only know that the watchers in Binger saw me stagger up into sight three hours after I had vanished; saw me lurch up and fall flat on the ground as if struck by a bullet. None of them dared to come out and help me; but they knew I must be in a bad state, so tried to rouse me as best they could by yelling in chorus and firing off revolvers.

It worked in the end, and when I came to I almost rolled down the side of the mound in my eagerness to get away from that black aperture which still yawned open. My torch and tools, and the handbag with the manuscript, were all down there; but it is easy to see why neither I nor anyone else ever went after them. When I had staggered across the plain and into the village I dared not tell what I had seen. I only muttered vague things about carvings and statues and snakes and shaken nerves. And I did not faint again until somebody mentioned that the ghost-sentinel had reappeared about the time I had staggered half-way back to town. I left Binger that evening, and have never been there since, though they tell me the ghosts still appear on the mound as usual.

But I have resolved to hint here at last what I dared not hint to the people of Binger on that terrible August afternoon. I do not know yet just how I can go about it – and if in the end you think my reticence strange, just remember that to imagine such a horror is one thing, *but to see it is another thing.* I saw it. I think you'll recall my citing early in this tale the case of a bright young man named Heaton who went out to that mound one day in 1891 and came back at night as the village idiot, babbling for eight years about horrors and then dying in an epileptic fit. What he used to keep moaning was *'that white man – oh, my God, what they did to him. . . .'*

Well, I saw the same thing that poor Heaton saw – and I saw it after reading that manuscript, so I know more of its history than he did. That makes it worse – for I know all that it *implies;* all that must be still brooding and festering and waiting down there. I told you it had padded mechanically toward me out of the narrow passage, and had stood sentry-like at the entrance between the frightful eidola of Yig and Tulu. That was very natural and inevitable – because the thing *was* a sentry. It had been made a sentry for punishment, and it was quite dead – besides lacking head, arms, lower legs and other customary parts of a human being. Yes – it had been a very human being once; and what is more, it had been *white.* Very obviously, if that manuscript was as true as I think it was, this being had been used for the *diversions of the amphitheatre,* before its life had become wholly extinct and supplanted by automatic impulses controlled from outside.

On its white and only slightly hairy chest some letters had been gashed or branded – I had not stopped to investigate, but had merely noted that they were in an awkward and fumbling Spanish: an awkward Spanish implying a kind of ironic use of the language by an alien inscriber familiar neither with the idiom nor the Roman letters used to record it. The inscription had read: *'Secuestrado a la voluntad de Xinaian en el cuerpo decapitado de Tlayub'* – *'Seized by the will of K'n-yan in the headless body of T'la-yub.'*